I WANTED TO SCREAM,
BUT NO SOUND CAME.

I needed to call the police, but I couldn't move. All I could do was stare down at my once-beautiful friend as the bile rose in my throat. As I tried to swallow, I saw the phone near her hand

Run. Get out of there. Escape. The message still wasn't getting to my legs.

My eyes traveled from the phone to a crimson scarf in her hand. The color of blood. It must have been the only thing she could grab as she reached out for a Peg-Board on the wall behind her to keep from falling. The Peg-Board had crashed to the floor, but the scarf she'd grabbed was like a beacon, pointing to a tiny scrap of paper that was also in her hand.

I couldn't leave now. Not with the awful fear that was growing in my stomach about the remnant of paper and what it looked like.

It was a torn fragment of computer paper from the top of the tickets we give to our customers to use when they pick up their clothes. I could see the letters "Dy" that were part of the name Dyer's Cleaners. The rest of the ticket for the Fortuny dress was missing.

D0834831

Dell Books by Dolores Johnson

TAKEN TO THE CLEANERS

HUNG UP TO DIE

A DRESS TO DIE FOR

A DRESS
TO DIE FOR

A Mandy Dyer Mystery

DOLORES JOHNSON

A Dell Book

Published by
Dell Publishing
a division of
Bantam Doubleday Dell Publishing Group, Inc.
1540 Broadway
New York, New York 10036

ISBN: 0-440-22355-5

Printed in the United States of America

Published simultaneously in Canada

October 1998

10 9 8 7 6 5 4 3

OPM

To my daughter-in-law, Mindy Pomper-Johnson, who's a welcome addition to our family. With thanks for the research on Fortuny that she did for me in Venice.

ACKNOWLEDGMENTS

I wish to thank homicide detectives Joe Tennant and Gary Hoffman of the Denver Police Department, who answered my questions about police procedures. I'm also indebted to information found in the book *Fortuny: The Life and Work of Mariano Fortuny* by Guillermo de Osma, as well as information about vintage clothing stores supplied by Suelynn Gustafson of Flossie McGrew's in Denver. Any errors in this book are mine and not the fault of the people mentioned above.

A special thanks for their help to members of my two critique groups—Lee Karr, Kay Bergstrom, Carol Caverly, Diane Davidson, Christine Jorgensen, Leslie O'Kane, and Peggy Swager; and Rebecca Bates, Thora Chinnery, Diane Coffelt, Linda Ensley Claflin, Cindy Goff, Donna Schaper, and Barbara Snook. As always, thanks also to my agents, Meg Ruley and Ruth Kagle, and to my editor, Jacqueline Miller.

CHAPTER 1

Most people think a trip to the cleaners is about as exciting as watching the spin cycle on the washing machine at the local coin-op laundry. Kate Bosworth wasn't one of them.

She always bubbled with enthusiasm when she brought me garments to be cleaned. On this particular Monday morning she was practically overflowing.

"You'll never guess what I found this weekend, Mandy," she said, leaning over the counter toward me. "You dream about this, and suddenly there it is where you least expect it."

I continued to let her bubble. She curved one hand around her mouth, and whispered, "I bought it for ten dollars, but the dress has to be worth at least five thousand."

"Five thousand *dollars*?" My voice was louder than I intended. "Does it have gold nuggets for buttons and ermine trim?"

She placed a round container on the counter. "Here it is."

My eyes widened. "Not a Fortuny?"

She nodded. "Can you believe it? I saw the hatbox, and when I looked inside, I thought I'd died and gone to heaven."

Years ago she'd told me about the Fortuny gowns and how they had come in their own special little hatboxes. I lifted the lid and looked at the dress, which was twisted up inside as if someone had just wrung the water out of it.

But according to Kate, that's the way they'd been sold back when a Spanish-born artist named Mariano Fortuny designed them just after the turn of the century. The gowns were meant to be twisted up and stored in the hatbox when they weren't being worn.

Kate removed the floor-length dress, a rich shade of blue, and miraculously the tiny silk pleats shook out as if it had been stored on a hanger all these years. It caught the light and shimmered, as if moon dust had been sprinkled on it to give it a silvery glow.

She looked at the gown in awe. "No one has ever been able to duplicate the way Fortuny could dye the silk so it would shine that way, or figure out how he put the pleats in it so they would never come out." She sighed. "I don't think I can ever sell it, Mandy. I'm going to keep it for myself."

Kate ran a vintage-clothing store, Past Perfect Fashions, and that's why she scouted the flea markets and garage sales on the weekends, searched attics, and went through steamer trunks, looking for garments of an earlier period. She also rented some of her merchandise as costumes for theme parties and other events that ranged from Renaissance weddings to sock hops.

"Maybe I'll have a Roaring Twenties party for Halloween this year and wear the dress." She held it up in front of her as she twirled around the call office, which is what we call the lobby of the cleaners.

It was only June, but Kate always planned the theme for her Halloween parties well in advance. Never mind that they weren't on Halloween. She held them in early October, so she could advertise her costume-rental business at the same time.

"It doesn't look like a Roaring Twenties dress to me," I said, although it might if she cut it off above the knees to look like one of the short flapper dresses of the era.

Kate shrugged. "Fortuny was a genius who didn't believe in changing styles every year. He designed the dress in 1907 at his studio in Venice, and the last one was produced in 1952, several years after he died. All the famous women of the time owned one."

So I guess whatever she wanted to call her party was fine with me. It was always the highlight of my social season. Of course my friend Nat Wilcox had said once that I'd let myself get into such a dating slump that a trip to Denny's was an occasion. However, things had improved considerably since Detective Stan Foster came back into my life. I'd met him when I became involved in a homicide investigation. Maybe I could talk him into going to Kate's party with me as one of the Keystone Kops.

Kate and I went way back. Well, not all that far because we're both only in our mid thirties. I'd just turned thirty-four, and Kate was probably a year or so older. We met in my Bohemian period, when I'd been an artist, doing charcoal sketches of people for five dollars a sitting. Kate had designed jewelry and always had a booth at the same street fairs where I set up my easel. Neither one of us could make a living at our art. Eventually she started her vintage-clothing shop, and I took over Dyer's Cleaners after my uncle Chet died and left me the business.

But we still saw each other occasionally, and I always gave her a discount when she brought in her vintage clothes to be cleaned. I'd even used her as one of the models for the mural my uncle commissioned me to paint on the wall of the call office. That was when he'd first built his new dry cleaners near the Cherry Creek Mall here in Denver, mercifully choosing to call it only Dyer's Cleaners instead of Dyer's Cleaners and Dyers, which he'd used at the old plant downtown.

The mural's a history of fashion from the turn of the century to the present, and I'd actually used Kate for my twenties' model in a short dress, long beads, and rolled silk stockings. I'd taken artistic license with her auburn hair, though, making it shorter than it really was.

Kate had always worn her hair long and straight, but she'd cut it a few months ago—"to match the mural," she'd said, because she liked the look. She always wore the same type of clothes she sold, mixing and matching them in a schizophrenic potpourri of the decades. I, on the other hand, had been forced to start dressing in the latest styles. If you're going to be a dry cleaner, you have to show your customers by example that you're up on the latest fashions and fabrics. I'd also cut my long dark hair and permed it, mainly so it wouldn't droop in all of the steam back in the plant or get caught in the equipment.

Kate had a healthy appetite but was still model-thin. In fact she probably didn't weigh much more at five-nine than I did at five-five. That's even after I'd lost the fifteen pounds I'd put on after my divorce, during the time when I went back to my maiden name of Dyer and took over the cleaners.

"Can I get a one-hour special on the dress so I can come back and get it this afternoon?" Kate asked, interrupting my thoughts about the unfairness of the way people burn calories.

"Give us until tomorrow," I said. "I don't want to rush with something that"—I lowered my voice—"costs five thousand dollars. Okay?"

She agreed, but she was so excited, she didn't seem to

want to leave. "Remember when we talked about going to Italy together someday when we both got rich and famous?"

I nodded. "I wanted to visit the Pitti Palace and the Uffizi Gallery in Florence, and of course the Sistine Chapel. You told me there was a museum in Venice for this artist named Fortuny, and that's what you wanted to see."

"We really ought to do it, Mandy, even if we aren't rich and famous yet."

"I'm a little short of money this week. Would you settle for an Italian dinner at Luigi's on Saturday night?"

Kate mulled it over. "That might work." She leaned toward me. "I probably couldn't afford Italy right now anyway. Evan wants me to buy out his share of the business."

Evan Carmody was her silent partner. I'd met him only a few times, but he was an elegant man whose looks were marred only by a crooked nose that would have looked like he'd been in a barroom brawl if it had been on anyone else.

I asked if Evan was having problems.

A look of sadness crossed her face. "I should have known better than to get involved with him in the first place—if you know what I mean." No, I didn't know what she meant. Was he a criminal, or on the verge of bankruptcy? Had the relationship turned sexual, then kinky or abusive? What? Before I could ask, she said, "I'll tell you all about it Saturday night." And then she seemed to perk up. "Maybe I'll even wear my new dress for the dinner."

This was going to cost me—in calories and clothes if nothing else. I'd have to find something fancy to wear if I were to compete with her Fortuny gown and I'd have to make sure to go swimming Sunday, which is how I'd lost the fifteen unwanted pounds in the first place—lap by excruciating lap.

"How's Nat doing these days?" she asked as she started to leave.

"Same old Nat," I said. "Unable to maintain a personal relationship because he's always out trying to uncover a scoop that will win him the Pulitzer Prize. He should have been born back in the Thirties when reporters actually did scoop each other."

Kate nodded.

She and Nat had known each other for years, thanks to my friendship with both of them. I'd even thought they might start dating at one point. They both should have lived in a different era, after all—Kate with her vintage clothes and Nat with his front-page mentality, but nothing had ever worked out. She'd been too devastated when the love of her life, Red Berry, broke up with her. He'd been a wannabe rock star with a band called the Sour Grapes to go with his obviously made-up name. He'd taken off for Hollywood about ten years ago, never to be heard of again, and she hadn't shown a real interest in anyone else until Evan Carmody came along.

"And this is for you, Mandy," Kate said, slipping something out of the big leather bag she always carried with her. "It was in the hatbox with the dress."

With a grand flourish she put a scarf on the counter. It was a wispy piece of crepe chiffon in a swirl of pastel colors, and when I started to unfold it, I realized it must be six feet long.

"It's beautiful," I said, "but you should keep it to go with the dress."

"No." She shook her head so that her reddish-brown hair glistened in the sun coming in the front window. "I want you to have it. Just don't go riding in a convertible with the top down when you're wearing it."

"Excuse me?"

"Isadora Duncan, the famous dancer, was strangled by a long, flowing scarf when it got caught in the spokes of an open roadster." She pushed the scarf toward me, grinning. "Her scarf was wool, though. This one would never kill you."

"Thanks. I think."

Kate waved at me from the door and said she'd be back first thing the next morning for her dress. By Thursday she still hadn't returned, and I began to worry about her.

CHAPTER 2

Granted, it had been only three days since Kate brought me her dress. Some people don't come back for their clothes for weeks. They seem to think our plant is a giant closet, set up for their personal convenience. If they don't have adequate storage space at home, why not just leave their winter wardrobes at the cleaners all summer?

But Kate had been too enthusiastic about the dress to do that. Unless she'd found a rich new lover and they'd flown off to Venice together.

I stared at the hatbox with the dress nestled down inside. It was on the shelf where we kept comforters and other household items, and I grabbed it and headed for the back of the plant.

"You'd have thought Kate would have been here by now to get her dress, the way she was so thrilled about," I said to McKenzie Rivers, my cleaner/spotter.

Mack had been excited, too, when Kate went around to the back door of the plant to tell him about it. He said he'd seen only one other Fortuny in all the years he'd worked for my uncle.

"Kate probably just got too busy with all the other things she does," he reminded me.

Mack's a big black man, who knew Kate because he's involved in community theater, and when he'd staged *Othello* a couple of years ago, she had helped find some of the costumes for the production.

"I'm going to take it over to her shop," I said, trying to feel reassured by his words.

Mack nodded. "Tell her I think she looks like a red-haired Theda Bara in that new, short hairdo."

"And who, pray tell, is Theda Bara?"

He grinned. "She was a silent screen star known as 'The Vamp.' "

"Okay, Kate ought to like that." It was the era she coveted, after all. "If you're gone by the time I get back, I'll see you tomorrow."

I'd been wanting to play hooky from the cleaners, and I finally had an excuse to get outside. It was a beautiful day with the temperature in the mid eighties, and I didn't even bother to go in my office and get the jacket to my peach-colored linen suit. I just took off.

I climbed inside what I called my "starter" car, a used Hyundai that I'd purchased recently. Before that I'd used the company van as my personal transportation, when it wasn't in service making our deliveries. With the Dyer's Cleaners logo on the side, I'd once looked at the van as advertising on wheels. To my regret I'd discovered several months back that advertising yourself everywhere you go can be downright conspicuous sometimes, not to mention incriminating, when the van had shown up at a crime scene.

I drove past the exclusive Cherry Creek Mall, turned south on University, and eventually wound my way to a cluster of shops in South Denver with a totally different style than Cherry Creek. They were in a neighborhood shopping area that has been turned into an eclectic bunch of artsy-crafty stores with simulated gas streetlights out front on the sidewalk.

Kate's store was between a bookstore and a doll-repair shop. It was located in its own separate Victorian building and looked like a giant dollhouse itself.

Parking was always a problem on the street, but I finally found a space a few buildings north of her shop. I walked back to it, holding the Fortuny hatbox as if I were a courier with a briefcase full of money.

Maybe Kate and I weren't rich and famous yet, but things were looking up, I tried to tell myself. She'd found the Fortuny, and my business was doing better now. Even though this was June—the beginning of the dog days for dry cleaners—the volume at the plant was up from last year, thanks to my delivery route, which I'd expanded to residential customers as well as businesses. Besides, I had a fellow, which had pleased my mother immensely when she visited me a few weeks before. And I'd even thought Kate might be falling in love with her silent partner, Evan Carmody, until she'd said she should never have gotten involved with him. I hoped she'd feel like talking about it when we went to dinner Saturday night.

I hurried up the four steps to the porch of Kate's shop only to find a CLOSED sign on the door. I set down the hatbox and cupped my hands around my eyes so I could look inside the store, which had once been the parlor of the house. There were no lights inside, but there was a shaft of sunlight coming in from a window on the south side of the building. It made the place look old and dusty, but I knew Kate kept it spotlessly clean. It was just the vintage clothing that gave it that feel, plus the mannequin near the front window, who wore a forties-style pompadour.

Maybe Kate had gone to lunch, I thought, although it was already three in the afternoon. I knew she couldn't afford any help except around Halloween, when she hired some part-timers. Perhaps she'd closed early because there was an estate sale somewhere.

I wasn't about to leave the Fortuny dress on the porch or with a neighboring shopkeeper, not the way Kate felt about it, but I wouldn't give up yet. If she'd gone to lunch, chances were she was eating in her apartment, which was on the second floor, above her shop. It had a separate entrance leading up to it from around at the side of the building.

Retracing my way down the steps, I took the sidewalk that led to the wooden stairway to the apartment. A rose bush was out in full bloom by the side of the building, and I could smell its fragrance as I went by. I would have stopped to smell the blossoms except that I was beginning to feel anxious. Besides, the bees that buzzed around the bush might not like my invading their territory.

At the foot of the stairs I came across the morning edition of the *Denver Tribune* where my friend Nat works as a police reporter. I took a look at the dateline, which is why I knew it was today's paper. Within the next half-dozen stairs, there were two more issues of the *Trib*.

"Kate," I yelled, feeling an increasing sense of alarm. "Are you up there?" I took the rest of the steps two at a time. I planned to knock, and if she didn't answer, start a canvass of the neighborhood. I never had a chance. When I got to the landing, I saw that the door was ajar. Just a little, but enough so that I knew it wasn't the way it should have been.

"Kate." I pushed open the door. "Are you home? What's the matter?"

The moment I looked inside, I knew it was something bad. The neat little apartment had been turned upside down. My stomach lurched. The drawers had been rifled in her desk and in the hutch in her dining room. Sofa pillows were tossed on the floor, and a lamp was upended. I set down the hatbox by the door and went inside. What I wanted to do was turn and run.

When I went to the bedroom door, the smell almost stopped me. I wasn't sure I could force myself to go inside. I could see clothes that had been torn off their hangers and thrown on the floor. Flies rose up from beyond the bed near the window, much as the bees had swarmed around the rose bush outside. I held my nose and willed my feet to move toward them.

I saw her when I got to the foot of the bed. She was on the floor between the bed and the wall, her short auburn hair still perfectly arranged as if someone had smoothed it down. That was the only thing that reminded me of the way she'd been.

A fringed scarf from some bygone era was pulled tight around her neck, so tight I couldn't even see the part that had choked her to death. Her eyes stared up at me unseeing, but with the remains of fear and disbelief still in them. Her body was bloated from the heat and covered with the flies. I was sure she'd been there several days, maybe even since Monday, when she'd come to the cleaners.

I wanted to scream, but no sound came. I needed to call the police, but I couldn't move. All I could do was stare down at my once-beautiful friend as the bile rose in my throat. As I tried to swallow, I saw the phone near her hand. It was all I could do to keep from grabbing it, but I knew I shouldn't do that. I needed to go to a neighboring shop owner and call for help.

Run. Get out of there. Escape. The message still wasn't getting to my legs.

My eyes traveled from the phone to a crimson scarf in her hand. The color of blood. It must have been the only thing she could grab as she reached out for a Peg-Board on the wall behind her in an effort to keep from falling. The Peg-Board had crashed to the floor, scattering the long neck-laces and scarves that had once been draped over it, but the scarf she'd grabbed was like a beacon, pointing to a tiny scrap of paper that was also in her hand. The piece of paper looked as if it was all that remained of a larger sheet that had been ripped from her grasp.

I couldn't leave yet. Not with the awful fear that was growing in my stomach about the remnant of paper and what it looked like.

I bent down closer to Kate's body, trying not to look at her, only at the ragged scrap of paper. I held my breath and squinted my eyes to focus on the paper. I was right.

It was a torn fragment of computer paper, and my worst fears were confirmed. It was from the top of the tickets we give to our customers to use when they pick up their clothes. I could see the letters *Dy* that were part of the name Dyer's Cleaners. The rest of the ticket for the Fortuny dress was missing.

CHAPTER 3

I turned and ran from the apartment, stopping only long enough to grab the hatbox with the Fortuny dress inside. When I reached the street, I turned north on the sidewalk to the doll-repair shop next door. A bell tinkled above the door when I opened it, and a plump, bespectacled man came out of a back room. He had wild gray hair that stood out from his head as if he'd recently been plugged into an electrical outlet.

"Can I use your phone? I need to call Nine-one-one."

"Of course." He motioned me to the phone, and I saw his faded blue eyes widen with fear as he listened to me tell the dispatcher about finding Kate's body.

"My God," he whispered. "What happened?"

The dispatcher had told me to stay on the line, so I didn't answer him. I didn't think I was capable of saying anything more anyway.

"Why don't you have a chair," he said. "You're white as a sheet. Let me get you a cup of tea."

I shook my head. I didn't want to sit down. I didn't want a cup of tea. All I wanted was to go outside. Try to get the smell of death out of my nose and off my clothes.

"It'll just take a minute." He ran his hands nervously through his hair, further electrifying it until I feared he might have a heart attack from the shock. He looked pale too.

"Maybe a glass of water," I said. "No, operator, I'm talking to someone here." The dollmaker nodded and went through a door to the back of the building.

I tried to think of something—anything—else, but everything reminded me of Kate. Even a dollhouse on a table at the side of the room. It could have been a miniature of houses in the neighborhood, almost like Kate's Victorian next door. A tiny replica of a real house, but a place where nothing bad ever happened. Hard as I tried, I couldn't help noticing the broken doll next to it that the man must have been working on. The head was detached from the body. There were dolls he'd put back together on shelves nearby. So easy with dolls. So hard with people. I couldn't stand it. I wanted him to put Kate back together.

"Here, have this," the man said when he returned, handing me the glass of water. His hands were shaking. "I can't believe someone was killed in this neighborhood. She seemed like such a nice young woman."

I took a few sips of water and handed the glass back to him. "Thanks." I covered the mouthpiece. "Did you see or hear anything strange at Kate's the last few days?"

"No." He lifted his thick glasses to wipe his eyes. "Well, I did hear some loud music when I went to the grocery store a couple of nights ago." He stopped to consider the day. "No, I guess it was Monday. I just thought she was having a party."

I heard the operator on the other end of the line. "Yes, I'm still holding. No, they aren't here yet." I covered the mouthpiece again. "What time was that?"

"About six, I'd say."

Six o'clock Monday. The day Kate brought the dress to me.

The man dropped his head. "I wonder if I could have done something." He sighed. "But there was a black pickup parked up on the grass. One with those big tires that looks like it belongs in a Monster Truck rally. It wasn't hers, was it?"

I shook my head. I knew she had a VW Bug.

"I didn't think so, but I just figured she had company. I haven't seen any sign of anyone over there since then, come to think of it."

I saw a patrol car pull up to the curb. "The policeman's here now," I said to the dispatcher. "I'm going to hang up and go talk to him."

"I'll go with you." The dollmaker followed me out to the sidewalk.

"I'm Arthur Goldman, the doll doctor, by the way."

By then the policeman was out of his car. He identified himself as Officer Werner and asked which one of us had called. I introduced the doll doctor and myself and explained that I was from Dyer's Cleaners and had brought a cleaning order to my friend, Kate Bosworth. "When her shop was closed, I went upstairs to her apartment and found her body."

"Why don't you show me where it is," the policeman said.

"Mr. Goldman says he saw a black truck over there Monday night," I continued, reluctant to go back to Kate's apartment.

"Okay, we'll talk to you later, Mr. Goldman," the cop said. "Just go back to your shop and wait for us there."

I led the policeman to the steps to Kate's apartment. Mercifully he said I could wait on the sidewalk while he went upstairs to take a look.

I still felt as if I were going to throw up. I tried to breathe in the fresh air, catch the scent of roses, but I still couldn't smell anything but decay. Would I ever be able to smell roses again without thinking of today? I hugged the round little hatbox in front of me as if it were a security blanket that could give me comfort, but it couldn't ease the pain.

I knew I had to turn it over to the police, that somehow it must be connected to the murder. I hadn't yet mentioned the ticket, but they would see it clutched in Kate's hand soon enough. Why had she had it in her hand? For my phone number? Surely she hadn't been trying to call me? She would have been trying to call the police, not me. No, her killer must have wanted the ticket because of the dress, and she'd been trying to keep it from him. If not, why else would he have torn dresses out of her closet and ransacked the apartment? Her shop hadn't appeared to be disturbed when I peeked inside; the killer must have known it wasn't there once he found the cleaning ticket. I squeezed the hatbox even closer to me.

I closed my eyes, but when I did, all I saw was Kate, the scarf wrapped around her neck so tightly that only the knot at the front and the fringed edges were visible. A scarf that made me think of the one she'd given me. I couldn't help remembering what she'd said about that scarf: It can't kill you as long as you don't ride in any open convertibles.

That's when I started to lose it. I gulped back the tears. I had to hold myself together so I could talk to the policeman again. All I wanted was for the police to find the bastard who had done this to Kate. I stared into the rose bush and tried to concentrate on that.

"Excuse me, ma'm." It was Officer Werner. "I need to get a statement from you now."

I hadn't even heard him come down the stairs. I noticed that another patrol car had pulled up to the curb, and the two men conferred for a minute before Werner pointed to his own car. "We can sit in there."

"Okay." I swiped at my eyes with my hand and hugged the hatbox to me even tighter as I followed him to the car.

I didn't want to hand over the dress. The police would keep it for evidence, stick it away in the bowels of the police department someplace, and never give it back. Not in time for Kate's funeral, anyway. It had meant so much to her. Somehow it seemed important to me that she be buried in that dress, but I knew it would never happen.

As I climbed into the car, I tried to get myself under control so I'd be coherent enough to tell Officer Werner what had happened. I started with Kate bringing the dress to the cleaners Monday morning and didn't stop until I was at the part about finding her body. I drew in a ragged breath. "Maybe you saw it," I said. "There was the top edge of a dry-cleaning ticket for the dress in her hand."

He stopped writing and looked over at the hatbox. "I'll have to take the dress."

I moved it away from him. "It doesn't have anything to do with the crime scene. I thought her family might want to—" Before I could blurt out something about her being buried in the dress, I had second thoughts. If the dress had something to do with her death, I wanted him to have it.

Werner didn't know this of course. "Look, I want you to wait here," he said. "I think the homicide detective will want to talk to you." He got out of the car.

I looked around, hoping Stan Foster would be the detective assigned to the case. After all, Stan and I had been dating recently, and I needed him now.

I didn't see him. I'd been vaguely aware of other people arriving—more police officials and paramedics, a TV camera crew and other members of the Fourth Estate like my friend, Nat Wilcox. Now I noticed that a crowd of spectators had begun to gather on the other side of the street.

And that's when I saw Nat, who looks a little like John Lennon with his granny glasses and shaggy dark hair. He was just crossing the street, a journalist intent on getting a story, and before I thought about it, I was out of the car.

"Nat," I yelled.

"Mandy, my God, what happened? What are you doing here?"

"Someone killed Kate." The words came out like a wail.

"Oh, God." He rushed over and hugged me. "I didn't realize this was her address until I got here."

Nat's a few inches taller than I am, but he was still in the street and I was on the curb. The hug was awkward, especially because I was still clutching the hatbox.

"What's that?" he asked, pulling back from me.

"It's a dress Kate found someplace over the weekend. I think it has something to do with why she was killed."

"Dammit, Wilcox, stay away from my witness until I've talked to her." The voice came from a huge, sandy-haired man who looked like a Broncos lineman but without the jersey, just a sports jacket and slacks.

I realized I probably shouldn't have said anything about the dress to Nat, but it was too late.

"Nat and I were both friends of Kate's," I said, trying to defend my actions.

The man didn't care. He pulled me away from Nat as Officer Werner came up beside us.

"This is Detective Reilly," Werner said as he consulted the statement he'd just taken from me. "And this is Amanda Dyer, who found the body."

Reilly took the statement and read it carefully. When he looked up, he seemed less angry. "I'm afraid we'll need the dress, Ms. Dyer. It might be important as to motive."

"I know." And if the dress would help catch her killer, I wanted the police to hold on to it as long as they wanted. I shoved the box at the detective with so much force that he looked surprised, probably because Werner had told him I was reluctant to part with it.

Somehow my decision to give up the dress helped me get through the next few minutes without crying.

"Where's your car?" Reilly asked when he finally finished questioning me.

"It's just a few houses down the street."

"Here, read over the statement and sign it. Then I'd better take you to the car or else the media will be all over you."

I did as I was told and tried to accept the idea of a police escort gracefully. "Will you tell Nat to call me?" I asked before Reilly closed the door on my Hyundai.

He nodded, but I doubted that he would. My anger about Kate helped me get back to the cleaners without having an accident. I would have liked to talk to Mack, but unfortunately he and the rest of the cleaning crew had already gone home by the time I arrived at the plant.

He had always been like a father to me, especially after Uncle Chet died more than two years ago. My own father, Chet's brother, had died when I was only a year old, and my uncle and Mack had been my father figures more than any of the stepfathers that were always passing through my life.

Never mind that Mack was black and I was white. Never mind that he was sometimes bossy and overprotective. He was the person who'd helped me get through Uncle Chet's death, and I guess I hoped he could help me through this new loss in my life.

I hurried up front to the call office, where my afternoon counter people were busy with customers who were picking up or dropping off clothes after work. I needed to warn them about the ticket, far-fetched though it seemed that the person who'd killed Kate would actually come into the cleaners and try to pick up the dress.

I waited while Theresa Emory, my front-counter manager, finished waiting on a customer. Theresa is a pleasantly plump woman who loves clothes and is great on the counter. I yearned for someone to give me comfort right now, but still I had to keep some semblance of control.

"Good hearing about your new granddaughter, Mrs. Jamison," Theresa said to the customer. "Your clothes will be ready after four tomorrow afternoon."

When the woman left, I motioned Theresa through the door that led to the plant. I knew she would remember Kate, who frequently came into the cleaners late in the afternoon after she closed her own store.

"Look," I said, "if anyone should come in with the ticket for Kate Bosworth's order, I want you to come and get me or Mack at once."

Theresa looked puzzled. "I thought the rule was that a customer's entitled to an order if he has a ticket for it. It's only when people don't have their tickets and we don't know them that we're supposed to check on their ID."

I hoped my voice wouldn't shake as I tried to explain. "Kate's dead. . . ." I had to turn away until I could get myself under control. "Someone killed her, and I believe it had something to do with that order she brought in Monday."

"That can't be true." Theresa drew back from me, and her round face began to crumple.

"I'm afraid it is." I was trying hard not to crumple too.

"That's terrible." She gasped suddenly. "That wasn't the dress that was in the hatbox, was it? The one that was supposed to be on a shelf with our household items, not on the conveyor?"

"Yes, that's the one."

"My God, Mandy, some man came in with the ticket Monday night just before we closed and tried to pick up the dress. He got really angry when I said it wasn't ready."

CHAPTER 4

The one thing I hadn't expected was that someone might already have tried to pick up the dress. I'd just assumed that the order wouldn't have been in the plant if someone had come in with the ticket. Thank God, the dress was still being cleaned when the man tried to get it, and I said another prayer for the fact that I'd finally fortified the building so that it was as secure as the bank down the street.

"You're sure it was Monday?" I asked.

Theresa nodded. "Yes, because I was going out for dinner that night, and I was anxious to close up. The man came in just a few minutes before seven."

"What did he say exactly?"

"That he was picking up a dress for Kate. He knew her name, and he had the ticket. When I told him it wasn't ready, he got upset, said we advertised one-hour service so why the hell wasn't it ready. I told him that some of the antique gowns Kate brought in took longer and suggested that he come back at the end of the week. I even offered to call you at home and let him talk to you, but he stormed out the door. I locked up just behind him."

I took a deep breath. "What did he look like?"

Theresa closed her eyes as if trying to conjure him up in her mind. "Well, he wasn't very scary. I remember that. Even when he got so mad, I wasn't really frightened of him."

"Good, but what did he look like?" Fortunately we urge our counter people to try to memorize something about a new customer, a tag so they'll remember the person the next time he or she comes in. Ordinarily, Theresa was good at it and must know ninety percent of our customers by name.

She opened her eyes. "Oh, Mandy, I don't know. He was kind of ordinary. Light brown hair, maybe my height, five-seven, and medium build. I think he had on jeans and a Rockies T-shirt."

Well, that narrowed it down—a Rockies T-shirt! Now that baseball season was in full swing, half the people in Denver wore Colorado Rockies logos on their clothes.

"Isn't there anything that was distinctive about him?"

Theresa looked upset. "I think maybe he needed a haircut."

"Okay, maybe you'll be able to think of something later, but I need to call the police and let them know about him. I'm sure they'll want to talk to you."

She nodded, and I went back to my office and called Detective Reilly. I left a message on his voice mail and told him about the customer who'd shown up with the ticket Monday night.

"I'm sorry about the description," I said to the recording, "but at least, this might help establish the time of death." I started to lose it on that last sentence and hung up without saying good-bye.

I needed to talk to a real live person, not some recorded voice. At the same time I had to maintain some semblance of dignity with my front-counter personnel. I returned to the call office, where, between customers, I managed to alert my other afternoon employee, Elaine, about the missing ticket. I flagged the order on the computer with a message to call Mack or me if anyone came in with the ticket.

There were no customers for the moment, and I turned to the women. "If Mack and I aren't around, push the panic button."

I was referring to the alarm button I'd had installed behind our counter as the result of a rash of robberies of dry cleaners around the Denver area. In case of a holdup, employees had orders to give the robber whatever he demanded and offer no resistance, but, at the same time, to press the button, which was hooked into our burglar-alarm system and sent a warning to our security company.

"You should try to keep the person at the counter until the police arrive," I continued, "and even if you can't, he might still be in the neighborhood if you can alert the police."

Elaine's jaw dropped, and I followed her eyes to the door. As if by magic, a patrol car had just pulled up outside and a policeman was getting out.

"I'm Officer Langley," he said when he came into the call office. "Detective Reilly asked me to talk to a Mandy Dyer. It's about a witness to a possible murder suspect."

"I'm Mandy," I said and introduced him to Theresa. "She's the one who talked to the customer."

"Is there someplace where I can take her statement?" the policeman asked.

I escorted them to my office with the intention of staying. Unfortunately the cop didn't want me in the room. Once again I was left without anyone to talk to.

I went to the break room, where there was another telephone, and called Mack. He answered on the third ring.

Thank God he was home and his answering machine didn't pick up.

"It's Mandy," I said, running my hands through my hair and hoping I could hold myself together long enough to tell him about Kate. "Remember how I was going to take Kate's dress to her this afternoon? When I got there, I found her body, Mack. Someone had killed her."

There was a stunned silence on the line. "Are you all right?" Mack asked finally.

"Don't you understand?" I could feel myself slumping in the chair. "Kate's dead." I didn't even give him time to respond. "And listen, Mack, she had the top of one of our tickets in her hand. I think someone killed her for that dress she brought in to be cleaned."

"Dear God." There was a sharp intake of breath. "What—how did she die?"

"Someone strangled her." I felt as if I were choking too as I strained to get out the words.

"Look, why don't I come over to your apartment? Are you home now?"

I glanced at my watch. "I'm still at work, but I should be there soon, and I'd appreciate the company."

"I'll grab a pizza from the Leaning Tower on the way."

I didn't want anything to eat, especially Italian food, not when I thought about the dinner Kate and I had scheduled at Luigi's for Saturday night. But I didn't refuse. Mack had to eat, and he loved the fare at his neighborhood pizzeria.

I sat up straighter in the chair when I saw Elaine at the break-room entrance.

"I locked the front door, and I'm leaving now," she said. "You coming too?"

I covered the mouthpiece. "No, I'll wait until Theresa gets through talking to the police."

Apparently Mack heard me. "The police? What are they doing there."

I waved good-bye to Elaine and went back to Mack. "Theresa says somebody came in Monday night with the ticket for the dress. The police are interviewing her about it now."

"Why don't I just come down and pick you up?"

"No, no." I squirmed in my seat. "I'll be home as soon as they're through, but Mack, you went with Kate to look for costumes a few times, didn't you? I wondered if she had regular rounds she made to flea markets as well as garage sales."

"I doubt it. I think she probably just hit the sales that sounded interesting."

"Well, she said she found the dress last weekend, and I think that might have had something to do with why she was killed. But do flea markets and garage sales have stuff like that? The dress was obviously valuable, and she said she got it for a steal."

"That's what those things are all about, Mandy. Finding something that's worth a lot more than what you paid for it."

"But do they even have clothes at flea markets?" I asked.

"Sure, they do, Mandy, but you're not going to start sticking your nose in where it doesn't belong again, are you?"

I heard the door to my office open. "Hold on a minute, will you, Mack?" I smoothed back my hair and went out into the plant. "Anything I can help you with, Officer?"

"No, that should do it," he said, closing his notebook. "If anyone comes in with the ticket again, call us immediately."

Theresa looked downcast. "I'm sorry I couldn't give you a better description of the man."

"That's okay, ma'am. I'll just let myself out." He started to the front of the building.

"I'm afraid we've closed for the night. Why don't you just

go on home too, Theresa. You can show him out the back door."

She left reluctantly, and I went back to the phone.

"Did you hear what I was saying?" Mack yelled. "Stay out of it, Mandy."

I began to ruffle my hair again. "But someone killed Kate, and I can't help feeling that we're somehow involved."

"What did Theresa say the guy looked like?"

"That's the trouble. Medium height, medium build, light brown hair."

"So if you want to be of help, why don't you get together with her and try to draw a picture from her description?"

"Oh, I don't know."

"That sketch you did last winter for the police was so good, someone said you ought to be a police sketch artist."

"Yes, but that was different," I argued. "I knew what the person looked like. I don't know if I could do a sketch from someone else's description, especially of someone nondescript."

"Try. Maybe that'll keep you out of trouble."

"Okay, I'll think about it, and I'll see you soon."

Despite my misgivings, I could feel myself taking on some much-needed energy. I was on my feet even before I hung up the phone. Theresa and I could at least try a sketch. But Mack's idea wasn't going to divert me from exploring the flea-market/garage-sale angle.

I dialed the phone and called Nat at his desk at the *Trib*. I reached his voice mail, but this time I didn't care. That's what those message machines are good for—relaying information and making requests.

"Nat, please stop by tonight. It doesn't matter how late it is, and will you bring me copies of the *Trib* for Friday through Sunday of last week?" As long as I'd already told him about the dress, I continued, "I want to check out the garage sales and see if I can find out where Kate found the dress. Thanks."

I hung up and went to get the suit jacket that I hadn't bothered to put on when I left for Kate's earlier. I grabbed my purse and was just starting out of my office when the phone rang. I figured it was Nat and grabbed it, not bothering to answer with our standard business greeting.

"Is this Dyer's Cleaners?" a man's voice asked.

I said it was.

"I'm trying to reach Mandy Dyer?"

"This is Mandy." The voice definitely wasn't Nat's.

"You may not remember me. I'm Evan Carmody, a friend of Kate Bosworth's."

Yes, I thought, and the silent partner who'd wanted her to buy back his share of the business.

"I was just over at her shop, and I found out what happened. A neighbor said you found the body and called the police."

"That's right." I waited for him to continue, but there was silence on the other end of the line as if he expected me to say something.

Finally he cleared his throat. "I'm in a state of shock, and I wonder if I could come by your cleaners and talk to you for a few minutes."

"I'm sorry, we're closed, but . . ." Should I wait around the cleaners to see what he wanted, I wondered? It didn't seem like a good idea now that I was alone in the plant, and besides, Mack would be arriving at my apartment before long. "Maybe we could just discuss this on the phone."

"What if I come to your house? I won't take up much of your time."

I thought about it for a minute and then agreed. Mack would be there, after all, and I was sure he would be as curious as I was about Carmody. I gave the man my address and told him to stop by about eight-thirty. That should give me time to straighten up the place and fill Mack in about Carmody's connection to Kate.

But try as I might, I couldn't figure out what Carmody would want that couldn't be discussed on the telephone.

CHAPTER 5

When I started up the final flight of stairs to my third-floor apartment near downtown Denver, I realized there was someone at my door already. I figured it was Mack, but when I got closer, I could tell by the silhouette that it wasn't. The man was too thin, and besides, there was no pizza box in his hand.

"Hello, I'm Evan Carmody," he said as I reached the landing. "I'm sorry I'm early, but I was in the neighborhood."

"We've already met," I said.

Frankly I couldn't imagine him in this neighborhood. Granted, a lot of young white-collar workers live in the old houses in the area, now converted into apartment buildings, but it has a reputation for being a high-crime area. In his expensive-looking suit, he seemed distinctly out of place on my landing; he seemed to belong in a Cherry Hills mansion or one of the fancy lofts that were a part of the redevelopment of Lower Downtown, where the old skid row used to be. He owned a couple of high-priced dress salons and had invested in Kate's business, she'd said, because he was interested in the history of fashion.

The man was just as handsome and sophisticated-looking as I remembered. All except for the bump on the bridge of his nose that had left his sharp Roman features slightly askew. I forgot about the broken nose, however, when I looked at the rest of him. He was tall and slender, with a touch of gray at the temples of his dark hair that matched the gray of his Armani suit. And his blue shirt was the same blue as the handkerchief sticking out of his breast pocket. So why did someone who could afford an Armani suit want to take his money out Kate's business?

I invited him in reluctantly. It wasn't that I was ashamed to let this elegant man see my apartment, which has all the ambience of an artist's garret. I love my apartment, even though it's just one big room. It has a skylight and lots of windows and makes a great studio for the rare times I can pursue my painting. I just wished Evan didn't have to see it with an unmade bed. I knew I should have put my Hide-A-Bed back together that morning when I left for work. The sheets and blankets were in a heap on top, and a few clothes were scattered on the floor beside it.

"I overslept this morning," I said, and was immediately irritated at myself for apologizing for the condition of the room. After all, he'd invited himself here, and had shown up early besides.

I went over and started to smooth down the blankets so I could push the bed back into its framework, but the chore was complicated by the fact that my long-haired yellow cat chose that moment to jump up on the pile of bedding.

"Get off, Spot," I yelled.

Spot's name was my uncle Chet's idea of dry-cleaning humor, and the cat with the disposition from hell ignored my command. I grabbed for him, but he deftly moved aside so that I almost fell flat on my face on the bed. I lifted myself up with as much dignity as I could muster and threw one of the blankets over him. I hoped he'd scoot out from under it and flee, but instead he hunkered down. When I removed the blanket, his haunches began to quiver as if he were about to attack a bird. But of course he didn't attack because Spot and I had never quite mastered the art of playful combat.

I started to fold up the bed, hoping he would jump off it and run into his closet retreat, but he dug his claws into the sheet and hung on for dear life. I was sorely tempted to shut him in the bed, but I finally decided the only surefire way to get him down was to lure him with food.

I tossed my purse on the floor. "You'll have to excuse me for a minute," I said, starting to the cabinet under the kitchen sink. "I have to get some food for—" Just then there was a knock on the door. "Oh, darn." I changed directions.

"It's just me," Mack said, holding the pizza box out toward me as soon as I opened the door.

"Come on in." I stepped aside to let him enter, but he stopped when he saw that I already had a visitor. I introduced the two men. "Evan was Kate's partner," I explained.

Carmody, who was still standing, nodded curtly. "I just stopped by to see if Mandy could tell me anything about what happened. I'm still in shock."

"We all are," I said. "Mack knew her too."

Mack was holding the pizza as if he didn't know what to do with it.

"Why don't you both have a seat." I motioned to the table and chairs that were across a counter from my minuscule kitchen, then checked on Spot, who was now bristled up on the bed, ready to bare his claws if anyone came near him. "I have to feed my cat before I do anything else," I said, proceeding to the kitchen, where I grabbed a can of Friskies tuna from underneath the sink and began to open it with my electric can opener.

That did the trick. As soon as Spot heard the electric

hum, he jumped down from the bed and padded over to his food bowl, but when I looked around, Mack had taken the cat's place at the foot of the open bed. Mack usually sat on the sofa when he came to my apartment, and I guess he'd decided he had a proprietary right to it, whether it was folded up or not.

I gave Spot some of the food, using the lid as a spoon. When I was through, there was nothing for it but to go over to Mack and tell him to move.

"Mack, why don't you put the pizza on the table?"

He was eyeing the stranger as suspiciously as Spot had eyed the lot of us. "Here." He handed me the box instead.

"Get off the bed," I said in a loud whisper that probably resounded around the room.

"Oh."

He moved over beside Carmody while I shoved the bed back into its day-mode, the heap of blankets and the stray clothing all stuffed inside. I slammed the cushions on top in a haphazard fashion, then straightened my skirt, tucked in my blouse, and joined my visitors at the table. So much for my housekeeping and attention to good grooming.

"Now, what was it you wanted?" I asked.

"I just wondered what happened to Kate," Carmody said. "I've been out of town since Sunday, but I talked to her just before I left and she was all right. Can you tell me anything?"

"I went over to visit her and found her body in the bedroom of her apartment. That's all I really know."

"How did it happen? Was she shot?"

"Someone strangled her. . . ."

I looked over at Mack, who was shaking his head and compressing his lips into a tight little bow. If we'd been playing Charades, I'd have said he was trying to act out "Zip your lip."

Carmody folded his hands in front of him on the table. "But who would want to kill Kate? She was such a loving, caring person."

I shook my head.

"When I talked to her before I left Sunday night, she'd been excited about a dress she'd just bought over the weekend. She wanted me to do some research on it for her."

Mack tensed on the other side of the table.

"Do you think that could have had something to do with her being killed?" I asked.

"Would anyone like a slice of pizza?" Mack opened the box and passed it around. I had a hunch he'd decided the only way to keep me quiet was to stuff my face with food.

Evan waved him off just as he did my question. "I was flying to New York that night, and I told her I'd talk to her when I returned today."

"Are you talking about the Fortuny?" I could see Mack's face. It was set in a permanent frown now, but I ignored it.

Carmody gave me a penetrating look.

"Well, I'm going to have a slice of pizza even if no one else does," Mack said. "I'll get us some plates in case anyone changes their mind."

"She told me about the dress too," I explained. "Do you know where she found it?"

"Sorry, no. She didn't really go into any of the details, just asked me to try to find out some of its history. I don't know if you know anything about Mariano Fortuny, but he supervised every detail of the production at his studio and later at a factory in Venice. However, to avoid paying a luxury import tax, he eventually entrusted a friend, Elsie Lee, to assemble dresses for the American market in New York from cut fabric. Kate wondered if those gowns would be worth as much as the earlier ones from Venice and how she could tell the difference."

"So did you see the dress?" I asked as Mack returned to the table with the plates.

"No, no," Carmody said. "In fact I was wondering if you have it. Kate said she was bringing it to you the next day to be cleaned because it had a spot on it."

Spot, the cat, hearing his name, came over to the table, swishing his tail across the pant legs of Carmody's suit and probably leaving a trail of cat hairs in his wake.

"I—" I tried to swat Spot's tail away as I decided what to say. Spot retaliated with a swat of his own. It went awry, and he snagged the leg of Carmody's expensive suit. "Oh, my God, I'm sorry. . . ." I reached down to try to extract Spot's claw. Carmody had already done it for me, but there was the telltale sign of Spot's wrath. A thread had been pulled out of the fabric. "Look, I'm really sorry." I got up and stomped my foot at Spot. "Bad cat." He took off in a huff as I resumed my seat. "Please, Evan, if you'll bring the pants into us, I'll have our seamstress fix it. She can fix it just like new."

Carmody frowned and shrugged off the offer. He was a man with a mission. "As I was saying, I was wondering if you might have the dress."

"Uh—no, I don't." Carmody had obviously realized I knew about the dress all along, so it was just as well I'd mentioned it earlier, despite Mack's frowns. "We cleaned it, but you know Kate. She wanted us to do a one-hour special for her. She hung around the store for a while and we talked."

I guess that was convoluted enough that Evan assumed she'd waited for it to be cleaned. Was I getting good at deception or what? In fact I was beginning to think I might have a gift of misdirecting and misleading without actually lying. It was a skill I'd developed lately to hide the fact that I'm a lousy liar with a tendency to itch when I do.

But the truth is I didn't want to say anything more in case

the police had decided not to reveal the information about the dress for a while. That, of course, was assuming that Nat, the loosest lip in the West, could be dissuaded from using the information in tomorrow's *Trib*. I should never have told him about the dress, even in the heat of stress, and I wasn't making the same mistake twice.

Instead I changed the subject. "You probably saw a lot more of Kate than I did, and I was wondering if you knew anyone who might have done this to her."

Carmody unclasped his hands, almost as if he was relieved I wasn't pursuing anything about the dress either. "Well, there was one boyfriend I met recently—a young man who seemed harmless enough. However, one time when I went over to the store about a month ago, she was wearing dark glasses, and when I asked her about it, she said some merchandise fell off a shelf and hit her in the face. She showed me the black eye, but I always wondered if the boyfriend gave it to her."

"What was his name? Do you remember?"

"Michael something. If I think of the last name, I'll let you know."

"I wish you would, and you should tell the police too."

Carmody nodded. "I'm not sure if she broke up with him after that, but I never saw him around there again."

Just then there was another knock on the door. This time it was Nat's signature knock—*dum-da-da-dum*. I hadn't thought he would show up until after he got off work at ten o'clock. We were fast becoming a party I wasn't sure I wanted to host.

I went over and opened the door. Nat was still in the same rumpled, wash-and-wear clothes he'd had on earlier in the day—a corduroy jacket, polyester shirt, and jeans, the antithesis of what a dry cleaner's friend should be.

He gave me a big hug. "I'm sorry about Kate."

"I know."

"I brought you the papers from last weekend so you can check out the garage sales."

I wasn't sure that was something I wanted to share with my other guests. I pushed him back so that he could see that we weren't alone. "Here's Mack, and this is Evan Carmody. He was another friend of Kate's."

Nat must have caught my nervousness at his earlier remark. "Hey, do I see pizza over there? I could go for some of that. I haven't had anything to eat all day."

"Sure," I said, trying to find my Martha Stewart voice. "Wouldn't you like some too, Evan?"

He looked from Nat to me. "No, but thanks anyway. I really didn't mean to take up so much of your time." He was on his feet by then, and I escorted him to the door.

"What did he want?" Nat asked as soon as Carmody left. The smell of his expensive aftershave lingered in the room.

"He was a silent partner in Kate's business, and he said he wanted to find out what happened to her," I said. "But I think he was looking for the dress. Once I said I didn't have it, he lost interest."

Nat squirmed in his seat. "How'd he know about the dress? The police want to keep it under wraps, and although it's against all my journalistic principles, I decided to go along with it—because of Kate."

I sat down, prepared to have the last piece of pizza before someone else took it. "Kate told him about the dress before he went out of town last Sunday."

I must have sounded skeptical because Mack nodded in agreement. "And didn't you think the gentleman protested too much about being in New York all week?"

Yes, and I couldn't help remembering how Kate had said

she should never have gotten involved with Evan in the first place. Was he projecting his own actions when he'd said that a boyfriend beat her up?

Before I had a chance to express my thoughts, there was another knock on the door. I jumped guiltily, afraid Carmody had returned and overheard our suspicions about him.

I put my fingers to my lips and hurried to the door, but instead of Carmody it was Stan Foster on the other side of the threshold. The thought that he'd heard our conversation was almost as bad as if Carmody had. He was a homicide detective, after all, with a pet peeve about civilians messing in police investigations.

For the moment, though, his face was filled with concern. "Are you all right?" he asked, worry lines making little darts between his eyebrows. "I just got back to town and heard about your friend and how you found the body."

So there hadn't been any chance of him being assigned to the case. He'd been out of town on one of those mysterious trips he took on his days off—the ones he never discussed. Only men who were tall, dark, and handsome were supposed to have mysterious pasts. Stan went against type. He was tall, blond, and handsome, and whatever it was that made him secretive also made him keep a certain distance in our relationship.

Until today, finding out what was behind his caution in our relationship had been a top priority on my list of things to do. Now finding out who murdered Kate took precedence, and all I wanted was to shed a few tears on his shoulder and have him hug me and tell me everything would be okay. But not in front of other people.

"I'm holding up," I said, motioning to the dynamic duo at my kitchen table who, unfortunately, looked as if they'd been caught in the middle of planning some clandestine activity. "Mack and Nat knew her too."

Unfortunately Stan had never met her, just heard me talk about her. But he did know my two closest friends, and he looked at them as if they were the Hardy Boys being lured into yet another undercover caper by the Nancy Drew of dry cleaners.

"Want a piece of pizza?" I asked, leading him to the chair recently vacated by Carmody.

He grabbed the piece that Nat and Mack hadn't eaten and put it on a plate.

"Has Detective Reilly found out anything more about Kate's murder?" I asked, knowing even as I posed the question that Stan wouldn't tell me anything Reilly hadn't.

Nat leaned forward in his chair, just in case the detective would impart some information, but Stan shook his head. He stopped with the wedge of pizza halfway to his mouth and stared at the classified section of the newspapers that Nat had brought me. I thought he was probably just mulling over what to say, but in case he was wondering about the week-old classifieds, I slipped the pile of papers off the table and put them on the counter behind me.

I don't think the newspapers raised Stan's suspicions as much as my furtive action to get rid of them. His blue eyes bore into me. "Be careful what you do, Mandy. Detective Reilly isn't as nice a guy as I am, and he doesn't take kindly to people messing in his cases."

I nodded, and Mack rose across the table from me. "I guess I'd better get going. I'll see you at work tomorrow morning."

Nat, however, had settled in for the long haul. By the time I got back from showing Mack to the door and thanking him for his moral support, Nat was at the refrigerator, helping himself to a beer.

"That's your last beer," he announced as he pulled the tab on it and came back to the table.

Nat had been responsible for bringing Stan and me together, as well he should have, after first misleading the detective into believing that he and I were live-in lovers. And he was willing to let the relationship develop, free from his prying eyes, but not tonight. Not when something might be said that would be grist for tomorrow's paper.

I guess Stan could see that Nat was in no hurry to leave, so, after finishing the wedge of pizza, he got up. "Look, Mandy, I'm really wiped out, and I have to get home and walk Sidearm. Okay?"

"Sure," I said as Nat nodded his approval, pleased that he'd outlasted everyone.

"Look, I'm really sorry about your friend," Stan said when I walked him to the door. "Want to have dinner tomorrow night and we can talk about it?"

"Fine," I said, knowing he wouldn't kiss me in front of Nat.

There were a lot of problems in this relationship, not the least of which was Sidearm, Stan's dog, who hated me.

I looked back at Nat, who was sipping his beer and staring at us. Was he wondering at the exact nature of my relationship with Stan? Maybe I should have him dig into the question of Stan's mysterious disappearances on his days off. I was shocked at myself that I'd even think of siccing Nat on something that was my personal problem.

That's when I kicked out the ace reporter and went to bed. I was exhausted, but I couldn't sleep. I wanted to cry, but I couldn't get the tears out. All I felt was anger and an overwhelming need to find Kate's killer.

CHAPTER 6

"If everything else fails, push the panic button," I said to my morning counter people about the procedures to follow if another person came in with the ticket for Kate's dress.

Ann Marie, who's the youngest member of the crew, began to giggle as if I'd asked her to go ballistic on me. Julia, her more mature partner on the morning shift, tried to hide a smile, but Lucille, who helps out at the counter only if we get busy, was on my side. She didn't think the remark was funny.

"Please, Ann Marie," I said. "Do you have to laugh every time I mention the panic button?"

Ann Marie was still giggling, and to tell the truth, I'd thought it was funny the first time I'd heard the security people call the warning device a panic button, but I didn't have much sense of humor today.

"At any rate," I continued, "if someone comes in with the ticket for Kate's dress again, try to stall him. Come back in the plant as if you're looking for the dress and notify me or Mack. We'll call the police."

I'd already checked with the three women to see if they remembered anyone else coming in with Kate's ticket after the incident on Monday night that Theresa had told me about. I didn't think anyone had returned a second time because the gown had been on the shelf in its special little box since Tuesday afternoon, when we'd finished cleaning it.

"You'll have to keep the person at the counter until the police arrive," I concluded. "Do you understand?"

"Yes," Julia said, now under control.

Ann Marie nodded and bit her lip in an effort to suppress her amusement. Lucille gave a tight little movement of her head and asked if she could go back to marking in the clothes. She doesn't like dealing with customers and always get a little surly when she's out front.

I told her she could go, and we both went through the door to the plant. I'd already talked to Mack, and he said he'd call the police in the event I wasn't around when and if someone showed up again about the dress. Frankly I thought it was about as likely to happen as the return of the bustle to the fashion scene, but I figured we should be prepared for all possibilities.

When I reached my office, I called Nat. "I was wondering if you'd like to go around to the garage sales and flea markets with me tomorrow."

"So you're really going to pursue this, huh?" Nat asked.

"Yes, and you're the only person I thought might go with me. Mack sure won't."

"Foster won't like it either."

I didn't even want to think about Stan's admonition to me to stay out of the investigation. "So what about it, Nat? Want to meet me here at the plant about eight in the morning?"

"You have to be kidding. Right? Me get up early on my day off."

"But you'll do anything to get a scoop," I said, knowing that was his weak spot.

"Seriously I'd like to go, but I'm going out of town on a follow-up to a story I did recently. The only time the person can see me is tomorrow."

"You aren't just saying that so you can sleep late, are you?"

"No, I'm really going out of town."

"What is it? Something about that woman who was killed up in the mountains during a break-in?" That's the only article I could remember him doing recently that was outside of Denver, and the only reason I remembered it was that she'd lived in a castle.

"Hey, I don't talk about my stories until they're in the paper."

"Okay, if that's the way you want to be about it." I changed the subject. "Is there anything new about Kate's murder?"

"The police think the time of death was sometime early Monday evening, and they're looking for a black pickup that was reportedly seen at her place."

That's what I'd already concluded, based on the time the man appeared here at the cleaners with the ticket and what the doll doctor had told me. Maybe I should talk to the doll doctor again and see if he'd remembered any more about the truck.

Nat signed off with his usual "Ciao," and I decided to leave the doll doctor until later. The main thing on my agenda for this afternoon was to get together with Theresa when she came to work and see if we could come up with a sketch of her mysterious customer Monday night.

I was pulling the sketch pad and pencils that I'd brought from home out of my purse when the phone rang.

"This is Evan Carmody again," the caller said when I identified myself. "I found something I thought you might be interested in."

I waited for him to continue, still suspicious of his motives.

"I thought maybe we could discuss it over lunch someplace in Cherry Creek."

I didn't really want to leave the plant when we were on Red Alert with the panic button. "Couldn't you just tell me over the phone?" I asked the way I had the night before.

"No, I have something I want to give you."

My curiosity won out over reason. "Okay, what time do you want to go?"

"How about twelve-thirty? I'll stop by at your shop."

Luckily I'd worn my best crushed-silk blouse and brown suit. They weren't even wrinkled yet. Maybe I'd still look like a halfway suitable companion for the Armani man by lunch.

"Mandy!" Ann Marie's eyes were like large round buttons as she ran into my office. "Someone's out there with the ticket, and he wants the dress."

I'd been planning to ask Carmody some more about what he'd found, but it would have to wait. I covered the mouthpiece of the phone. "Stall him," I said to Ann Marie, and went back to Carmody, "I have to go now. I'll see you at twelve-thirty."

When I hung up, I realized Ann Marie was still standing at the door. "Hurry, and just remember what I said: Go back out there and tell him someone is looking for the order, but it will take a few minutes. By the way, it is a *he*, isn't it?"

Ann Marie nodded.

"I'll call the police." I picked up the phone.

She seemed glued to the floor, unable to move.

I covered the mouthpiece as I tapped in 911. "Get out

there, will you?" I fanned the air to indicate that she should get moving.

"But he's just a—a kid. You know, like junior high."

That surprised me, but it didn't change anything. A dispatcher came on the line, and I gave her the information about the kid and the ticket for Kate's dress. "I'll try to keep him here until the police arrive," I said. Fortunately Ann Marie had disappeared when I hung up.

I detoured by Mack's spotting board. When I told him the situation, he put down his steam gun. "I'll go around on the outside of the building and stop him at the door if he tries to leave."

"Good." I hurried to the front of the building, but met Ann Marie when I was halfway there. "He's getting—like, really nervous," she said. "What'll I do now?"

I had to think fast. "Well, I guess we'd better give him a dress since that's what he came for. Tell him we've found it, and someone's bringing it up to you. I'll be there in a minute."

Ann Marie went back to the counter, and now I had to find a dress. I wasn't about to give him a customer's dress and risk losing it; I decided I'd better give him something of mine. I checked the computer to find the location of my own cleaning. Good, I had a blue linen dress and a beige suit. The dress was even the right color for the Fortuny. I started the conveyor and ran it until I found the correct slot and yanked my order off. I'd be darned if I'd risk losing two outfits, since I was woefully short of good work clothes as it was. I scooted the suit out from under the poly garment bag, set it aside, and ripped off my ticket before I headed for the counter with the dress.

"Here it is," I said, trying to smile nonchalantly at the boy, who looked like an underaged paramilitarist. He was wearing a khaki T-shirt, a baggy pair of camouflage pants, and combat boots, and his hair was cut about an inch from the scalp all over his head. "That'll be eight-fifty, but I wonder if you'd take a look at the dress to see if you're satisfied that we got the stains out."

"It was supposed to be in a box," the kid said.

"Oh, I'm sorry. We always package our garments on hangers. The only thing we put in boxes is our shirts if the customer wants them folded."

"But I think—uh—Mom had a box for it when she brought it here."

"I'm sorry. Let me go back and check with my cleaner to see if he knows what happened to it."

"Naw, that's okay." He started to take the dress from the rail where I'd hung it.

I held on to it. "About the stain. We always ask the customer to inspect the garment to make sure he's satisfied with the work before he leaves."

I could see the kid was getting even more edgy now than he'd been before. I started to lift the bag to let him inspect the dress, but as I did so, I let go of the hanger. He snatched the dress and took off. I should have been more careful, but fortunately Mack was waiting outside the door. He grabbed the kid, who began kicking and screaming.

"Help, somebody," the boy yelled. "I'm being mugged."

I was afraid a passerby would come to the kid's aid once people saw him being attacked by a big black man. Never mind that he looked like an escapee from an army stockade for delinquent teenagers. I joined the fray and was smacked in the nose for my efforts.

"Dammit," Mack screamed as he let go of the mini-Rambo.

The boy took off, and since the police hadn't arrived yet, there was nothing for it but that Mack and I take off after him. No way was I going to lose him. This was no time to be concerned with image. I hiked up my skirt in order to run at full speed.

"The stupid kid hit me," Mack puffed, and the way he was running doubled over, I had a good idea where the blow had landed.

As the kid sprinted ahead of us, the garment bag with my dress inside floated out behind him like a sky-blue sail covered in Handi-Wrap. I think it may have slowed him down a little, but Mack and I were falling behind.

The boy raced up our side street toward Second Avenue and what's called Cherry Creek North—a bunch of upscale shops that go with the fancy mall nearby. He turned the corner and ran west on the sidewalk, then darted across the next intersection on a red light, narrowly avoiding being hit by a couple of cars. I ignored the red light too, but luckily, the cars had already come to a screeching halt for the kid, so I made it across the street in one piece. He swung south. I was afraid he was heading for the mall, where I'd lose him for sure. Instead he ducked into a parking garage. By the time I got there, I could just make out the blue dress sailing over his close-cropped head as he headed for the ramp that led to the second level.

I was afraid I'd never catch him now, not if I had to keep up with him on the incline. Luckily he seemed to be running out of steam himself, and I still had him in view when he reached the second floor of the garage. I was puffing so hard, it felt as if my lungs were being pulled out of my chest with a pair of pliers, but I kept going. Mack was somewhere behind me.

Midway up the ramp I could see the boy come to a stop by the second-floor railing. He handed my dress to a man who was waiting there, but the guy didn't fit Theresa's description of Monday night's visitor. He was a big dark-haired guy with a swarthy complexion—at least from what I could see of him from a distance, and he wasn't planning to let me get any closer. He took one look at the dress, threw it down, and disappeared from view.

I was almost at the top of the ramp by then, and I had to make a choice—the guy who'd rejected my dress or the kid playing G.I. Joe. I took off after the man, but not before I saw the kid run over to the elevator and squeeze into it behind a young couple and a little girl.

I leaned over the railing and yelled at Mack. "He's in the elevator, and it's coming down."

Mack nodded and turned around.

I thought I'd lost the man for a moment between all the parked cars, but I finally spotted him. He was just getting into a black pickup with big wheels on it like the ones the doll doctor had seen at Kate's Monday night. I headed toward the truck, but I figured the best I could do was slow it down and get the license number as he drove past me.

He backed out of the parking space, put the truck in first gear, and hit the gas pedal, aiming right at me. I moved to one side to let him pass but with my eyes fixed on the license plate, ready for the numbers to come into focus.

The driver veered toward me. I started to jump between two parked cars when suddenly, from out of nowhere, someone hurtled toward me.

"Watch out," a man yelled. He tackled me at shoulder level, and we seemed to fly through the air, landing on the hood of a BMW. The truck's license number was forever unrecorded because the Good Samaritan had his body rammed into my back.

"Good thing I came along right then," he said. "You could have been killed by that crazy driver. It was like he didn't even see you."

Of course the guy who'd saved me could have killed me too when he pinned me to the hood of the car. He lifted himself off my bruised body. That's when I saw the make of the car and its metal emblem. If my face had been squashed against the grillwork, I'm sure the name would forever have been embedded in my forehead.

"Are you okay?" he asked, squinting at me through half-closed eyes.

"I think so." I brushed myself off and thanked him, even though it was my opinion that I could have saved myself without his help. No need to go into that with someone who had been trying to do a good deed.

He stood back and took a better look at me through what Mom used to call "bedroom" eyes, but which I called sleepy instead. "Want me to go into one of the stores and see if we can get you some first aid?"

I shook my head and was glad that he wasn't a really big bruiser. In fact he was kind of skinny with short brownish-blond hair, and an alligator shirt and jeans. He didn't look like the hero type.

"No, I'll be all right," I said finally. "I'm just a little shaken."

"I think you skinned yourself when you landed."

That's when I realized I had a cut on my arm. It felt as if I might also have twisted my knee, and my nose was beginning to swell where the kid had sucker-punched me in the face.

"Thanks, though, for your help," I said and hobbled over to the railing. What else could I say to a man who'd been trying to save my life, even if I was now a whole lot worse for the wear than I'd been before? I moved my nose back and forth to see if it might be broken. I couldn't decide.

I looked down at the first floor and spotted Mack right away. He had attracted quite a crowd of people, who must have come out from inside one of the stores. He'd corralled the kid somehow and had him in a choke hold.

When I glanced back to my would-be savior to reassure him that I'd be all right, he'd disappeared. I limped around the corner to the ramp, noting with irritation that the guy in the truck had run over my dress, which was where he dropped it. Tire treads were on the plastic, and unfortunately they'd made a pattern on the dress where the plastic had fallen away from it. I decided to leave the dress where it was in case the police could get some tire prints from it that would help identify the truck and its driver.

By the time I reached the main floor, there was a security guard on the scene, and he was putting handcuffs on the boy. How Mack had been able to explain the situation to the security guard while holding the kid is more than I could understand, but comprehension isn't always necessary. I was just glad Mack had caught the kid.

Once the guard had the boy handcuffed, he took out his walkie-talkie and told command central to call the police.

The kid spotted me. "Hey, lady, I didn't mean no harm. Honest."

Oh, right, like I'm going to believe that. "Where did you get that ticket for the dress?" I asked, not feeling it was necessary to go into the fact that it wasn't even the right dress.

"Some guy said he'd pay me fifty bucks if I picked it up. I was going to pay you for it, but I got scared. I figured somethin' was wrong or he'd have gone and got it himself."

Smart of the boy to figure that out now. "What was the guy's name?"

"I don't know, lady. I swear. I never seen him before."

Unfortunately I couldn't pursue my interrogation. A uniformed cop arrived on the scene. I explained the situation to him about Kate's murder and the earlier visit to our cleaners by a man looking for the dress. "It didn't look like the same man, however," I added. "This guy was dark, and the other man supposedly had scraggly, light brown hair."

"Where's the dress?" the policeman asked.

I pointed to the second level. "It's not the right dress, and the man dropped it as soon as he saw it. Then he ran over it with his truck. It has some tire tracks on it that might help you identify the truck."

The policeman looked at me as if that were doubtful, but he went up the ramp to take possession of the dress.

I guess that's the risk you run when you use one of your own dresses as a decoy. The police would probably keep the dress longer than they'd hold the kid.

"Lady, why don't you tell 'em I didn't mean no harm?" the kid's voice trailed back to me as he was hauled away.

I went over to Mack. He was doubled up, still trying to get his breath or recover from being kneed. "Dammit," he said. "If I'd known this was part of the job description, I'd have gone into another line of work."

CHAPTER 7

We hobbled back to the cleaners like bruised and battered soldiers in the Revolutionary War. The only things missing were a fife and drum.

Mack was still out of breath and bent over. I hated to think of his wound. I was nursing my scraped arm and sprained knee, and my nose was beginning to swell. My hose were ripped, and my skirt was covered with dirt from being pushed into the hood of the BMW. You'd think a guy who owned a car like that would at least keep it clean.

What was worse, I had only forty-five minutes before my lunch with Evan Carmody. I grabbed my beige suit from the front of the plant where I'd set it aside when I tried to pawn off my dress on the kid, then continued to my office. Mack followed me.

On our way to the plant I'd given him a brief account of the guy in the pickup, but he wanted the unabridged version once we got to my office.

"Who was the Good Samaritan?" he asked when I reached that part of the story.

"What?"

"Who was the Good Samaritan?"

"Oh, damn," I said. "I should have found out, shouldn't I? Maybe he wasn't trying to be my savior after all. Maybe he was trying to keep me from seeing the license plate."

Mack nodded, but he didn't rub it in. I was doing enough mental lashing for both of us. He did insist on taking a look at my nose, wasting valuable seconds of my limited time. He agreed with me that my nose probably wasn't broken but suggested I put an ice pack on it to keep down the swelling.

I told him I'd do it when I returned from my lunch date. I was beginning to sound as if I had a head cold, and I wasn't sure he understood me.

Apparently he did. "Who you going out with? You never go out for lunch."

"I don't thin' tha's any of your concern," I answered with as much dignity as a person can muster when the inside of her nose is beginning to close shut.

"It's about Kate's murder, isn't it?"

"It's with Evan Carmody, if tha's what you mean. He said he had somethin' to show me." I escorted Mack out of my office and closed the door so that I could change into the suit. The good thing about owning a cleaners is that you always have something to wear. Just get it off the conveyor, and voilà, you're a whole new person. Unfortunately the bruises made a lie of the old axiom that clothes make the woman.

Beige—with a red blouse of mine that I'd found to go with the suit—didn't do a thing for me today or for the bulbous nose, which, I feared, would make me look like W. C. Fields in drag. On the bright side, maybe the damage could be used as a way of finding out how Carmody had broken his nose in his dark, distant past.

Once I was dressed, I took some ice out of the refrigerator in our break room and wrapped it in a clean towel from our rag pile. I actually had a few minutes to apply the cold pack, and I think it helped the swelling. The pain had subsided by the time Julia from the counter knocked on my door.

"Someone's here to see you," she yelled.

"I'll be right there." My voice sounded almost normal.

I took a quick check of my appearance in the employee restroom. The ice had brought out the red on my injured nose, giving me a Rudolph the Red-nosed Reindeer glow that I tried to cover up as best I could with an application of makeup. It was as good as it was going to get for the time being, so I ran a comb through my hair and set forth for my luncheon engagement.

Carmody looked as suave and debonair as he had the night before. This time his suit was a dark gray with a pale yellow shirt and a gray-and-yellow striped tie.

I tried not to limp too much as I walked around the counter and joined him in the customer area of the call office.

"Excuse me for asking, but are you all right?" he asked.

"Just a little accident." I touched my nose self-consciously. "I'll be fine."

He held the door for me. "I thought we could just walk someplace in the neighborhood, but let me drive my car around and get you."

I protested, thinking maybe it wasn't a wise idea to get in a car with a man who could be Kate's killer. He insisted, and my curiosity won out over caution.

I stood on the curb until a fire-red Ferrari pulled up beside me. Why didn't the guy just sell his car instead of calling in Kate's IOU if he was having a cash-flow problem?

I climbed inside, and he whisked us away to a fancy restaurant with valet service. No danger involved. He gave the keys to an attendant, took a briefcase from the car, and we went inside.

A hostess, whom he called by name, seated us quickly even though there were other people waiting. She gave us a huge menu but without any photographs of the food.

"You know, you ought to have your nose looked at by a doctor," he said. "I broke my nose playing racquetball one time, and it didn't heal properly. You see the results." He touched the knob on the ridge that I'd thought might give a hint to his criminal past. Instead it explained only his slender but well-conditioned physique.

And actually the nose added interest to his too-perfect features, but it disappointed me that a revealing story wasn't attached. That still didn't mean he wasn't a member of the Mafia, though.

"So what was it you wanted to talk to me about?" I asked.

Just then a waiter approached to see if we'd decided what we wanted. Neither one of us had looked at the menu, but Evan said he'd take a glass of Chardonnay and the veal scallopini. I said I'd take soup—whatever it was—and coffee. When Evan protested that I should order more than that, I had to confess that I wasn't even sure I could enjoy the soup. I didn't seem to be able to smell very well at the moment. Fortunately if I still smelled grungy after my skirmish with the dressnapper, I didn't know that either.

The waiter departed, and I repeated my question about the purpose of the luncheon.

"Well, as you already know, I was part owner of Kate's business," he said. "In any event the police took down the cordon and let me into the shop this morning. Of course they'd already gone over everything. I'm afraid the dress Kate told us about wasn't there, but I did find one thing of interest."

"What?" I hoped it was a receipt for the dress that would lead the cops to the killer, but I'm always overly optimistic.

"Here." He reached into the briefcase and pulled out

some pages from the newspaper. On top I could see the classifieds from the *Trib*. "They're from last Saturday's papers, and Kate had tied them up and taken them over to be recycled by her friend at the bookstore." He pointed to the ads. "Kate had apparently circled some of the garage sales that she planned to attend over the weekend."

There were indeed circles around half a dozen want ads on the page I could see.

"I thought you might be interested in following up on them," he said. "I overheard what your friend said last night, and I was hoping this would be of help."

"Thanks." I accepted the papers from him, but I couldn't help wondering if Kate had really circled the ads or if Evan had done it himself. What better way to send me off in the wrong direction than give me a guide to where she hadn't gone instead of where she had.

"I'd look into them myself," he said, "but I'm too busy this weekend, and frankly I can't imagine that the newspaper or the dress could have had anything to do with her death."

The waiter returned with Evan's wine and my coffee, and I waited until he left. "Did you make a copy of the ads for the police?"

Evan looked surprised. "No, it didn't occur to me."

"I'll see that they get it, then." I waited for him to say something, but when he didn't, I asked "So what do you think could have been a motive for someone to kill Kate?"

"I don't know, but I did remember the boyfriend's name— Michael Morrison—and of course I told the police about him." Before I had a chance to consider Kate's new boyfriend, Evan turned the question back on me. "Do you have any ideas about problems she was having?"

I shrugged, and was disappointed to note that my shoulder was getting sore where I'd been slammed into the hood of the car. By tomorrow I wondered if I'd be able to walk, much less tromp through the flea markets of Denver.

But I must admit that I was so convinced her murder had something to do with the dress that I hadn't really considered other possibilities. Except for her relationship with Evan himself.

"Actually," I said, thinking of the big love of her life, "she had a blowup with one boyfriend, Red Berry, but that was years ago. Did she ever mention him to you?"

Evan shook his head. "No, but that doesn't sound like a real name to me."

"It probably wasn't. He didn't even have red hair, but he had a band called Red Berry and the Sour Grapes." I took a deep breath, although it was hard to do because of my swollen nasal passages, and plunged ahead. "The two of you went out together for a while, didn't you?"

I watched him carefully, and he looked surprised. "Where on earth did you get that idea, Mandy? Kate and I had a strictly business relationship." If he was lying, his nose didn't even twitch the way mine does when I lie. Maybe now that I'd bashed it in, my nose would become as insensitive to lies as it seemed to be to smell.

I tried to look innocent. "I guess I just assumed you did. Kate said you wanted to end the relationship."

Evan laughed and took a sip of his wine, first sniffing it to savor its bouquet. "Oh, you mean because Kate was planning to buy out my share of the business?"

I nodded, taking heart from the fact that my sense of smell might also return someday.

"That was Kate's idea—not mine," he continued.

I was pretty sure he was lying now, but I had no way of proving it without any twitching or itching on his part. I made a mental note to check out Kate's will. I wondered if Kate had left everything to Evan in an agreement where the surviving partner inherits the business. But would that involve enough money to kill someone?

"So do you know if Kate was having any financial problems?" I asked, figuring I'd gone as far as I could on relationships.

"Well, like any new business, it didn't do very well at first, but it was beginning to turn a nice profit. That's why she wanted to buy out my interest." He paused. "You know, I think Kate said she had an appointment sometime over the weekend with a woman who wanted to sell some of her grandmother's old clothes. Maybe that's where she found the dress—not at a garage sale."

Could I be wrong about where she'd found the dress? Well, yes, but she'd said she found it "where you least expect it," and a prearranged appointment didn't sound as if it qualified. Maybe Evan was simply trying to misdirect my efforts in another way.

"Any idea what the woman's name was?"

"No, sorry. As I already mentioned, I wasn't involved in the day-to-day operation of the business."

Since he couldn't remember the woman's name, there didn't seem to be much else to say, but luckily our orders arrived right then, so I sampled my soup. Clam chowder, of course, because it was Friday. And I was right. I couldn't taste a thing, although in my nose's defense, clam chowder has never seemed especially flavorful to me.

"Personally I have the feeling that she found the dress through some private party who contacted her or at an estate sale somewhere," Evan continued as he sliced a piece of veal.

Why, oh why, hadn't I asked her at the time? All I had to

go on was that one vague statement Kate had made, and I didn't want Evan to confuse me with other options.

"So," I said, "you mentioned that Kate wanted you to research the Fortuny. What did you find out about it?"

Evan took a bite before answering, and I noticed that he ate in the European style, never transferring his fork to his right hand but using it upside down with his left instead. Was it affectation or did it imply a foreign background that wasn't apparent in his accent? I also noticed that he didn't have a wedding ring on his left hand, but that didn't mean he wasn't married.

"Well, the one thing I can tell you is that it was almost impossible to tell the year one of the dresses was made," he said finally. "Fortuny was an artist who thought of fashion as art, and he produced almost the identical dress—with only slight variations—for over forty years, although his factory was closed during World War Two. And he was never accepted by the couturiers of his time because, even then, the designers and the stores that sold their fashions would go out of business if the styles didn't change every year."

"I'm surprised he didn't change his design too," I said after swallowing a spoonful of soup.

"He wasn't a couturier, as I said before. He was an artist who appreciated the beauty of the human form. He thought it should be covered in something that wouldn't encumber the body and would allow for free movement."

I could relate to that. As a dry cleaner I sometimes became irritated myself by the changing styles every year. They made it a semiannual learning experience to find out how to clean the new fashions and fabrics.

I watched Evan take another underhanded bite with his fork before he continued. "The design of his gown coincided with a movement by the artists and aesthetes of the time to free the body from the strictures of the corset. There was even an organization called the Realistic Dress Society, which had its own publication and advocated a more liberating dress code for women both on the stage and in everyday life."

When I stopped to think about it, a rational dress society wasn't so hard to believe. Wasn't that part of women's lib back in the sixties when everyone was burning bras? Maybe we dry cleaners should have tried to organize consumers a few years back when designers came out with those beaded gowns—the ones that had little care labels like "Do Not Dry Clean. Hand Clean Only," or even worse: "Do Not Dry Clean. Do Not Wash." They might as well have said "Wear Once and Throw Away."

Evan shook his upside-down fork at me. "You might be interested in this. Fortuny and the woman who began to assemble the dresses for him in New York City actually asked that the dresses be shipped back to them for cleaning." He lowered the fork to stab a piece of zucchini squash. "At any rate, the members of the Realistic Dress Society even wanted to get rid of the tutu and the square-toed shoes of the ballerina, saying that they were inhumane. In fact there was a move afoot among dancers like Isadora Duncan to free them from the restraints of such clothes."

Isadora Duncan? That's who Kate had mentioned when I saw her for the last time. She'd said the famous dancer died when her long wool scarf became entangled in the spokes of a car. It seemed eerie that Evan would mention her too, and I shuddered involuntarily at the memory of Kate with the fringed silk scarf around her neck.

Fortunately Evan didn't seem to notice. "In fact that's how Fortuny became interested in fashion in the first place. He did a lot of set designs for the theater, and he began to sketch clothes for the actors." He paused for another bite before he continued. "He actually patented the design for his dresses, which he call the Delphos robe, and it was their very simplicity that made the socialites of the time covet them. The dresses never went out of fashion."

I'd wondered all along if he might be deliberately trying to divert me from the subject of Kate's death, but I suddenly sat forward in my chair. "Kate said the dress might be worth five thousand dollars. What do you think?"

"That's probably a good estimate."

I shook my head. "It sure doesn't seem like enough money to kill someone for. But what if the dress had belonged to some famous person? Would that increase its value, do you think?"

Evan gave me what seemed like a condescending smile. "It would be almost impossible to trace the—" He paused, as though considering his choice of words. "—the lineage of the dress." He made the Fortuny seem like a living thing with a questionable family tree. Maybe the word he wanted was *provenance* if the dress was truly a work of art. So there, Evan Carmody. Don't patronize me.

"But what if the dress belonged to, say, Rose Kennedy," I continued, "and she handed it down to her favorite daughter-in-law who had her picture taken in it so that one of the slight variations you mentioned would show up? I bet then it would be worth something."

"Perhaps you're right, but of course you'd need a photograph of the person in the dress and then you'd have to compare it with the actual gown." He gave me a suspicious look. "Are you really sure you don't know what happened to the dress, Mandy?"

"No." I began to shake my head even before the word was out. "No, no, I don't have any idea." Oh, damn. I guess the fact that I'd bruised my nose wasn't going to keep it from itching when I lied. I put my hand up and rubbed it as inconspicuously as I could. Evan might not have noticed except he probably saw me wince in pain. Now I had a nose that not only itched but hurt as well.

Eventually he flagged down the waiter and paid the bill with a Gold Card, which of course is exactly what he would do if he were having cash-flow problems. I let him do it. My credit card wasn't in the same category.

I grabbed the newspapers he'd given me, and he hailed an attendant to fetch his car when we reached the entrance to the restaurant. As he sped me back to the cleaners, I looked at the ads that were circled in the paper. I noticed one that said "clothes for sale" and wasn't even marked. You better believe I was going to check the circled classifieds against the others when I went home that night. Just in case Evan was hoping to send me off on a wild-goose chase.

I tucked the newspapers in my purse when I got back to work. For the time being I had other things on my mind. One was to reapply an ice pack to my nose, but first I summoned Theresa to my office. She seemed puzzled when she arrived.

"Remember how I did that sketch last winter of the woman who disappeared?" I said. "It was pretty good, if I do say so myself, and Mack suggested that you and I try to do a sketch of the guy who came into the cleaners Monday night."

"Oh, I don't know." She shook her head.

"Let's just give it a try."

I'd set up an easel I'd brought from home and attached a sheet of paper from a sketch pad to it with a clip. I'd already drawn an egg on it for the shape of the human head. Normally I just started with the eyes, but that was when I was drawing a person from memory or when they'd posed for me back in the days when I did sketches of people at street fairs. I didn't really have any idea how to start something like this. But hadn't the woman who'd made a sketch of the Unabomber drawn a pretty good likeness from an eyewitness who'd spotted the man seven years earlier?

Theresa stared off into space as if trying to conjure up the man in her mind. "Well, his eyes were pretty close together," she said.

I put in some generic eyes, not as far apart as I would ordinarily make them. Then we went through the various other features: an ordinary-looking nose, a mouth with not too much upper lip showing, a round chin, and shaggy light brown hair that came down to his neck.

"I think the upper lip was longer," Theresa said.

I erased the lip and dropped the mouth a few centimeters.

She squinted her eyes as she looked at the face. "I think the eyelids were a little droopy."

"You didn't tell me he had droopy lids." I sounded more accusatory than I intended, but that was a great facial tag. I wished she'd remembered it earlier. I sketched in the droopy lids, but I was beginning to have an uneasy feeling about this.

Theresa nodded her approval. "That's really beginning to look like him."

"Maybe the chin was a little sharper," I said, definitely uncomfortable now, and I sliced a little off the sides of his face.

She looked at me in surprise. "How'd you know that? It's the guy. I'm sure of it."

I put my hands up to cover his hair. It was the guy, all right. Her last customer Monday evening had gotten himself a haircut sometime during the week and turned into a Good Samaritan this morning.

CHAPTER 8

I ran off copies of the circled ads in the classifieds and of the sketch I'd just drawn before I put in a call to Detective Reilly to tell him about them.

Actually I'd have given them to Stan when I saw him later that evening, but I was afraid he might connect the ads to the uncircled classifieds I'd had on the table the night before. Since I'd acted so furtive about them, he might put everything together and become suspicious that I planned to do a little investigating on my own. No sense upsetting him about it.

He'd said he would pick me up at eight at my apartment, but just as I was getting ready to leave work, the phone rang.

"Dyer's Cleaners," I said, picking up in the call office where I'd been giving Theresa instructions about turning over the ads and the sketch if a policeman showed up for them.

"Mandy Dyer, please," someone said in a gruff male voice.

"This is Mandy."

"This is Jim Bosworth, Kate's father. My wife and I just got into town, and we wondered if we could talk to you."

"Of course," I said, my insides knotting up as I agreed. I'd never met Kate's folks, but I probably should have found out their phone number and called them the night before. All I'd known was that they lived in Michigan.

"Kate often spoke of you, and the police told us you're the one who found the—" The gruff voice got even gruffer. "—found her."

"Yes." I couldn't even get out any words of comfort at the moment.

The man cleared his throat. "We're staying at the Brown Palace, and we were wondering if it would be convenient for you to stop by tonight."

I took a deep breath, steeling myself for the encounter. "Of course, and I can't tell you how sorry I am."

We agreed that I'd come to the hotel at seven-thirty. I called and put a message on Stan's answering machine that I'd be late and would call him when I got home. Then I left Theresa to close up the cleaners and hopefully to deliver the sketch and ads to the police.

When I got downtown, I went around the block several times. I told myself I was looking for a parking spot on the street near the hotel. But who was I kidding? I was just trying to delay the inevitable.

I finally parked in a lot and waited through three "Walk" lights to cross Broadway to the hotel. I thought about climbing the huge curving staircase and then taking the emergency stairs all the way to the fifth floor, but I finally opted for using the elevator like any mature adult would do.

When I knocked on the door of 521, a man answered immediately as if he'd been waiting on the other side for my arrival. He had a big build that matched his gravelly voice and a mane of silvery hair that looked as if it surely belonged on a senator. Now I knew where Kate had gotten her height.

"Mr. Bosworth?" He nodded. "I'm Mandy."

He gave me a hug as if we'd known each other for years.

I saw a woman rise from a sofa inside the room, which must be a suite. She was tall too, with the same regal grace and burnished hair, now going gray, that Kate had had.

"This is my wife, Emily—Kate's mother," Bosworth said.

I went over and hugged her too. "I'm so sorry . . . ," I said.

Out of the corner of my eye I saw a younger man get to his feet from a chair next to the sofa. I thought Kate had a brother, and I expected Kate's parents to introduce him to me.

"This is Michael Morrison," Mrs. Bosworth said. "His parents are friends of ours in Michigan, and Mike recently moved here to Denver."

It was a good thing I wasn't still hugging Kate's mother or I'm sure she would have noticed my body tense. Michael Morrison. That was the name of the boyfriend Evan Carmody had mentioned just hours earlier—the man Kate had been dating, the man who might have beaten her up. I'd expected a brother, and here was a possible batterer. I didn't know what to say.

"I'm sorry we have to meet under such tragic circumstances," Michael said, extending his hand. "Kate often spoke of you."

"Hello." I shook his hand and wished she'd spoken to me of him. I looked away, afraid my thoughts would somehow show in my face.

We all sat down, Kate's parents on the sofa, and Michael and I on either side of them. I'd forgotten all the things I'd planned to say. I took furtive looks at Michael. He was medium height—not the way Kate had always liked her men—with dishwater blond hair and glasses. And he seemed a little too nerdy-looking for her—with neither the elegance of Evan nor the hippie craziness of Red Berry and some of her earlier boyfriends.

"Mike works for a computer company," Mrs. Bosworth said, "and Kate had been showing him around Denver since he's single and didn't know anyone here."

"We'd been friends since we were kids," Michael added.

I nodded mutely. Did the Bosworths know that this man, the son of their good friends, might be a woman beater? I doubted it, or Kate's mother wouldn't have let him squeeze her hand affectionately. Or maybe the whole thing was something Evan Carmody had made up to divert my suspicions away from him? Michael Morrison didn't look like an abuser, but who does?

"We wondered if you could tell us something about the way Kate died," her mother said.

I looked over at her and wished I could say that Kate hadn't suffered for long, but I knew she had. "It's still hard for me to talk about," I said finally, "but I think it happened quickly." I was lying through my teeth, but I didn't care.

Mrs. Bosworth nodded as if that was a small comfort. I could see that her father knew better, and he changed the subject. He said Michael was going to help them put together a memorial service for Kate. "Could you supply him with the names of some of her friends?"

"I'll do what I can." I glanced over at him, and Michael seemed to be staring at me. I wondered if he thought I knew something about his alleged abusive ways and would tell Kate's parents. "But I'm afraid we were both too busy to see that much of each other the last few years." I could have sworn he looked relieved.

"Maybe we could get together in a day or two," he said.

"Fine." I would have to try to figure out how to ask him about the abuse charge at that time. There were so many things I wanted to ask Michael and Kate's parents, but I wasn't about to do it when they were together.

Instead we talked about Kate the last time I'd seen her alive—how happy she'd been and how we'd discussed that fantasy trip we were always going to take to Italy. Mrs. Bosworth's eyes teared up, and I wished I hadn't mentioned the trip we were never going to go on now.

"I think her business was turning a profit," I said, quoting what Evan Carmody had told me, "and she was really happy about a—" I didn't know if I should mention the dress. "—about the way her life was going."

I wanted to help ease their pain, but I didn't know how to do it. I was afraid I might start crying if Kate's mother did. I looked over at Michael, shaking my head as if I could shake away the tears.

"It must have been an attempted robbery, don't you think?" he asked.

I twisted a Kleenex I didn't even know I'd brought out of my purse. "Maybe."

Kate's father interrupted. "The police have given us the details." He obviously didn't want to talk about it.

"I'd better get going." I got up quickly and went over and hugged Mrs. Bosworth again. "Anything I can do, please let me know."

"Maybe you could join us for dinner later on," Kate's father said, escorting me to the door.

I agreed, but I wanted to say I'd do it only if Michael wasn't along.

Michael rose and came over to the door as well. "I'll call you later about the memorial service."

I nodded and fled to the elevator and out to the street. I was glad this first meeting was over, but I didn't feel relieved. All I felt was an ongoing sadness. I wanted Stan to comfort me and tell me everything would be all right.

As soon as I got home, I fed Spot and then called Stan. He said he'd be over in half an hour. Meanwhile I knew the best thing to do was keep busy. I changed into a pair of brown slacks and a bright yellow cotton sweater. Then I hauled out the copy I'd made of the classified ads Kate had circled and began to read them, checking off the garage sales that listed clothes for sale, whether Kate had circled them or not.

I jumped when someone pounded on the door. Thirty minutes couldn't have gone by already. I grabbed the copies I'd made from the table and tried to decide where to hide them.

"I'm coming," I yelled as I headed in the opposite direction and shoved the ads in the drawer with my silverware.

When I reached the door, I looked up to where Stan's head should have been. I kept dropping my eyes until they settled on a woman about my height, five-five.

"Yes?" I asked, bewildered.

My landlord needed to start putting more than 40-watt bulbs in the light fixtures above the landings. I peered at the woman in an ill-fitting pants suit, her gray hair cropped close to her head. Solicitors seldom came all the way up to the third floor, and this woman's battered suitcase didn't look as if it were filled with Avon products.

"You don't recognize me, do ye, Mandy?" she gave me a gap-toothed grin.

That's all it took for me to make the connection. It was Betty the Bag Lady. I couldn't believe it.

Her name had always had a double meaning because she'd worn plastic bags over her clothes to shield her from the elements. She'd gotten me involved in an earlier murder case where I'd first met Stan, and I'd wondered what had happened to her ever since. Mack finally told me to quit worrying about her because she'd probably headed to a warmer climate after the murder was solved. I'd always hoped he was right.

"Did you mean what you said at Christmas about giving me a job at your place?" she asked.

Well, yes, I had, but the offer had been made half in jest and half in the euphoric state I'd been in after the murderer was apprehended in that other case. I'd never meant it as a standing offer to be acted on when and if she chose. Besides, I'd never expected her to take me up on it at all. I also hadn't expected her to show up on my doorstep with, dear God, her suitcase in hand, ready to move in with me. Okay, so I'd let her stay with me once—but that had been an emergency situation. This wasn't.

She continued to grin at me, pleased with herself that I hadn't recognized her at first without her Hefty bag.

"Hi, Betty," I said finally. I thought about adding that this wasn't a good time, but instead I moved aside and let her in. "I'm expecting company, but I have a little time before he gets here." Dreamer that I was, I thought maybe I could give her something nonalcoholic to drink and send her on her way.

She stomped into the room in a polyester pants suit and a scuffed pair of walking shoes.

"How about a cup of coffee?" I asked.

"Got any doughnuts to go with 'em?" That had been what I—and my uncle before me—had given her when she used to show up at the back door of the cleaners looking for a handout.

"Sorry, no doughnuts," I said.

"Well, then, coffee will have to do, but to tell you the truth, what I really need is a good night's sleep." She plopped down on the overstuffed chair by my neatly folded up Hide-A-Bed as if she owned the place.

It was the chair where Spot had once terrorized her to

the point that she'd threatened to leave. Where was he now? As if he'd caught my telepathic messages, the cat padded out of the closet and positioned himself at Betty's feet, ready to leap into her lap.

"Still got old Spot, huh?" she asked. She gave him a pat on the head and said, "Didn't I tell you we were both tough old alley cats, boy, and that I wasn't going to let anyone kill you?"

Spot cocked his head as if he remembered her, but he didn't jump on her lap, just sat there and looked at her adoringly. I swear he knew she'd saved his life last winter, and it was as if they'd made a pact to give each other their space.

I gave up any hope that he would chase her away, and went into the kitchen to put water on for instant coffee. "Maybe I can call around and find you a bed at a shelter," I said hopefully.

"I'm really tuckered out, Mandy, so if it's okay with you, I thought maybe I could just crash here for the night." It was as if that ended the discussion.

There was another knock at the door. This time it was Stan, and I pushed him out into the hall so we'd have a little privacy. He gave me a kiss, but I drew back. It was because of my bruised nose, not Betty or lack of desire.

"What happened to your nose?" He touched it gently.

I'd been hoping he wouldn't notice, but I told him about getting sucker-punched by the kid who'd come to the cleaners for the dress. "I'm sure that dress had something to do with Kate being killed, Stan."

He nodded and gave me a hug, then propelled me into the room. That's when he saw Betty. I could tell he didn't recognize her.

"I didn't realize you had company," he said.

For the first time I thought this might be fun. "This is a friend of mine." I motioned between them. "Betty, this is Stan. Stan, Betty."

He came over, apparently to shake her hand, but then he took a better look. "Betty the Bag Lady," he said in surprise.

Betty squinted at him and then recognition dawned. "You're that cop fellow who scared the bee-jesus out of me last winter, ain't you?" Maybe Betty's dislike of cops would send her on her way even if Spot hadn't. "What you doin' here?"

"Thanks to you, Betty, Stan and I became friends," I said.

She snorted her disapproval as I sat down on the couch and patted for Stan to join us. Spot scooted away as soon as Stan approached. Maybe the cat didn't like cops either, but I suspected it was because he knew Stan had a dog.

I decided to take my hostess role seriously. "Betty just got into town from—where was it, Betty?"

She frowned at me for trying to extract information from her, then shrugged. "You might say I wintered in Florida and points in between, but I got to tell you, it gets hot enough down there in the summer to melt a witch's tit." She gave a Betty-like cackle, and although I might not have recognized her at first in her new togs and short hair, I'd have known that laugh anywhere.

At that moment the kettle began to whistle in accompaniment to Betty's laugh. I started to get up to get the coffee, but Stan said he'd get it for us. I think he just wanted to regroup from this unexpected turn of events, so I let him do it.

He took three mugs out of the cupboard, although he might have preferred something stronger than coffee, but it wasn't until he went for a spoon in the drawer that I reacted.

Whoops. That's where I'd stuffed the list of garage sales to go to the next morning.

I was on my feet and heading toward him before I knew it.

"What's this?" he asked, staring at the sheaf of papers.

"Uh—" I stopped as I rounded the counter into the kitchen. I was in big trouble if he found out my plans to go hunting for the source of Kate's Fortuny gown.

"I didn't know you were into garage sales," he said with a puzzled look on his face.

"Uh—" I repeated. "Usually I'm not, but Betty and I are going to some tomorrow to get her some new clothes so she can come to work for me."

"Good," she said from the couch. "I need some new duds if I'm going to work for a high-falutin dry cleaner."

Damn. Now what had I done? As soon as the words were out, I realized I was going to have a problem making my rounds the next day without taking Betty with me. Not only that, but I'd actually said I would have her come to work for me.

CHAPTER 9

Maybe this wasn't such a bad thing, I tried to tell myself as I grabbed the classifieds away from Stan and put them on top of the refrigerator. After all, I'd wanted someone to go hit the garage sales and flea markets with me, but I'd been thinking of Nat, not Betty.

And it sure wasn't what I'd had planned for the evening. No nice dinner with Stan, no chance for a private conversation, no romantic interlude afterward. Instead we ordered in Chinese, which Betty, in no uncertain terms, told us she didn't like. I'm not that fond of it myself, but I was tired of pizza. Still it was a scary thought that Betty and I might have similar taste buds and lack of dexterity with chopsticks. We both used forks.

After dinner Stan seemed anxious to leave. I didn't blame him. He said good-bye with a bemused look on his face, half-suspicious of my reasons for taking Betty to find clothes and half-amused that I'd fallen into the Betty trap again. Fortunately he hadn't noticed that the ads he'd found for garage sales were for last week's offerings. He hadn't brought up anything about Kate's death either, which was fine with me. Betty didn't need to know.

Once he was gone, I set up the rollaway bed behind the screen where Betty had slept the other time she was here. That time I'd feared for her life, which is why I took her in. This time I had no rational excuse.

I strongly suggested that she might like to "wash up" and handed her a towel, a washcloth, and one of my oversized T-shirts in the likely event she didn't have any sleepwear. She glowered at me, but I heard the shower running as I pulled out my Hide-A-Bed and pondered this latest turn in my life. I think I'd fallen asleep by the time she came out of the bathroom, but I had more trouble once she started snoring.

I dragged myself out of bed the next morning and took a shower to soothe my aches and pains. My knee was actually better, but my nose was still sore. Then I fixed some toast and mugs of coffee and put them on the counter for Betty and me. She'd slipped into the same polyester pants suit which, for all I knew, was the only thing she had. The thought of replenishing her wardrobe helped me rationalize our planned trip for the day.

She hiked herself up on one of my stools and slathered grape jelly on a piece of toast. "Well, it ain't doughnuts," she said, "but I've got to tell you, it sure beats some of the breakfasts I've had." She scarfed down the toast and grabbed another slice. "Looks like we're in for some rain," she continued as she looked out one of the windows at the overcast sky. "Sure you want to go out on a day like this?"

"Yes, I want to go, and what's more, I don't think it's going to rain." I knew about these things. I'd lived in Denver all my life, and I was sure the haze would burn off in a few hours, but more than that, I couldn't imagine what Betty and I would do to each other if we were cooped up inside together all day.

She chuckled and put more jelly on her toast. "Well, we

better take some Hefty bags with us just in case." That's one of the reasons she'd been called Bag Lady, of course, although she generally preferred the lightweight poly garment bags from the cleaners in the summer.

"I have a couple of *real* raincoats we can use," I said, "but believe me, it's going to be nice today." I finished my first piece of toast and told her she could have the second one I'd made for myself.

She nodded happily, and I went to the closet and dug out the plastic raincoats in their own little plastic bags. Just in case my infallible weather sense failed me.

"Here," I said, handing one of them to her as I headed for the door.

"What's the hurry?" She got off the stool, the third piece of toast in her hand. "I have to tell you I'm a little slow to get going in the mornings."

I'm not a morning person myself, although no one would ever know it because I'm normally at work by seven o'clock, but it was a scary thought that Betty and I might be kindred souls in more ways than one.

"Well, you'd better get used to rising early, Betty, if you're going to work for me, and besides, I'm told that you have to get to these flea markets at the crack of dawn if you're going to find anything good to buy."

"Flea markets—I thought we were going to garage sales," she said, then shrugged as she trailed after me down the stairs to my car.

I'd decided during the night, while I listened to Betty snore, that I'd start at the flea markets. After all, I was only planning to go to houses where garage sales had been held the previous weekend, places where Kate might have found the Fortuny. Betty might get suspicious of that and tell Stan, and I certainly wasn't going to tromp around to sales in progress.

I'd have to find a way to lose her for that portion of my trip. Maybe I could ask Mack to help me this afternoon by finding her a place to live. Something far enough away that she wasn't a regular drop-in at my apartment but could still get to work on her own. I wasn't looking forward to asking Mack for the favor, much less telling him that she was going to be working for us, but what are plant managers for if not to help out in emergencies and to train new employees?

I was wearing a pair of jeans and an all-white T-shirt, the better to fend off the bright rays of the sun, which I was sure would be beating down on us in no time. Rain, ha!

In the daylight I could see that Betty's pants suit was a bilious shade of green, and whether she'd slept in it or used my old T-shirt was something I didn't need to know. But it definitely shouted out for a new wardrobe. I was even willing to pay for it, too, but I told her it was coming out of her wages, providing she hung around long enough to earn any money.

"By the way," I said once we were on the road, "if you're going to work for me, you're going to have to stay sober. No drinking or not showing up for the job."

She grinned at me. "Hey, I've decided to turn over a new leaf. I been on the wagon for four months now. I don't intend to hide my troubles in a bottle no more."

Well, that was a good sign. It made my decision to hire her seem almost sane. I hoped Mack would agree.

"I told you so." She chortled with glee when the first drops of rain hit the windshield as we headed east to what was to be our first stop of the day—the Plains and Mountains Flea Market, which, as far as I could tell, was a whole lot more plains than it was mountains. I finally managed to get off work for the day, and I'm on my way to the wheat fields of eastern Colorado—not to some wonderful stream in Rocky Mountain National Park. And it's raining besides.

I wondered if I'd be able to find the flea market easily. No problem with that, as it turned out. I could see brightly colored roofs in a garish combination of reds, yellows, and aquamarines as we approached the correct mile marker on Interstate 70. The buildings were off in the distance to the south and looked like the midway of a traveling carnival but without any Ferris wheel looming over it. There was also a steady stream of cars turning off the freeway to an exit ramp, so it was impossible to miss.

Suddenly I had to slam on my brakes as I came to a complete stop in the right-hand lane of freeway traffic. A twenty-car pileup looking for a place to happen, it seemed to me. We poked along for the next hundred yards until the other cars en route to the flea market slowly wound their way up the exit ramp and onto a county road. A woman in a yellow raincoat was motioning us all to turn right. What a sissy. It was hardly even sprinkling.

The parade of cars crept down the road a quarter of a mile until more parking attendants, holding up signs, directed us into a huge paved parking lot. Thankfully it wasn't dirt, or it would turn into a sea of mud should Betty's prediction of an all-day rain come true.

Fortunately the brief shower had stopped. "See, I told you it wasn't going to amount to anything," I said as I climbed out of the car. I grabbed the raincoat anyway, just to be on the safe side. I also noted the lot number, aisle number, and space number where I parked the Hyundai. Otherwise I might never see my car again. I thought we'd be the first ones here, but obviously "early" meant something different to bargain hunters than it did to me.

As we approached the flea market, we had to weave our way through tables and canvases laid out on the ground where every imaginable kind of item from garages and attics was for sale. Some of the people, who had cars and vans backed up to their spaces, had canopies over them to shield themselves and their wares from the sun, which I was sure would break through the clouds at any moment with a fierce intensity. What the others planned to do in case of rain or searing sunshine was beyond me.

I didn't see any clothes anywhere, so we continued on to the center of the flea market on paved walkways that were conveniently marked with street designations. Nothing—clothes or anything else—caught my interest as we made our way past some lean-to-type buildings to the midway.

"I don't see any clothes here either," I said to Betty, looking back at her.

She wasn't there. Oh, good grief.

I retraced my steps and found her at a table with psychic wares—crystals, tarot cards, and books on fortune-telling and pyramid construction.

"We aren't buying any of this stuff," I said when I reached her.

"I was just looking," she said, holding up a crystal on a chain. "Pretty, ain't it?"

"Yeah, sure." I sighed, and picked up a package with a couple of balls inside. The information on the front said they were "Chinese therapy balls—good for relieving carpal tunnel, arthritis, and reducing stress." I looked at Betty and then back at the balls. I could sure use something to reduce my stress level at the moment, and I decided the balls were a steal at three dollars. So what the heck. I forked over the money, took the balls out of the plastic wrap, and tried to roll them around in my hand the way the instructions said to do.

It wasn't as easy as it sounded. You were supposed to roll the balls around in a clockwise or counterclockwise direction, but one of the balls fell out of my hand and went rolling along the pavement.

A four-year-old boy grabbed half of my therapy treatment. "Look, Mama, I found a little ball," he said.

"Give it back to the lady," his mother said.

"No." He stomped his feet.

"Give it back."

With that he took the ball and hurled it as hard as he could. It hit Betty, and she picked it up and looked as if she were about to deliver a ninety-five-mile-an-hour fast ball back at him.

"Don't even think about it." I grabbed it away from her.

"It hurt," she said.

I stuck the balls in my shoulder bag. So much for relieving stress.

Betty pointed up ahead of us. "Look, there's some dresses."

"They're kids' clothes," I said as we neared the space where a woman was hanging tiny garments on a movable rack similar to the ones we had at the cleaners.

"No, over there."

I glanced to the other side of the street.

"Mandy," someone yelled. "Mandy Dyer, is that you?"

I looked around to see who was calling me. It was the woman with the used-kids' clothing. It wasn't until I was right up to her that I thought I recognized her.

"Luella?" I asked finally.

"That's me," she said as she wound a rubber band around her long brown hair to get it back from her face. "I haven't seen you in years. How you doing?"

"Fine. How are you?" I hadn't run into her since we'd worked the People's Fair together back in the old days. She'd peddled her macramé plant hangers and wall hangings at the same street fairs where Kate sold her jewelry and I did my sketches.

"I just read about Kate, and I couldn't believe it," she said. "I might not have recognized you, but I'd been think-ing about you. It said you were the one who found her."

This was not what I wanted. Another person interested in talking about Kate's death and how I'd found her body. Except that Luella was a connection to that earlier life I'd shared with Kate. Maybe she sold expensive vintage gowns under the counter.

Betty yelled at me from the middle of the street. "I'm go-ing over there to look at those clothes."

"Fine," I said. "I'll catch up with you." I turned to Luella.

"Do the police know who killed her?" Luella had stopped working and was waiting for me to answer.

"Not yet, at least not as far as I know." I looked around her stall, but all I saw were boxes of kiddie clothes, ready to be unpacked. "What are you doing these days—do you work out here every weekend?"

"I'm married and have a couple of kids, and I have a little store over on Thirty-second Avenue where I sell used chil-dren's clothes." She took a business card out of her purse and handed it to me. "On weekends my husband runs it, and I come out here."

That didn't sound like a person who would be selling Fortuny gowns, but maybe she knew of someone at the flea market who dealt in vintage clothes. I asked her about it, but she didn't know of anyone.

"No, most of the stuff around here is pretty new," she said.

"Did you ever run into Kate out here?" I asked. "You know she had a vintage-clothing store, don't you? I thought maybe she came out here looking for merchandise."

"I did see her once in a while, but not for a long time."

So maybe this was an exercise in futility. I looked around for Betty as I started to leave.

"But you know," Luella continued, "it's almost like old-home week here today. You'll never guess who I saw not half an hour ago."

I shook my head.

"Guess," she said.

I hated it when people wanted me to play games I couldn't possibly know the answer to. "I have no idea," I said.

"Red Berry. Remember him?"

Of course I remembered him. Kate's old boyfriend. The love of her life. The man I'd just been talking about with Evan.

"You're kidding," I said. "Does he sell stuff out here or what?"

"No, I've never seen him here until today. I thought maybe he was in town for Kate's funeral, but he hadn't even heard that she was dead. I really felt awful being the bearer of bad tidings, and he was blown away by the news. Said he hadn't seen her in ten years, and he'd even been thinking about calling her up while he was in town."

"Why is he here? Do you know?"

"Nope, but I guess he's a big music producer in Los Angeles now or something."

"Where's he staying?"

"He didn't say."

Was this a coincidence or what? Her old boyfriend showing up just when Kate had been murdered? I went for my therapy balls and rolled them around inside my bag to see if they would calm me down. If this was a coincidence, then it was a really weird one.

I didn't really see how there could be a connection between Red and Kate's murder, but . . . "That's too bad you don't know where he is," I said, more to myself than to her. "I'd really like to talk to him while he's here."

Luella had gone back to hanging little-girls' dresses on the rack. "You know, if you'd like to see him, he said he was going over to one of the pawnshops. They're in some of the permanent buildings over there." She pointed to the next street. "Said one of his friends runs it, and he wanted to see him while he was in town."

"Which one? Do you know?"

"No, he didn't say, but I bet if you scoot right over there, you might be able to find him. If you hear when they're going to have the funeral for Kate, let me know."

I nodded. "I'll give you a call."

Before I went searching for Red, I needed to collect Betty. I found her on the other side of the street inspecting the inside of one of the dresses. You'd have thought she was Lucille making an inspection at the dry cleaners. That was a surprise.

"Look, I heard that one of my friends is here, and I want to see him. Do you want to meet back here in an hour?"

"Nope." She turned the dress right-side out again. "I've seen better stuff at Goodwill."

This was a whole new side of Betty, one that I'd never seen before—her being particular about what she wore.

"The seams are so skimpy, they'd unravel the first time you put 'em on," she said.

"Really." I'd have to explore this area of her expertise at a later date. Maybe she was an eastern socialite who'd gone on the skids. "Okay, come on, but if I find my friend, I need a few minutes alone with him. Okay?"

She winked at me. "Gotcha. I could probably go have something to eat if I had any money."

That sounded like blackmail to me, but why not? She

was a recovering bag lady after all, and I was sure there was a high recidivism rate with them.

We'd reached the other street. Sure enough, there was a row of pawnshops. I wouldn't have expected to find pawnshops here, but I'd seen everything else—stalls selling Indian jewelry, western hats, redwood signs, vacuum cleaners, incense and perfume, even tires. Why not a pawnshop?

I glanced in at the open front of the first pawnshop and didn't see Red, although there were several customers in the store and a guy who looked like a cowboy behind the counter.

At the next store there he was. I probably would have gone right by him without giving him a second look except that I'd been tipped off that he was here. I watched him from outside the store as I felt a few big drops of rain.

"Told you it was going to rain," Betty said.

"Here. Go get yourself some lunch and meet me back here in an hour." It probably wouldn't take that long, but I needed a little time to myself. I handed her a five-dollar bill from my purse once I could convince my hand to let go of my therapy balls. They weren't doing a thing for my stress anyway, now that I'd seen Red, whose face hadn't changed that much from the old days. It was as if Kate would pop around the corner at any moment and join him at the counter.

Only reason I could tell ten years had gone by was that his hair was beginning to turn gray and it was no longer in a ponytail. It had always been a medium brown, never red the way you'd have expected of someone with a name like that.

He was still tall and slender, about the same height as the heavier man behind the counter, who looked vaguely familiar. The clerk had a ponytail, although he was almost bald on top, and he had a beer belly under a T-shirt that said ARCHIE'S PAWNSHOP . . . WE GIVE YOU A FAIR SHAKE. Ugh. The shirt gave an address on East Colfax, so this must be a weekend location only.

"Red," I said when I reached the counter.

He turned around and gave me a blank look.

"I'm Mandy Dyer, Kate's friend. Remember me?"

I could tell he recognized me then. "My God, Mandy. I just heard about Kate, and I was telling Archie about her." He motioned over to the other man. "Do you remember Archie? He was my drummer back when I had my band, and we called him Bones."

A scary name, and I wondered how he'd gotten it. From the drumsticks, or from something more ominous? Then it came to me. He'd been the guy who was all "skin and bones." Boy, had he changed, which made it even more embarrassing that he didn't seem to remember me. I like to think it was because I'd gotten better.

Red gave me a hug and then drew back. "Is it really you? I just ran into Luella Rainey, and she was telling me that you were the one who found Kate. I couldn't believe she was really dead."

"I still can't." I waited for him to say something, but when he didn't, I continued. "Do you have time to have a cup of coffee?"

"I was just about to suggest it." He took me by the arm and yelled back at Archie. "I'll see you later."

By then it was pouring rain outside. Betty had been right after all. I was sure she would gloat about that later. Red and I both took time to don our rain gear—me the plastic raincoat, which luckily came with a hood, and him a Burberry trench coat that he'd had over his arm. Pretty expensive threads for a guy who had been a wannabe rock star the last time I'd seen him.

Then we braved the storm and made a mad dash for the concession building, which luckily was right across the way.

Out of the corner of my eye I saw a figure step out of the overhang in front of the pawnshop next door.

I glanced back as the rain pelted my face. Good grief. It was Betty, and she was following us like a two-bit detective in a crime novel.

CHAPTER 10

Luckily I hadn't lost complete control of my senses, or I might have thought I was following myself. Betty had the hood pulled down over her face so that it was hard to tell us apart in our look-alike plastic raincoats. They were so long that I couldn't even see the bilious green legs of Betty's pants suit sticking out from under the raincoat of the would-be stalker.

Red insisted on getting the coffee while I saved us a seat. It was a lucky thing because hordes of people were descending on the small building to seek shelter from the rain. I deliberately avoided looking around to see where Betty was because the best way to make her go away, I decided, was to ignore her.

The place felt like a sauna, but I decided it was partially because my plastic raincoat didn't breathe. I removed it as I watched Red return to the table with coffee, hot dogs, a squeeze jar of mustard, and some packets of relish.

"I figured it was about lunchtime, so I might as well get us something to eat too," he said as he sat down and handed me one of the hot dogs. "Now, tell me about Kate.

Do the police have any clues as to who could have killed her?"

"If they do, they aren't telling me." A truer statement was never spoken.

"I just flew into town this morning on my way to New York," he said. "I'm a music producer these days. Did Luella tell you that?"

I nodded. "How long are you going to be here?"

"Till tomorrow. I have to be in New York Monday. Why?"

"I think there's going to be a memorial service for Kate next week, and I thought you might like to go."

"I don't think so, Mandy. Kate and I said our good-byes ten years ago. I prefer to remember her the way she was with that long red hair"—he looked nervously at his watch—"and that beautiful smile of hers."

"You never saw her again?"

"No." He shook his head sadly. "I was even thinking about paying her a visit this trip." Red picked up his hot dog, put relish on it, and took a bite.

Somehow his attitude chilled me. How could he speak so calmly of someone he'd once loved? I picked up the mustard and tried to squeeze it on my hot dog. It wouldn't come out, so I turned the container upside down.

I still felt that chill along my spine, and I looked around. Betty was standing against the wall a couple of tables away. She hadn't even bothered to get anything to eat with the five dollars I'd given her. Instead she was staring at us in rapt attention. No wonder I'd had that eerie feeling down my spine.

I wondered if she was trying to hear what we said above the roar or if she thought she was my guardian angel, ready to spring to my aid at the slightest provocation. But hey, I didn't need any help when it came to self-defense. I turned around haughtily and gave the mustard jar a mighty pat with the heel of my hand. Unfortunately I was in the process of turning it right-side up again as I squeezed down on it. Maybe I thought it was Betty's neck. Mustard squirted out as if it was being shot from a cannon. It made a neat little arc across the table into the safety net that was, unfortunately, the left lapel of Red's expensive Burberry trench coat.

Was I just an accident-prone klutz—usually at someone else's expense—or was this some deeper psychological problem that made me ruin other people's clothes so they'd have to bring the stained garments to Dyer's Cleaners?

"I'm sorry." I half rose out of my chair with the napkin that Red had so thoughtfully provided in my hand. I tried to get the dollop of mustard off the lapel, but I was only making the stain worse. I sat back down amid loud guffaws from the back wall, where Betty was making her amusement known.

"I'm really sorry," I said.

Red grabbed his own napkin and began to stab at the mustard.

"Actually," I confessed, "I think you should probably just let it dry and then scrape off what you can. Mustard's really tough to get out—so why don't you take it to your dry cleaner when you get home and send me the bill?"

Red waved off my offer, his mustard-stained napkin still in his hand. "Forget it, Mandy. It's all right."

No one could assuage my guilt if I didn't want them to. "Look, I inherited my uncle's cleaners, and I could take it down there and get it out for you. Where are you staying? I could return it to you tonight."

Fortunately Betty's enjoyment of the whole thing had been reduced to only a few infrequent snickers, but I could still hear her.

"It isn't necessary, Mandy, really," Red said. "I'm doing well enough these days that I can swing for the dry-cleaning bill."

Actually I'd had an ulterior motive. I wanted to know where he was staying. "Well, if you won't let me do that, at least let me take you out for dinner tonight to repay you."

He held up his hand to stop me. "That's nice of you, Mandy, but I already have dinner plans."

"A drink, then? What if I buy you a drink?"

"No, it's okay—really. There's a band here in town that I'm checking out, so I'm busy tonight. That's why I stopped off here in Denver this weekend."

"Okay, Red. I understand." But if he wasn't going to accept my invitation or let me know where he was staying, I tried another approach.

"You know, I always wondered where you got that name, anyway. You don't even have red hair. Was Red Berry just a stage name like—uh—Bones?"

He took a bite from his hot dog and finished chewing before he answered. "You are the curious one, aren't you? If you must know, my name's really Redmond Von Fursten-berg, Jr., which just didn't sound like a name for a rock star. I decided to keep the Red, though, because that's what my family always called me."

I still wanted to know where he was staying. "How about breakfast tomorrow?" Good grief, I was beginning to sound like a person desperate for a date with someone who didn't want to have anything to do with me.

He shook his head. "Sorry, Mandy, but my plane leaves for New York at eight in the morning and I have to get the rental car checked in and be at the airport by seven."

Well, that eliminated the possibility of my offering to take him to DIA, I supposed, so I finally gave up. I'd tell the police about him, and if they wanted to talk to him, they could check out what airline he was leaving on and be waiting for him at the gate before eight o'clock. At least I knew his real name now. Who could make up a fictitious name like that?

Red finished off his hot dog and looked at his watch again. "I really better get going."

I grabbed my uneaten hot dog with one hand and tried to slip into my raincoat with the other.

"No, please, just stay where you are and eat your lunch," he said, rising quickly. "I'm glad we ran into each other, but I'm devastated by the news of Kate."

If he was devastated, why had he just told me that he'd said his good-bye to her years ago as if that ended any feeling he had for her? I'd have to think that one over. For the time being, we said our own good-byes, and as soon as he was out the door, I joined Betty at the window with my hot dog. We watched as he hurried back across the street to the pawnshop.

"Who was that guy anyway?" Betty asked.

"An old friend."

The rain was still coming down, and the windows had steamed up from all the moisture. I wiped a spot clear to get a better view as I debated whether to wait until Red came out of the pawnshop and try to follow him. That might be difficult to explain to Betty, but I'd get to that when the time came.

"Here," Betty said. She picked up another bottle of mustard from a table that was just being vacated. "I hate to say it, but if that mustard had been a bullet, your old friend would've been dead by now." She let out one last chortle and handed me the bottle. "Maybe you'll have better aim this time."

I grabbed the bottle irritably and put a line of mustard

across the top of the hot dog. Then I sat down at the table closer to the window and returned my gaze to Archie's pawnshop.

"You goin' to spy on the guy?"

It irritated me that she'd read my mind because I thought I was doing it a whole lot more subtly than she had, and I felt a desperate need for my therapy balls. "While we're on the subject, why were you following us?" I asked, my eyes still glued to the pawnshop.

"To tell you the truth, Mandy, I had the feeling that someone was following us earlier today, and I wanted to see if any suspicious-looking characters came in here after you did."

That was a remark guaranteed to make me lose my concentration. "What are you talking about?" I asked, looking at her. "What did the person look like?"

Betty shrugged. "I don't know. It was just a feeling."

Just a feeling? Was this the paranoia of a bag lady or the vibes of a person who was a lot more observant and intuitive than I was?

"Well, did you see someone suspicious come in here?"

She dropped her head. "I hate to admit it, but I got so distracted when you zapped the guy with the mustard that I forgot about it."

I might have felt sorry for her, but I realized that she hadn't dropped her head in shame. She was trying to hide her amusement, but her shoulders were shaking with silent laughter. Why me? Why did I listen to her in the first place? I went back to staring out the window.

"I think I'll go get my lunch while you're staking out your friend," Betty said.

I waved her off and kept my eyes on Archie's place. When Red hadn't come out of the building by the time

Betty was back with a corn dog, I began to wonder if he'd snuck out during the time she'd been telling me about her "feeling."

"Let's go," I said finally.

" 'Bout time." Betty got up and left me to clean off the table. I had to stop to put on my raincoat, but Betty had never bothered to take hers off. How had she been able to wear it with all the heat and humidity in the building? I realized that was a stupid question even to ask myself when I remembered the Hefty bags and the poly garment bags from Dyer's Cleaners that she used to wear on a regular basis.

Once we slogged through the puddles to the pawnshop, I looked inside. No Red Berry, a.k.a. Redmond Von Furstenberg, Jr. I saw Archie, whose girth made a mockery of his old nickname, Bones. He was over by some musical instruments that people had apparently hocked. He had enough pieces, including a set of drums, to have his own jam session right here.

I left Betty under the overhang of the building with an admonishment to stay where she was while I went inside.

"Archie?" He glanced over at me, but he didn't recognize me until I pulled my hood back from my face. "What happened to Red? I thought he came back over here, and I wanted to get his address to send him a program from Kate's memorial service. Do you have it?"

The man hiked up his trousers as he stared at me. "No, sorry. Red came racing back in here and said he had to get going and that he'd call me later if he had the time."

I looked around the pawnshop and saw a back door. Either Red had sneaked out that way or he'd left during the time that Betty had been spinning her yarn about how she thought we'd been followed earlier. At least I always knew where I could find Archie.

I put the hood of my raincoat up over my head before I went outside in the rain again. Betty had wandered a few stores away, but it was easy to spot her because she looked like me. She was just finishing off the corn dog when I corralled her.

We eventually bought a few outfits for her at another storefront—some slacks and tops that I said she would need if she was going to work at the cleaners. But I finally gave up on finding any vintage clothing, and said we might as well leave.

Betty stopped to buy another corn dog for the road. That was fine with me. It might keep her occupied on the trip home. I hustled her away from the temptations of the unpredictable items that might catch her interest en route to the car. Of course who had bought the therapy balls?

Betty was right behind me as I started to the parking lot through a decidedly thinned-out group of people hawking their wares out of their cars. They must have been scared off by the rain, but it had stopped again. The sun was finally breaking through the clouds, just as I'd predicted it would, and steam was beginning to rise off the parking-lot pavement.

I'd taken off my raincoat by then, and I was giving the therapy balls one last try by rolling them around inside my purse. "See, I told you it would be sunny today," I said, looking back for Betty as if we'd put a large amount of money on it and I'd won the bet.

But damn her ornery hide. She had disappeared again. Maybe she'd been drawn back to that psychic booth because she'd decided she needed some help to hone her questionable skills for sensing when there was bad karma around.

I returned to the booth, but she wasn't there. I thought

about seeing if I could get a refund on the therapy balls since they weren't doing much right now to reduce my stress, but maybe I hadn't tried them under the right circumstances. Maybe I needed to be alone to make them work.

I'm ashamed to say that I was tempted to head back to town without Betty. After all, she'd gotten along without me all these years. I was sure she could find her way back to my apartment on her own. In fact now that she knew where I lived, she seemed to have developed the homing instincts of a carrier pigeon.

But much as I wanted to, I couldn't quite bring myself to dump her. What if she was lurking under the overhang of one of the buildings trying to confirm her premonition—for lack of a better word—that someone was following us? And what, God forbid, if she was right? I couldn't very well abandon her here if she had my best interest at heart.

I looked up and down the street where the psychic booth was located, but I didn't see her. That's when I decided to go back to the main drag. The tallest building at the flea market was there. It was all of two stories high and had restrooms on the first level and steps and a ramp leading up to second-story offices for the complex. I'd seen the sign pointing to it earlier. There was also a deck out in front, the better to see when trouble broke out at the flea market. Maybe it would help me spot a missing bag lady.

In a worst-case scenario I could always ask someone at control central to put out a call over the P.A. system for Betty to meet me there. I was sure it wasn't the first time someone had gotten lost at the flea market—although more often than not it was probably a child, not a middle-aged bag lady.

I headed through the passageway that connected the two main streets. I was pleased that I'd thought about having management send out an S.O.S. for Betty. I needed to find her as quickly as possible instead of wasting time looking for her. I still had to get to the garage sales. Okay, the places where garage sales had been held the previous weekend.

The problem was how to accomplish this. First, I had to find Betty and then I'd call Mack—oh, please, let him be home—and see if he'd take her off my hands for a while. Then I'd go over to his apartment and drop her off so that I could begin the rounds I'd so carefully charted last night before Betty changed all my plans.

I was deep in thought as I made my way past the concession building and turned to the right on Main Street. It took me a minute to realize that a crowd was blocking the stairs leading to the flea market offices at the end of the block.

I started to veer to the other side of the building so that I could take the long ramp that led to the second-floor deck, but my eyes were drawn to the knot of people at the foot of the stairs. I couldn't see what was attracting the crowd. Perhaps it was a wannabe rock star like Red Berry who had made it big and was making a guest appearance at the flea market. No, that didn't sound right. Well-known entertainers probably didn't perform at flea markets. Or did they?

Curiosity got the best of me, and I went over to the crowd and stood on tiptoe to try to get a glimpse at what everyone was looking at. I couldn't see a thing, and I started to turn away. That's when I spotted the remains of a corn dog that had been trampled by the throng.

Dozens of corn dogs had probably been sold at the flea market that day, but I was beginning to have a bad Betty-kind of feeling about this. I started to elbow my way through the spectators.

"I'm sorry," I said. "I need to get through."

I didn't stop elbowing until I reached the front row and saw a man bent over someone in the middle of the circle. The person was lying on the ground, and I couldn't see her face. All I could see were some bilious green pant legs sticking out from under a raincoat exactly like mine.

CHAPTER 11

"**W**ill you get the hell away from me? I already told you I was okay."

Betty's angry voice warmed my heart and relieved my mind. She sounded as if she was her usual cantankerous self, and hopefully none the worse for the wear.

I bent down so I could see more than her legs. "What happened to you, Betty?"

She raised her head to get a look at me. "Hey, Mandy, I'm glad you're here. Will you tell this guy to let me up?"

I looked over at the man who was kneeling beside her. He was in uniform and was apparently one of the security guards at the flea market. "What happened to her?"

He motioned with his head toward the flight of stairs to the left. "I guess she tripped and fell down the steps."

"Fell, hell," said Betty. "I was pushed." With that she gave a mighty push herself, nearly knocking the guard on his backside as she struggled to a sitting position.

He managed to rise to his feet. "Did anyone see what happened?" He looked around at the assembled crowd for an answer.

No one volunteered any information, but a few people shook their heads.

"Come on. Somebody must have seen something."

Finally one man near the steps came forward. "There were a lot of people on the steps right before she fell because a group of kids had just gone up, and that interfered with the people trying to get down. The kids were almost at the top when suddenly this woman comes sailing right past me down the stairs."

I looked over at the speaker. "Did you see if anyone pushed her?"

"No, sorry."

"Dammit, will somebody help me up?" Betty was still sitting on the ground, her legs splayed out in front of her.

The guard and I both jumped to attention. We each grabbed an arm and pulled her to her feet. She winced as she stood up.

"What's the matter?" the guard asked nervously. "I thought you said you were okay?"

"I musta hurt my ankle." She limped to a bench as the onlookers began to wander away. I tried to help her, but she brushed me off.

"Do you suppose we could look around for the person who pushed her?" I asked the guard before he vanished too. "You just sit here and catch your breath, Betty. We'll be right back."

The guard kind of rolled his eyes, but I guess he decided anything was better than having us bring a lawsuit. We went up the stairs and into a hallway that led to a bunch of offices. One at the front had a cashier's booth, where a sign said that this was the place to buy seller permits.

"Who are we looking for?" the guard asked with a touch of sarcasm in his voice.

"I don't know—anyone who looks suspicious." Sure, like there was a police profile for the type of person who pushed women down stairways. The only people I saw in the hallway didn't look like that kind of pusher. There were a few women, plus a heavy-set man in one of the offices. The group of kids had disappeared.

But I certainly didn't want to tell the guard that I was looking for someone I recognized: Red Berry or Bones, Evan Carmody, Michael Morrison, or the guy I'd drawn the sketch of the day before. Maybe even the guy who'd tried to run me over with the black pickup. Or how about Luella of the kiddie clothes? The list was endless, but I didn't see a soul I knew.

The other thing I didn't want to admit even to myself was that the person who pushed Betty down the flight of stairs might have thought he was pushing me. Maybe as a warning to me to quit poking into Kate's death. After all, hadn't we both looked alike with the hoods pulled up on our long raincoats? Even I could hardly tell us apart, much as I hated to acknowledge it.

And by looking for someone I recognized, I guess I was admitting to myself that Betty might have been shoved down the stairs because of me. Guilt formed a little black cloud above my head that had nothing to do with the rain that had plagued us most of the day.

Dear God, I didn't want to feel responsible for Betty's injuries, but I did. And if I had to let her stay with me until she recovered, would she feel beholden to me forever? What a scary thought.

When the guard and I returned through the hallway to the deck, I went to the railing and took one last look up and down the midway. There was no one even vaguely familiar among the mob of would-be bargain hunters, although it would be hard to pick anyone out from the crowd that had magically reappeared once the sun came out.

"If someone actually pushed her," the guard said finally, "I'd guess it was some rowdy kid who was trying to give a friendly jab to one of his buddies."

"You're probably right," I said, but why couldn't I convince myself of that? I guess it was a whole combination of things—Betty and her bad vibes as well as me running into so many of Kate's old friends.

We retraced our steps to the bench where Betty was sitting.

"How you feeling now?" the guard asked, a slip-and-fall lawsuit foremost in his mind.

"I could use another corn dog," she said. "The one I had flew out of my hands when I took that header and went rolling away to Lord knows where."

"I'll go get one for you," the man said, eager to satisfy her every want as long as it didn't cost much money.

Betty smiled, seemingly pleased with herself for conning a corn dog out of the man.

I sat down beside her. "Do you think you'll be able to get to the car?"

She nodded. "Soon as I get some fortification."

"What were you doing up on that deck anyway? I thought you were right behind me when I started to the car."

"I figured I'd take one last look around the place, see if anyone followed you out to the parking lot. You know, because of that feeling I had all day. I'd about decided the whole thing was my mind playing tricks on me when, wham, bam, I got blindsided from the backside."

"Are you sure someone knocked you down the stairs?"

Betty gave me a disgusted look. "When push comes to

shove, honey, this old broad can tell the difference between tripping over a step and being smacked in the back."

The guard and I helped Betty hobble to the car, and during the slow journey I began to notice my own leg hurting too. Maybe it was sympathy pains, but probably it was from my derring-do the day before when Mack and I went after the kid who'd come to the cleaners for Kate's dress. The leg had felt okay this morning. However, I'd probably overdone it with all the tromping around at the flea market. I gritted my teeth and willed myself not to limp. I'd be damned if we'd both look alike in that way too.

The guard saw us to my car, and once Betty was safely fastened in to her seat belt, he hurried away in obvious relief.

"Where we goin' now?" Betty asked, grabbing the corn dog I'd carried for her to the car.

I hated to tell her my plans because I remembered what a fuss she'd made once before when she wound up in the hospital. "I thought I'd take you to an emergency room," I mumbled, "just to check out your bruises and make sure you're all right."

I saw her going for the seat belt even before I finished. "Unh-unh. No siree. I ain't going to no hospital."

It was about time I put my foot down. I stomped on the gas and screeched out of the parking place. "Yes, Betty, you are going to the emergency room, so I don't want to hear any arguments about it." I could be as stubborn as she could, and my guilt over her injuries probably strengthened my resolve. I didn't want her unattended wounds on my head.

She looked at me in shock that I'd countermanded her decision. "Don't get your nose all out of joint. Okay?" I'd almost forgotten about my wounded nose, and I gave it a little self-conscious tweak as she continued, "I'll go. You don't need to get all huffy about it." I lifted my nose in a haughty victory gesture, glad that by now it hurt only when I touched it. Betty locked the seat belt back in place and picked up her corn dog. "But I got to tell you, Mandy, there's something mighty weird going on here. What's the matter, anyway?"

I still didn't want to go into Kate's death with her. "Nothing's the matter except that I'm concerned that you were pushed down the steps."

She chuckled. "Maybe they thought I was you. We did look kinda alike in those raincoats, didn't we?" Dear God, was it apparent even to her?

I decided to take her to one of those storefront emergency clinics where, luckily, there weren't many emergencies this time of day. I thought they were going to refuse to treat her at first because she didn't have any insurance. I said I'd swing for the bill, and a receptionist reluctantly agreed.

The woman gave me a clipboard with a form to be filled out, and I handed it to Betty when I reached the chair where she was sitting. She gave me a dirty look but wrote in the name Betty *Smith*. Yeah, sure. For her address she put down "Care of Mandy Dyer" and handed it back to me to fill in my last known place of residence. I might have to move if things didn't get any better.

I was in the process of returning the form to the receptionist when a nurse opened the door. "The doctor will see you now." She was looking straight at me, and I realized I was limping again.

"No, not me. She's the patient." I pointed at Betty and bit my lip as I tried not to favor my sore left knee as I went to help the actual patient from her seat.

The nurse offered to let me accompany Betty inside for the examination, but I declined. Instead, free to limp to my heart's content, I went outdoors to a pay phone I'd seen by the store next door. My original intent had been to call Mack as soon as we left the flea market. I'd been hoping to coerce him into taking Betty out to find a place to stay. I had the phone off the hook to call him when I realized I couldn't very well ask him to do that now that Betty could hardly walk.

Instead I fumbled around in my pocket until I found Detective Reilly's number at the Denver Police Department. When I dialed it, I reached his voice mail. Frankly that was fine with me. I didn't particularly want to answer questions about the message I was about to impart: "I just ran into a man named Red Berry, who was Kate Bosworth's boyfriend ten years ago, and I thought you might like to know."

I went on to explain that I hadn't seen him in all those years and it seemed too coincidental that he'd shown up in Denver just after Kate was murdered. I provided what little information I had about him, including his real name and what time he was leaving town the next morning. The rest was up to the police if they wanted to pursue it.

I returned to the waiting room to mull over the reemergence of Red Berry in Denver. What did it mean? Had he or Bones pushed Betty down the steps, or was it that invisible person Betty had thought was following us earlier in the day? What had made Betty decide to come back to Denver and change her ways from a bag lady to a potentially productive member of society? Why wasn't anything seriously romantic developing between Stan and me, and did it have anything to do with his frequent trips out of town on his days off? I guess those last few questions were way down on my list of things that needed to be answered right now, but all the unknowns in my life seemed to swirl above my head like gigantic question marks within my personal black cloud.

I grabbed for my therapy balls, and I'd finally reached some sort of nirvana in which my mind went blank. That's when a doctor appeared in front of me with Betty in tow. "There don't seem to be any broken bones," he said.

That was the best news I'd had all day. Maybe I could have Mack take her out apartment hunting after all.

"I told her to get right home. . . ."

The doctor kept on talking, but all I heard was the word *home*. Betty had no home. I was the only one who had a home.

"—she should stay off her feet for a few days until the swelling goes down," he continued.

"What was that other part you said?" I asked. "I missed something."

"She needs to lie down and elevate her leg as soon as she gets home . . ." That word again. ". . . and put ice on the sprain to keep down the swelling."

"See, I told you it wasn't nothin' to worry about," Betty interjected.

"Okay, thanks, doctor."

I knew when I was licked. I paid the bill, and we were on our way. No use calling Mack now, although I needed to talk to him sometime over the weekend to tell him what I'd committed us to in the way of a new employee. And for the time being, this could work out—except for the obvious inconvenience of having a roommate who wasn't a hoped-for lover like Stan.

The main thing I'd been concerned about for the immediate future was getting rid of Betty while I went to the garage sales Kate had circled from the previous week's papers. With Betty ordered by the doctor to stay off her feet, I didn't need Mack. I would just take her back to my apartment, get her fixed up with an ice pack and a couple of pillows on the rollaway, and be on my way. How bad could it be?

There was a tense moment when we reached my apartment and Betty proclaimed that she could sure use a "nip of the old grape" to ease the pain.

I gave her a dirty look and told her I was fresh out of wine or anything else alcoholic. Luckily it was true. Nat had drunk the last beer I had Thursday night.

"Besides, the doctor gave you some pills to take for the pain." I went to the sink and poured a glass of water and brought her the pills. I'd already fixed her up in her favorite overstuffed chair, her leg propped up with pillows on the sofa across from her.

"Can't you take a joke?" Betty asked. "I told you I gave up drinkin' when I decided to come back here and get a job with you."

Spot had come out of his hiding place in the closet. He was watching my feverish activity as I tried to make our guest comfortable. The two of them—both old alley cats, as Betty had said, were cut out of the same cloth, and I wasn't sure I could trust either one of them.

But in this case I guess I had no choice. I fed Spot and left them to fend for themselves. Then I started on my rounds of last weekend's garage sales. I knew it was apt to be a fruitless search, but maybe I'd already found out what I was looking for when I saw Red Berry and Bones at the flea market.

Still I plowed on. My technique was to go up to a door and ask the residents about their recent garage sales. "My friend told me you had some wonderful old clothes for sale last weekend," I would say. "I wondered if you had any of them left."

The answers ranged from a woman who slammed the door in my face to people who wanted to sell me their leftovers that no one else had wanted to buy. One man even lectured me on how the city would allow him only one garage sale a year and it pissed him off. "Some people outside the city limits can have as danged many garage sales a year as they want," he said.

It was nearly six-thirty by this time, and as I headed back to the inner city, I passed a place called Cottonwood Mobile Home Park and slammed on the brakes. It had advertised a community garage sale the previous week. I'd checked it off in the newspaper because it listed clothes for sale, but it hadn't been one of the ads Kate had circled. The thing that was interesting to me was that it was on a direct line between two of the other sales she'd marked. What's more, Kate had said she'd found the dress where "you would least expect it." Who would expect to find an expensive Fortuny at a mobile home park?

There was no sign of a garage sale this weekend or even trampled grass where it might have been. I drove into the complex and parked my car by a sandy area with swing sets, a teeter-totter, a slide, and a dilapidated merry-go-round.

A woman was pushing a little girl on a swing while two older kids went up and down the slide. I went over to her and asked about the garage sale.

"I heard it went pretty good," she said, "but I didn't have anything to contribute. We just lost everything in a fire, and that's why we're living here."

I told her I was sorry and barged ahead in my one-track way. "Do you know who organized the sale?"

She pointed down the street. "See that trailer with the yellow shutters? Mary Lou, the lady who lives there, planned the whole thing."

I thanked her and started to leave, then turned back. "Do you have enough clothes for your family?"

"Not really. Why?"

I told her I ran a dry cleaners, and we always had some clothes that people never bothered to come and get. "Maybe we can find some things for you and your kids."

She said that would be wonderful and gave me her name, Joanna Sandell, and the space number of their trailer. I made a mental note to put that on my growing to-do list.

I found Mary Lou frying hamburgers on a grill under the awning of her mobile home.

"Someone just told me that you arranged the garage sale last weekend," I said. "A friend of mine said you were selling some old clothes and jewelry at it." I just threw in the jewelry so my question wouldn't sound so suspicious. "I wondered if you might have anything else you'd be interested in selling."

The woman shook her head. "Nope, it wasn't me. I was mainly trying to get rid of the stuff from the house where we used to live. It was just too much junk for a trailer."

"Well, I didn't mean you specifically. Was anyone else selling that kind of stuff?"

"No, sorry." I thanked her and was halfway to my car when she yelled at me, "You know, come to think of it, I think Shirley Sawyer had some old stuff for sale. Things like an old brooch that nobody wears anymore."

I hurried back to her. "Could you tell me where she lives? I'd like to talk to her."

"Down the block. The last trailer on the right."

I was so excited, I almost didn't hear her parting words to me as I started off in the direction she'd indicated.

"But I'd make sure that her boyfriend isn't there. He's a real troublemaker. Always drinking and beating her up."

CHAPTER 12

For a moment I fantasized that the truck with the oversized tires that had tried to run me down the day before might be parked in front of the place. In that case I would head for the nearest phone. But things are never that easy. There was no vehicle of any kind outside the trailer when I got there.

Then another scary thought occurred to me. What if her battering boyfriend was Michael Morrison, the mild-mannered computer nerd I'd met last night? What if it was Evan Carmody? No, I couldn't see Evan in a place like this, even though it was actually quite nice with towering cottonwoods overhead. But why should I be surprised at the trees when I was at a place called the Cottonwood Mobile Home Park?

Most of the mobile homes had well-tended miniyards in front—all except for the one at the end of the street. The tiny yard had gone to weeds, and it didn't look as if anyone lived there. I walked past it and then back again. I was sure no one was home, but then I heard the noise of a television inside. I went up to the door and knocked.

"Come on in. It's open." Fortunately it was a woman's voice.

She sounded as if she was expecting company, and I knew it wasn't me. I thought about knocking again, but finally I grabbed the knob and let myself in.

"Who are *you*?" A thin, dark-haired young woman was at the sink, and her eyes, already emphasized by dark eyeliner, widened when she saw me. They reminded me of the eyes in the paintings of children that an artist named Walter Keane used to paint. They'd been popular with our next-door neighbor when I was a child, but those eyes and the ones on this woman all seemed frightened to me.

"Don't be scared," I said. "I'm just here to see if you have any more of that jewelry and those old clothes you were selling at the garage sale last weekend."

"No." Her answer was a little too abrupt. She must have realized it too. "I mean, no, I never had any jewelry or old clothes in that sale. You must have been mistaken about who was selling stuff like that." She looked nervously around the tiny living room/kitchen as if she were afraid some tell-tale trinket was still around the place.

"You're Shirley Sawyer, aren't you?"

Her eyes had dark circles under them, which made her seem older than she probably was. "Yes," she said, "but what's that got to do with anything?"

"Well, Mary Lou down the street said you had some neat stuff like a brooch that you were selling." I thought she might be less nervous if I mentioned the name of the garage-sale organizer instead of some mythical friend who'd sent me here.

"Mary Lou was wrong. I just had some old clothes I wanted to get rid of because I'd lost weight since I bought them." She wiped her hands on her jeans and came over toward me as if she meant to keep me from coming any farther into the trailer.

Too bad. I was already in, and she'd invited me here. I was staring at a picture on a little table beside a brown tweed sofa. I couldn't take my eyes off it. I'd have sworn it was a picture of the guy Theresa and I had just sketched the day before. The man—before he'd cut his hair—who'd acted like a Good Samaritan to push me out of the way of the truck in the parking garage.

I went over and picked up the photograph. "Who is this?" I realized, as soon as I asked, that I probably shouldn't have reacted to the picture. I should have made a quick getaway and called Detective Reilly about my suspicions.

Shirley grabbed the photo out of my hands. I didn't really blame her. I was getting awfully pushy, but once I'd seen the photo, I'd acted on impulse.

"The picture came with the frame," Shirley said. "I been planning to put my folks' picture in it."

No way was I going to believe that. The last time I'd looked at frames, the manufacturers put pictures of handsome hunks in them, not guys with sullen looks and droopy eyelids.

I heard a noise from the other room, and her head jerked around toward the sound. "You'd better go now."

The hairs stood up on the back of my arms. Was this the scary boyfriend that Mary Lou had warned me about? Was he going to come out of the bedroom and throw me out of the place? Worse yet, was he going to recognize me from yesterday in the parking garage and keep me here?

I was already halfway out the door when I glanced back and saw a black-and-white cat come meandering out of the back room. It wasn't an irate boyfriend at all, but another pesky feline like Spot.

I managed to hand her one of my business cards as she herded me to the door. "Well, if you ever do have any jewelry—"

"You'd better leave now or I'm calling the police."

Unfortunately I didn't think she would make good on her threat, so I decided to call them myself. As soon as the door slammed, I saw a curtain close at a mobile home across the street. I wondered if it was a friend of hers or the neighborhood busybody. I hurried down the street, not looking back. When I reached Mary Lou's place, I stopped and asked her if I could use her phone.

"Did Shirley have anything else?" the woman asked as she flipped a hamburger on the grill. A man had joined her on the patio and was sitting on a picnic bench nearby.

"No, I guess she sold everything she had," I said. "But a friend told me of someone else who might have some jewelry. I need to call her."

Mary Lou told me to help myself to the phone. I went inside, where a surly-looking teenager was sprawled on a couch reading the comic strips.

"Where's your phone? Mary Lou said I could use it."

He looked at me in that distrustful way teenagers have and motioned to a counter that separated the kitchen from the living area. I dialed Detective Reilly's number. This time I wanted him to answer, but I got his voice mail again. The boy was watching me over the top of the comic strips, and I didn't want to spell out the whole story with him listening to what I said. For all I knew, he might be a friend of Shirley's. She didn't look much older than he did.

I tried Stan's number instead, first at work and then at home. To my relief, he picked up just as I thought his answering machine was about to kick in.

"Could you meet me at the Cottonwood Mobile Home

Park?" I gave him the address, which I remembered from the classified ad.

"What's the matter?"

It was a legitimate question, but I didn't feel like sharing it with the curious teenager on the couch. "Look, it's important or I wouldn't bother you about it. I'll tell you when you get here."

I heard the sound of a car coming down the graveled road, and I stretched the phone cord so I could lift the curtains at the kitchen window and see it. There was a woman driving a minivan, and I gave a sigh of relief. I didn't want Shirley's boyfriend to come along and whisk her away before Stan arrived.

"Okay," Stan said, "but you'll owe me dinner."

That was fine with me. It would make up for the aborted dinner last night when Betty showed up and we had to settle for take-out Chinese.

I hung up and thanked Mary Lou on the way to my car. It was still parked by the playground, where the first woman I'd talked to was now pushing another child on the swing.

"Can I get out back there?" I motioned to the far end of the road where Shirley's trailer had been.

"No, this is the only way in or out." She pointed in the direction where I'd entered the park.

Just as I was getting in my car, I thought to ask her for her children's sizes. I said I'd be back with some clothes, then turned the car around and drove to the entrance. I parked across the street on the shoulder of the road and scooted down in the seat to watch the comings and goings in and out of the trailer park. If the guy I'd sketched the previous day showed up, I'd spot him on his way to Shirley's. If she left alone or with anyone else, I'd be able to see that too. I would have to follow them, I decided.

Meanwhile I waited for Stan and hoped I didn't have to take off in pursuit of anyone now that I'd asked him to meet me here. That wouldn't make him happy. In fact, I'd dare say, it would leave me with a major mending job to do.

The earlier rain had moved out of Denver, and I could see the mountains to the west in jagged outline. It was going to be a beautiful night—except maybe for me personally. It was only as I sat there, finally with time to think, that I began to worry about calling Stan at all.

How was I going to explain my trip to the trailer park when he'd specifically said I should stay out of Reilly's way? Well, hopefully the information I had to share with him would more than make up for my ignoring his warning. And who could prove, anyway, that I hadn't been out for an afternoon of clothes hunting for the bag lady when I ran into Shirley? Yeah, right. He wouldn't buy that idea for a minute since there was no garage sale going on here today. I tried to think of a creative explanation, except my mind had decided to go blank again, and without any help from the therapy balls this time.

I don't know how long it was before his unmarked car pulled up behind me. He was out of the car and coming over to my driver's-side window before I realized it.

The window was already rolled down, and he leaned over toward me with no hint of his lovable lopsided grin. "So, are you going to tell me what's so important that I had to meet you out here?"

This was going to be harder than I thought. "I think I found a woman with a connection to that guy who came into the cleaners with the ticket. . . ."

"Go on." Not even a look of excitement about the information I'd just imparted.

"Well, I was out looking for clothes for Betty like I told

you I was going to do last night, and I ran across this woman with a photo of the guy."

He looked up and down the street and across the road at the trailer park. "So where's this mythical garage sale?"

I had a sudden idea, and I tried it out. "Well, they've already closed, but it was back there in the trailer park." My nose began to itch, and I rubbed it with the back of my hand. That itching was always a tip-off that I was lying, and unfortunately Stan had figured that out by now.

"Come on, Mandy, there wasn't any garage sale here today. What's the real story?"

I sighed, and got out of the car. "Okay, if you must know, this is one of the places I think Kate must have come last weekend. The woman who ran the sale said a neighbor had been selling some old clothes, and when I went up to her door, I saw the picture."

Stan glared at me, his beautiful blue eyes icing up as if it were the depths of winter. "And how did you know where Kate went last weekend?"

I put up my hands in mock protest. "I didn't. I just looked in the newspaper for garage sales that advertised clothes for sale." I'd already turned over the information about the sales Kate had circled to Detective Reilly. No need to get another detective riled, and besides, I'd found this garage sale by myself. Kate hadn't even marked it.

"So what do you want me to do about it?"

"I thought maybe you could go back there with me and talk to the woman. I bet you could get her to admit what she knows."

"Look, Mandy, this is Reilly's case. . . ." But I thought I was beginning to wear him down.

"She could be gone forever by the time we get ahold of him. I already tried to call him."

He was mulling it over, but I took it as a yes.

"Good," I said. "Do you want to walk, or should we drive back there and I can show you where the place is?"

"Drive," he said, "because when we get there, you're going to sit in the car." He obviously meant his car because he was heading in that direction.

That was fine with me. I went over to the car and got in, trying hard to hide the smile on my face. After all, he had agreed to talk to the woman, and he hadn't seemed as irritated with me as I'd expected.

I pointed out the trailer, and he made a U-turn at the end of the block and parked in front of the little paved sidewalk that led up to the trailer.

"Stay here."

"Sure." I smiled agreeably.

He climbed out and slammed the door. Well, maybe the way he shut the door indicated a suppressed anger. I watched him go up to the porch and knock. No one came to the door. He knocked again. Nothing.

He walked down the steps and returned to the car. "Sorry, there's no one home."

I was out of the car before he finished. "There has to be. A woman told me that the only way in or out of the park is the way we came in. I've been watching the entrance, and she didn't leave."

"Well, maybe you scared her so much, she went to a neighbor's to hide out. Did you ever think of that?"

"She was waiting for someone. I don't think she'd leave." I started up the path toward the door.

"What do you think you're doing now?" he asked.

"I'm going to try again. Maybe she saw a tall, handsome man outside her door and that scared her." I turned around and gave him my most ingratiating smile. "Did *you* ever think of that?"

At least he grinned, and seemed to give a tacit approval for me to make one last attempt.

I knocked and waited. Still nothing. "Shirley," I yelled. "I think maybe I left my keys in there when I picked up that photograph. Could you let me in so I can see if they're there?"

Shirley didn't know that I began to itch when I lied, so I rubbed my cheek and knocked again. When there was no response, I went over to the window and looked inside.

"What are you doing now?" Stan yelled from his car.

I shaded my eyes to get a better look. The picture had disappeared from the table where she'd set it down before I left the first time. I was so irritated that the "evidence" was gone that I lost control of myself for a minute. I went over and tried the doorknob. It wasn't locked.

"What the hell do you think you're doing?" Stan got out of the car when he saw me open the door. "You can't go in there when she isn't home."

I returned to the car so we wouldn't alert the whole neighborhood. "What if she's hurt or something and can't get to the door? I should be able to go in then, huh?"

"Not with me along—and not without a warrant."

Dang. I wished I'd never called him. Here was the perfect opportunity to snoop around the place a little, and I had to have a by-the-book policeman with me.

"Not even if the door isn't locked?"

"Not even then." He climbed back in the car.

The curtain moved at the trailer across the narrow road-way. An elderly woman was looking out her window again, apparently roused by our earlier yelling. I waved at her and started across the street before Stan could stop me. The woman ducked away from the door, but I was unde-terred. Maybe Shirley was inside, or else the woman was the neighborhood busybody, in which case she might know if Shirley had gone to another trailer while I was gone.

When I reached her porch, I tapped on the door. "Excuse me, but we're looking for the woman across the street. I was over there a few minutes ago, and I think I left my keys in her place. I wonder if you know if she left in the last few minutes."

The woman didn't appear at first, and I heard something scraping across the floor. Finally she showed up, moving slowly on a walker. She was heavy-set with gray hair and glasses. I didn't think she was probably Shirley's bosom buddy.

I tried to look friendly and sincere. "Did you happen to see the woman across the street leave in the last few minutes?"

The woman sniffed her disapproval. "It would be fine with me if they left permanently."

"But did she go someplace right after I left?"

She peered at me above the glasses. "You a friend of hers?"

I could tell by her earlier remark that I wouldn't get any points if I were. "No, I'm the Avon lady," I said. "She bought some lipstick from me the last time I was here, but she didn't pay me for it." It would serve me right if I had to buy some special lotion for the permanent rash I was going to develop because of all the stories I'd been telling.

"Figures," the woman said.

"So do you think she's around here someplace? I need to find her because I think I might have left my keys over there."

The woman began to shake her head. "I'm afraid you're out of luck, honey. She took off the minute you left and went hightailing it out of here."

I motioned to the entrance. "I thought there was only one way out."

The woman opened her screen door and pointed in the other direction. "She went that way—on that trail that cuts through the field back there to the Seven-Eleven out on the main road."

Despite my stakeout, Shirley Sawyer had escaped. I didn't think she'd gone to the 7-Eleven for a quart of milk.

CHAPTER 13

"She got away," I said when I flopped into the seat of Stan's car in disgust. "The woman across the street said she took off on foot as soon as I left."

Stan didn't say anything, just turned on the ignition and drove me out to the main road to my car.

"Well, thanks anyway," I said, "and please tell Detective Reilly about this so he can follow up on it."

He motioned to his police radio. "I already called it in, but I certainly appreciate the suggestion."

"Okay," I said. "I deserved that." I climbed out of his car and headed for my Hyundai. "I'll see you later."

He leaned his head out the window. "Aren't you forgetting something?"

I looked back at him in bewilderment.

"You promised you'd take me to dinner."

"Oh, yes, I forgot." I walked back over to the car. "Where do you want to go?"

"There's a place called Adam's Ribs on the way back to town. How about going there?"

"Okay." I didn't even have the energy left to tell him that I resented eating at a place with a name like that. Frankly I wasn't looking forward to the meal either. I had a feeling that Stan, who had been pretty laid-back about my activities thus far, was planning to barbecue me over dinner.

"Do you want to follow me?" he asked.

"No, I know where it is, and I saw a Seven-Eleven down the road. I need to stop and get some—uh—Clorets." Couldn't I do any better than that? "And some candy I promised to get for Betty."

"All right. I'll see you in a few minutes." Stan took off, and I climbed in my car.

At the 7-Eleven I decided to forgo the Clorets, but I did pick up a Hershey bar for Betty. "Was there a young woman in here a little while ago—about five-six, long dark hair?" I asked the clerk when I paid for the candy bar.

"You mean Shirley from the trailer park?"

"Yes." I nodded excitedly. This was a whole lot better than I'd expected.

"She didn't come in," he said, "but I saw her outside making a phone call not too long ago. Then she went out to the road and waited until someone in one of those high-riser trucks picked her up."

Damn and double damn.

"Was it black?" I asked.

I knew it was, and the attendant confirmed my suspicions.

"Did you happen to know the person who was driving?"

"Nope, couldn't see that far."

I couldn't believe my bad luck. I'd been onto something, and I'd let Shirley slip away.

By the time I got to Adam's Ribs, Stan had already found us a booth, and he'd ordered us both a beer.

I took a swallow and tried to calm down. "Shirley called

someone from a phone booth outside the Seven-Eleven, and the person came and picked her up in a big black truck like the one that was seen at Kate's the day she died. It was also like the one that tried to run me down in the parking garage. I told you about that last night, remember, when I explained how the boy with the ticket had punched me in the nose?"

Stan nodded and gave me a long-suffering look. "I figured you had some ulterior motive for going to the Seven-Eleven. I thought breath mints were a little much."

"The neighbor said she'd headed in that direction."

Stan twirled his glass. Okay, here it came. "Mandy, you have to quit checking into this. It's a police matter, and you're screwing it up."

"What do you mean? I didn't see Detective Reilly out looking into any of last weekend's garage sales."

"I should have known you were up to something last night when you said you were taking Betty to garage sales. Where is she, by the way?"

"She's home." I stopped jut short of telling him how she'd been pushed down the stairs at the flea market. "We *did* find her some clothes, and she needed to get off her feet for a while." At least that part wasn't a lie. "But you have to understand, Kate was a friend, and someone killed her for a dress he thinks I have. Next time he may come to the cleaners with a gun and use it on one of my employees."

"But Mandy, why didn't you trust me enough to tell me all that in the first place?"

I thought the answer was obvious, but I said it anyway, "Because you would have tried to stop me if I did."

The waitress came up to the table right then and wanted to take our order. Stan said he would take the baby back ribs, and I said I'd take them too. I hated to get the same thing he did, but after all, that was the specialty of the house.

"You need to stay out of it, Mandy, and you need to be honest with me," Stan said as soon as she left.

"Oh, you think so, huh?" I thrust back my shoulders, ready to do battle. "Well, while we're on the subject, you don't seem to trust me either. You're always disappearing on your days off and you've never once said where you go or what you do."

A hurt look flickered across his face. "What does that have to do with what we were discussing?"

I was sure he could see the connection. "Well, trust works both ways, you know." I was probably being a little overly dramatic as I pointed back and forth across the table with my knife. "And besides, you always seem to draw back any time we get close to sharing our feelings."

"I had a bad experience before I met you . . ."

Okay, maybe we were getting somewhere. It was the first time he'd said anything remotely personal about his life, at least in the recent past. Oh, we'd talked about how he and his brother had played cops-and-robbers when they were kids. His brother, who was two years older, had insisted on playing the bad guy, which is why Stan said he'd probably become a policeman when he grew up. He'd gotten used to the part. His brother became a lawyer in California. I don't know if there was a connection between that and the "bad guy" roles of their youth, but at least I knew Stan had a brother. I didn't know anything about the women in his life, other than the fact that he'd never been married.

". . . and I'm not ready yet for a commitment," he said.

I leaned forward. "Who's talking commitment? I'm not sure I want a commitment either, but I would like to explore the possibilities and I'd like to know what's going on in your head."

The waitress brought the food, and it seemed to break up any chance we had for a heart-to-heart conversation.

"This wasn't what we started out to talk about," Stan said and drank the last of his beer. I didn't know how he could do it with clenched teeth.

I pushed my plate away because I'd lost any appetite I'd ever had. "Yes, it was. It was about being honest with each other, and just once I would have liked it if you had mentioned what you do on your days off." Of course I hadn't acted interested so maybe it was partly my fault.

"It's a personal problem I'm trying to work through."

"It sounds to me as if there's a girlfriend someplace else." God, I hated it when I acted like a jealous shrew, which is probably why I hadn't asked in the first place.

"I can't talk about it now. I'll tell you later."

"Fine, and I'll tell you exactly what I plan to do every minute of every day when you feel like confiding in me." I waved at the waitress. "Could I get a doggie bag?"

"I gather you're leaving," Stan said.

"Don't worry. I'll pay for the meal like I promised." I was standing by then, and when the waitress returned with the Styrofoam box, I swooped the baby back ribs, French fries, and cole slaw into the separate little compartments of the box. I'd planned to stop and get something for Betty on the way home, and this ought to work out just fine.

"Never mind," Stan said, and I could see the muscles in his jaw as they tightened again. "I'll pay for it."

His offer didn't phase me. I grabbed the ticket and stopped at the register only long enough to put down thirty dollars. That ought to cover it. Then I was gone.

The last I saw of Stan, he was scowling at the door and he still hadn't started to eat.

Well, that was sure a swell way to divert the conversation away from my nosing around in police business, I thought to myself as I drove away from Adam's Ribs. I should have told him how offensive I found the name of the place while I was at it.

I wavered between anger and depression all the way home. Embarrassment too. I'd wondered about his mysterious trips, and I'd planned to ask him about them sometime, but not in such a combative way and certainly not with the accusations about another woman in the mix.

Oh, well, I'd decided by the time I pulled up in front of my apartment building, if we were going to end our relationship, why not end it now instead of drawing it out painfully over several months—or even years the way I'd done with my ex-husband, Larry, another lawyer. Maybe I should apologize for my outburst; otherwise I had a feeling I'd never hear from Stan again. He hadn't exactly tried to stop me when I took off from the restaurant.

I grabbed the doggie-bag dinner, which I'd decided by now that Betty was going to have to share with me. After all, I hadn't had anything to eat all day except for a slice of toast and that one lousy hot dog. I started up the stairs to the front door. I noticed I was limping again. I probably should have had the doctor take a look at my leg too, but maybe Betty and I could just elevate our feet and sit there all night with our separate ice packs. Whoopee, what a fun evening.

Just as I opened the door, someone nearly ran over me. I reeled from the impact and looked up in surprise. It was Mack, and he was out of breath. Oh, boy, I was in trouble now. I hadn't gotten around to telling him about Betty, and he must have found out about her and blown his top. He grabbed me by the upper arms and pushed me away from him as if he were trying to see what made me tick. For a man in his sixties, Mack was really strong, and I'd always suspected that he'd been a bouncer in another life. He gripped me so hard, it hurt.

But no, I could see that it wasn't irritation in his eyes. It was fear.

"What's the matter?" I asked as he held me at arm's length.

"Thank God, Mandy, you're all right."

"What are you talking about?" If he'd discovered that Betty was sharing my apartment, maybe he was looking at me to make sure I hadn't completely flipped out.

"God, I'm glad you're here. I thought sure something had happened to you."

"Mack, dammit, what's wrong?" He wasn't making any sense, and I decided maybe he was the one who'd flipped out at the sight of the bag lady.

He let go of the viselike hold on my arms. "I was afraid something awful had happened to you. I looked all over to see if you were hurt or dead."

I still didn't know what was going on, but I had a sinking feeling in my stomach. "Please, Mack, what's the matter?"

He took a deep breath. "Somebody broke into your apartment and trashed the place."

CHAPTER
14

Mack's words didn't sink in for a minute.

"I already called Nine-one-one," he said.

"A break-in at my apartment?" I couldn't possibly have heard him right.

He nodded. "I was just coming down here to wait for the police."

I still couldn't comprehend, and I had to see it for myself. I pushed past him and headed up the stairs, but I stopped halfway to the second floor. My heart felt as if it had stopped too. "What about Betty and Spot?"

"What about who?"

I didn't have time to explain about Betty right then. "What happened to my cat?"

"He must have escaped. The door was wide open when I got here."

I took the steps two at a time until I reached the third floor and stared into my apartment. Mack was right. The place had been torn apart. Betty and Spot were nowhere in sight. I knew neither one could be hiding in the closet because the door was open and most of its contents had been thrown out to the middle of the floor. The screen I'd set up had been tossed aside, revealing Betty's empty bed.

I looked in the bathroom, even pulled back the shower curtain. Nothing. The place was empty and pretty much destroyed.

I was terrified for Betty and the cat. Then a terrible thought occurred to me. What if Betty had done this? She was a bag lady, after all, and I was probably nuts to have taken her into my apartment, not once but twice. At least that's what Mack had thought the first time I'd invited her to come stay with me. Now he was going to be filled with I-told-you-sos.

But why would she have trashed the place? If she'd been looking for liquor, she'd obviously been out of luck, and if she'd wanted to leave, why not just get up and disappear again? She'd done that often enough before. And why take Spot with her, which it was beginning to look as if she'd done? A cat seemed like a major inconvenience for someone who lived on the street all the time. Besides, I hadn't thought she liked him all that well, even though she'd once saved his life.

"Here, Spot. Here, kitty, kitty." It was my last hope—that he would come sneaking out from the debris around me. I knew it wouldn't do any good to call Betty because there really weren't any places for a grown woman to hide.

Nothing made any sense, and I didn't have time to analyze it any further because I heard voices coming up the steps. Mack entered the room with a young policeman, who looked around at the mess.

"Is anything missing?" he asked.

"Who can tell? I just got home."

"How did someone get in?" He went over to the window, opened it, and looked out. "Was the window locked when you left?"

I shook my head. "I don't know." I had to tell him about Betty, even if Mack would have a fit. "There was someone staying with me, and she could have opened it. She and my cat are both missing."

The cop turned around and came back over to me. "You mean we have a possible kidnapping?"

"Maybe."

Mack couldn't contain himself any longer. "Who'd you have staying here?"

"Yes," the policeman said, "what's the name?"

I hesitated a minute. "Uh—her name is Betty."

"Betty what?" The officer had pen in hand.

Mack exploded. "Not Betty the Bag Lady?"

I nodded my head.

"I thought I didn't hear you right when you said it the first time," Mack continued, shaking his head.

The policeman waited expectantly, still prepared to write down my houseguest's full name.

"I'm sorry, Officer, I don't know her last name. The only thing people call her is Betty the Bag Lady." I looked over at Mack, who had an appalled look on his face. "But she said she'd reformed and was ready to come to work for us in the laundry. Remember how I promised her a job last Christmas before she disappeared?"

Mack threw up his hands as he went over to my over-stuffed chair and collapsed in it. He popped right back up again. "What the devil?" he asked holding up a leaking Bag-gie of water that had once been Betty's ice pack.

He went in the kitchen and tossed the Baggie in the sink. Apparently he didn't even think the subject of why it had been in the chair was worth pursuing. I could see that the seat of his pants was wet, and I was glad he didn't decide to sit on my Hide-A-Bed. Probably that was because the pil-lows were tossed helter-skelter around the room, so he chose a stool at the counter between the kitchen and the living room.

"Well, it looks like your bag lady might be the perp," the cop said. "Did you have any money or alcohol around that she could steal?"

"Well, a little money in that cookie jar over there." I pointed to the counter where Mack was sitting. He was still shaking his head. He stopped long enough to dip his hands in the jar. He came out with a handful of coins.

The policeman looked at me as if he expected me to say there'd been a lot more money in there the last time I looked.

I almost hated to admit that those few coins were the extent of my cookie-jar cache. "That looks about right," I said.

The policeman had me check around to see if anything appeared to have been taken. I didn't see anything obvious, but I was getting madder all the time. He told me I could file a report if I discovered something missing later. He finished his report and started to leave, then glanced down at the door handle.

He ran his hands along the wood frame. "It looks like someone forced the door open with a crowbar."

Mack and I both went over and took a look at the door.

"I didn't even notice it because the door was open," Mack said as he rubbed his hand down the door. "The wood is all splintered along the edge."

"Then it wasn't Betty, was it?" For a second I was relieved because it validated my decision to let her stay with me. "She could have walked out without doing anything to the door."

"So you think maybe it was a kidnapping, after all?" The policeman came back in the apartment.

My stomach knotted up. "I don't know." Relief turned to

fear for both Betty and Spot. It was impossible to tell if they'd put up a fight, what with the condition of the room, but at least there was no blood.

The policeman said he'd take a look around the neighborhood for any traces of Betty and let us know if he found anything. It was not a comforting thought.

Once he left, Mack went over to the table and sat down again. "I could use a beer."

"Luckily I don't have any," I said, "or I'd have thought Betty drank it up and went on a tear."

"What about coffee?" Mack asked. "I need something."

I went over and zapped a couple of mugs of water in the microwave. Then I poured instant coffee in them, doctored up Mack's with milk and sugar, and brought them over to the table. "I was going to tell you about Betty tonight," I said as I sat down beside him.

"I would hope so."

"I really thought she could work out in the laundry, helping Juan at the washers."

Fortunately Mack didn't voice his skepticism, but I could see it on his face.

I picked up the Styrofoam box with Betty's dinner in it and put it in the refrigerator. I felt as if I was going to cry, and when I came back to the table, I started searching for a Kleenex in my purse. "Mack, I'm never going to be able to forgive myself if something happened to Betty and Spot. . . ."

I couldn't find a Kleenex. All I could find were my therapy balls. If there was ever a time to see if they worked, it was now.

Mack patted my hand with the therapy balls inside. "You can't blame yourself."

"Yes, I can. I bet someone was looking for Kate's dress, and they thought I had it here at home. I wish the police had released the information about it, and then this wouldn't have happened."

"You don't know that they were looking for the dress."

The balls were clinking around in my hand like castanets. "Yes, I bet they were." I paused to lay further guilt on myself. "Betty even asked me if something weird was going on, and I said everything was fine. Then I brought her home, and this happens."

Mack watched me with a worried look on his face. "Why don't we go out and drive around the neighborhood as soon as the cop comes back. Maybe we can find her."

I sank into a deeper despair. "I don't think she could get away. She hurt her ankle and she could hardly walk." Suddenly I heard a tap, tap, tap. At first I thought it was me having an out-of-body experience with the therapy balls. I stopped rolling them around and listened. I heard the noise again. It was coming from the fire escape.

I dropped the balls on the table and went over to the window. I tried to look outside, but I couldn't see anything. Suddenly something moved on the other side of the pane. I jumped back in fear. When I recovered from the initial shock, I put my nose up to the window and shielded my eyes to get a better look.

That's when I saw Betty and Spot. Their noses were up against the pane on the other side. Relief swept over me, and I started to open the window. It was locked. The policeman must have hooked the catch on it. I unlatched it and lifted the lower part of the window.

"Who locked me out?" Betty asked, and let go of Spot. He vaulted across the ledge and took off for the closet. He was in for a surprise; there was no place to hide.

Betty hoisted her leg across the sill, and Mack and I helped her into the room. I had a feeling Mack was as happy to see her as I was. Well, maybe not quite, because now he'd have to help train her to work in the laundry.

She hobbled to the overstuffed chair and flopped down in it before I remembered it was wet.

"Shit," she said. "Don't tell me I was so scared, I wet myself?" She struggled back up, and I helped her to the kitchen table.

"It was the ice pack for your leg, Betty. It melted."

"Good, I didn't think I was getting that bad."

"What happened to her leg?" That was Mack.

"She sprained her ankle."

"Yeah, someone pushed me down a flight of stairs at the flea market," Betty said.

"Good God, Mandy, I thought I talked you out of going to the flea markets and garage sales."

"I'll tell you about it later." I sat down across from Betty and leaned toward her. "Now, tell us what happened tonight."

She gave me a penetrating look. "Then you have to tell me what's going on around here. I knew my feeling was right about the danger."

I said I'd tell her everything, but first she should tell us what happened in the apartment while it was fresh in her mind.

She leaned back and closed her eyes. "Well, I was sitting here just like this, minding my own business." She opened one eye and motioned with her head to the chair. "Except I was over there, and the lights were off. Guess I'd fallen asleep, but I had my leg up on the pillow and the ice pack on my ankle like the doc told me to do." Both eyes were open now. "All of a sudden I heard a noise at the door, and someone was fooling around with the lock. Well, I knew it wasn't you because I heard men's voices, and one of them said he'd have to pry it open, and if that didn't work, he'd bust it down." She stopped to catch her breath.

"Go on," I said. "What happened next?"

She made a movement as if to lift herself up from the chair. "Well, I wasn't about to sit here and wait to be raped or somethin' worse, so I grabbed Spot and skedaddled to the fire escape. We been out there ever since, and I got to tell you, it's no fun sitting there holding a cat that doesn't want to be held."

I could understand that. I couldn't even hold Spot for a minute without him scratching me.

"Did you see anything?" Mack asked. "Did you look inside the window while the men were here?"

"You out of your mind? I wasn't about to look in the window and have them spot Spot or me." She gave a little snicker, apparently at her choice of words. "So I just hunkered down at the back of the fire escape and waited it out."

"I'm sorry, Betty." I started to take her hand and noticed it had a scratch on it. No doubt Spot's work. "And thanks for taking care of my cat."

"Don't thank me for that. I wanted to kill him myself. He put his claws in me, and I had to let him go. But would he leave? No. He just kept hanging around, and for a while I thought he was going to jump on the ledge and start meowing to get back inside. I knew the jig was up if that happened."

I got up to get something to put on her scratches.

Mack had been pacing, but he sat down in a chair beside her. "So what was this about being pushed down a flight of stairs?"

I heard her telling the story as I went to the bathroom and started looking through the cabinet for something to put on her wound. I was beyond caring if Mack knew the story. He'd probably be as irritated as Stan about my nosing around, but hopefully it wouldn't be the end of our friendship the way I thought it might be with Stan.

I finally found some rubbing alcohol and started back to the living room with it. God, maybe I should dump it after I administered to her wounds. Didn't alcoholics drink anything they could find, even rubbing alcohol? Or maybe it was a good sign that she hadn't gone looking for it already? I continued to the living room, applied some to her wound, and asked if she wanted a bandage. She declined.

By then, she was at the part of her story where she'd lost her corn dog and the guard bought her another one. "I had a bad feeling all along that something else was going on out there at the flea market," she concluded, looking over at me. "You going to give me the straight dope on it now?"

I nodded and told her how my friend, Kate, had been killed and that I thought it had something to do with a dress she'd bought the previous weekend. "So I thought we'd combine the two things—looking for some clothes for you and seeing if there might have been anyplace out there where she could have found the dress."

She snorted suddenly. "I got to tell you, Mandy, you lead a very scary life for someone who cleans clothes for a living."

Mack was watching me, and I was suddenly self-conscious. "What?" I asked. "What's the matter?"

"You look like Captain Queeg rolling those dumb balls around in your hand."

"What do you mean?" I looked down at my hand. I hadn't even realized I'd picked up the therapy balls again.

"The balls—they remind me of Captain Queeg, although I think he was playing with a couple of ball bearings when he fell apart on the witness stand."

"Oh, you're talking about *The Caine Mutiny Court Martial*." That was a play Mack had been in a few years ago. It had also been a movie in which the captain is removed from his command after he goes off the deep end when he thinks his strawberries have been stolen from aboard ship.

Mack grinned, and ham that he was, pretended to be rolling ball bearings around in his hand. " 'Ah, but the strawberries!' " he said, pulling his upper lip down over his teeth in a good imitation of Humphrey Bogart. " 'That's— that's where I had them. . . . I proved beyond a shadow of a doubt, and with geometric logic, that a duplicate key to the wardroom icebox did exist.' "

Betty guffawed at his takeoff on Bogart. I was miffed, however, and if my therapy balls were going to make people think I was a nut case, I was going to deep-six them forever.

I got up and threw them in my purse, fully intending never to use them again. But I must say, the distraction about the infamous strawberry incident had brought back my appetite. I went to warm up the ribs, which I figured we could split three ways.

CHAPTER 15

I had just put the ribs on the table, two for each of us, when I heard a knock on the door. It was the policeman, who'd come back to tell me he couldn't find any trace of Betty around the neighborhood.

"We found her," I said, pointing to the table. "She was hiding on the fire escape."

"I looked out and didn't see her," he argued, coming into the room.

"I scrunched up against the wall and grabbed the cat when I heard someone open the window," she said as she gnawed on one of the ribs.

"Oh, you thought I was still the burglar?"

"Somethin' like that." Betty nodded as she wiped the back of her hand across her barbecue-stained lips and continued to eat. I had a hunch that she may have known it was a cop and not wanted any more to do with him than she had with the crooks.

He took a statement from her, and then I told him about Kate's murder and the Fortuny dress and how I thought the break-in must have been another attempt to get the dress. As he left, he said to let the police know if I found anything missing later. I realized that this would probably be the end of the investigation. Break-ins happen all the time, and the police can't devote a lot of time to the ones where nothing is taken.

I went back to the table, where I discovered that Mack had taken the last two ribs. My ribs. I decided not to point this out to him. If a couple of ribs were going to make Mack accept Betty graciously into our dry-cleaning family, I decided to let him have them.

Betty smacked her lips and threw down her second rib, chewed clean. "I think maybe I could use another one of those ice packs. My ankle is throbbing again."

I went to the refrigerator, grabbed some more ice, and put it in a new Baggie since the earlier one had been destroyed when Mack sat on it. I was muttering to myself as I did it because I had an apartment to clean up and I didn't feel like playing nursemaid permanently.

"Maybe you can help me get to bed, and then I can elevate the leg," Betty said. "I'm really tuckered out after spending all that time on the fire escape."

Guilt, of course, overcame my desire to ask who among this intrepid crew was going to help me clean up the place. While Betty was in the bathroom, I remade the rollaway bed, which had been stripped of its sheets by the burglars. Then I set up the screen to separate the bed from the rest of the room. Luckily the burglars hadn't slashed it since it was one of my best works of art, with a picture of the Denver skyline painted on it.

Mack had a look of amusement on his face the whole time. It especially irritated me because he was still chewing on one of the ribs. My ribs. I was attempting to be gracious about it, but he was trying my patience.

I found a couple of pillows so that Betty could elevate her

foot, then helped her to the bed, and came out from behind the screen to see if there were any baked beans or cole slaw left. No such luck.

"Why did you happen to come over tonight?" I asked.

Mack wiped his mouth on a napkin that he'd grabbed from the napkin holder on the table. "Theresa said you'd told her you'd be down to the plant tonight to close up, and when you didn't show up, she called me," he said. "I went down there, and then I stopped by here to see what had happened to you. I have to tell you, Mandy, that you gave me a scare when I saw the apartment."

I'd forgotten all about closing up because I'd gotten so engrossed in the surveillance at Shirley Sawyer's place. "Thanks, Mack, I really appreciate it, and I'm sorry you were frightened when you saw the apartment."

He prepared to leave, having devoured all four ribs. "What you going to do about the door?"

"I'll pull the chain on it and put on the dead bolt. That should do until I can get someone out to repair it."

"I would suggest that you come over to my place if you didn't have this—uh—problem." He got a silly grin on his face as he motioned to the screen that hid Betty from view.

I waited until we were out in the hallway. "Why do you have that dumb smirk on your face?"

He broke into a wide grin. "This reminds me of *The Man Who Came to Dinner*."

"And who, pray tell, is that?"

"*The Man Who Came to Dinner*—it was a movie."

Well, of course, why wouldn't it be? Mack was a movie buff, after all, and he had a movie quote for every occasion. I'd known about *The Caine Mutiny*, but I had to admit that this one stumped me.

"And so?" I asked.

"Well, the movie's about this famous, middle-aged radio celebrity. He's a thoroughly unlikable fellow named Whiteside, and while he's the dinner guest at the home of a family he has never met before, he falls and breaks his hip. He then proceeds to terrorize and intimidate the family because he has to stay with them until he recovers."

Okay, I got the point. He was saying that Betty, now that she had a sprained ankle, would be with me forever.

But now that Mack was on a roll, he wouldn't stop. "His private-care nurse finally says, 'After one month with you, Mr. Whiteside, anything I can do to help exterminate the human race will fill me with the greatest of pleasure.' "

I couldn't very well ask Mack to go with me to find Betty an apartment after that. He was already taking entirely too much pleasure in my dilemma. Better to act as if I were having a great time with my houseguest.

"Good night, Mack," I said.

He gave me a worried look. "Promise me you won't go checking out any more flea markets or garage sales."

"You have my word on it."

Betty was already snoring by the time I returned to the room and secured the place. I didn't even have to take the cushions off my Hide-A-Bed in order to pull it out. They were already on the floor, but apparently the burglars hadn't opened the bed. I yanked it open and fell on it.

But I couldn't go to sleep, and I didn't have the energy to get up and clean the apartment. All I felt was anger at being violated this way. I tried to think of what I'd learned today about Kate's death, but then my mind kept switching over to my personal problems: my outburst at Stan, and what I was going to do with Betty. Not only did I need my own space, but I didn't want to be worrying about her safety when I wasn't here.

It didn't make sense that the burglars would come back

again. They had to realize that the dress wasn't here by the time they got through trashing the place. And it had to be the dress that they were looking for. Why else would they have broken in? Was it just coincidence that they'd done it tonight, or had Shirley Sawyer sicced the burglars on me, knowing that I was staked out at the mobile home park?

In the morning I'd tell Betty it was too dangerous for her to stay in the apartment with me any longer, that I didn't want to jeopardize her welfare by having her here. But first, of course, I needed to find another place for her to stay while she recovered from her sprained ankle.

And then I had a thought. My most brilliant thought of the day. Well, I actually had two. First, I remembered the candy bar I'd bought for Betty, and I retrieved it from my purse. I made as little noise as possible—in case Betty would hear me and want part of it. I wasn't into any more sharing tonight. Me and Captain Queeg.

I'm sure my second brilliant thought came as a result of elevating my blood sugar level. I suddenly thought of a woman I'd met a few months earlier when one of my employees disappeared. Her name was Mrs. O'Neal, and she lived in an apartment building just off Broadway and had been my employee's baby-sitter.

I'd come to think of the middle-aged woman as Mrs. Santa Claus because of her white hair, roly-poly build, and round red cheeks. She was a caregiver-type if I'd ever seen one. If there was a vacancy in her apartment building, wouldn't it be the perfect solution to move Betty there and hire Mrs. O'Neal to take care of her? Just until Betty was back on her feet and ready to come to work for me. I cringed at that last thought, but one problem at a time.

My leg was feeling better the next morning as I drove over to a King Soopers supermarket. I bought some doughnuts for Betty. Better to tell her that she'd have to move over her favorite food. Unfortunately she was still asleep when I returned, and I'd already eaten two chocolate-covered doughnuts by the time she roused. Well, give me a break. I'd had only a piece of toast, a hot dog, and a candy bar the day before.

Betty limped to the kitchen table, her face lighting up at the sight of the doughnuts.

"So what we goin' to do today?" she asked, grabbing one.

"You're going to stay off your feet like the doctor ordered, and I'm going out to try to find you a safer place to stay."

"Obviously you don't know some of the places I've lived before."

I hoped she wasn't going to give me any trouble about this, but I'd discovered one thing the day before. If I put my foot down, she gave in to me. Hadn't I gotten her to see the doctor? "I don't want any arguments, Betty, and I don't want to be worrying about you when I'm not here."

She shrugged. "Okay. I can't say that I like being around here all that much anyway. Bad things just seem to have a way of following you around, if you don't mind my saying so." One thing about Betty was that she never ceased to surprise me.

Just as I was about to leave, the phone rang. It was Michael Morrison. Kate's childhood friend wanting to know if we could meet for dinner at seven o'clock that night to discuss her memorial service. He suggested a place in LoDo, a revitalized and now-trendy area in Lower Downtown near Coors Field, where I had visions of the crowds that would be celebrating after the Rockies baseball game in the afternoon. It would be too noisy to hear each other, much less talk about a memorial service, so I suggested we meet at a restaurant on Speer Boulevard on the way to LoDo.

As soon as I hung up, I told Betty to lock the door after me, and I departed for the boxlike apartment building in South Denver where Mrs. O'Neal lived. There was even an APARTMENT FOR RENT sign on the front lawn, so maybe this was going to be my lucky day. I was due for a little luck.

I thought I'd check with the caregiver before I consulted the building manager, so I rang the bell for Mrs. O'Neal's apartment. When she answered, I said "This is Mandy Dyer. Remember me?"

"Oh, yes, the young woman who liked my cinnamon rolls so much." I wished people wouldn't remember me only for my voracious appetite for sweets, but I let it go. "Just a minute, I'll let you in." She buzzed the door, and I grabbed it and went down the hallway.

The woman, still looking like a perfect mate for Santa, even in the midst of summer, gave me a big smile and ushered me into her cluttered, doily-filled apartment. "I was just getting ready to fix myself some French toast," she said. "Will you join me?"

"Thanks, but I've already had breakfast." No way was I going to be remembered by her as "the young woman who liked cinnamon rolls and French toast too."

I told her about my need to find an apartment for a woman I knew and that I wanted to hire someone to help the woman for a few days until she recovered from a sprained ankle.

Mrs. O'Neal beamed. "I could help her," she said as if it were her idea. "And I wouldn't want any money for it."

Together we went down the hallway to the manager's apartment. I'd met the manager before too, and I remembered her mostly because she had a baby girl with very little hair but a magical bow that stayed on top of her head as if it were attached to her scalp.

The manager opened the door. She looked almost as ha-
rassed as she had on the other occasion when she'd had the
crying baby on her hip. The woman, her long brown hair
uncombed, was wiping an orange substance from her face.
"Yeah, what do you want?"

Mrs. O'Neal stepped forward, all smiles at the thought of
having someone to take care of. "You remember Mandy
Dyer, don't you?" She pointed at me. "She was here a few
months ago looking for one of her employees, and now she
wants to see about renting an apartment for a friend of
hers." Well, *friend* was a little strong, but I didn't correct her.

"Sure, come on in, and I'll get the key." She moved aside,
and I could see the baby in a high chair. "I'm sorry but Jes-
sica just threw her strained carrots at me." Little Jess lobbed
another spoonful across the room, reminding me of the way
I'd launched the mustard at Red Berry's Burberry trench
coat. The child had grown some curly brown hair to match
her mother's since the last time I'd seen her, and she was still
wearing a big pink bow on the top of her head.

"Still using Karo syrup, I see," I said.

"Uh?" the manager/mother asked.

"Don't you remember? I couldn't figure out how the bow
stayed on top of her head even when you bent down with
her to get a pacifier off the floor. You said you stuck it on
with Karo syrup."

"Oh, yeah."

"So are you still using Karo syrup to hold the bow in
place?"

The woman looked at me as if I weren't too bright. "No, I
don't have to do that anymore." She grinned suddenly, and
it lit up her face. "She has hair now to attach it to."

Dumb me, but at least the conversation seemed to help
reestablish a rapport, and we later sealed our relationship
with a handshake and my personal check to rent the apart-

ment as of the next morning. I tried to give Mrs. O'Neal some money for her help, but she waved me off. Of course, she hadn't met Betty yet.

I was almost euphoric when I left. I'd found Betty a furnished apartment and a "caregiver" at the same time. And I was way ahead of schedule besides. I wasn't about to go home yet. I guess I just wasn't ready to face cleaning up the apartment after the break-in. Why not stop by the doll doctor's repair shop instead?

The shop wasn't far out of my way. The street was deserted on a Sunday morning because most of the stores were closed. However, just as with Kate's apartment above her vintage-clothing store, I'd gotten the impression that "Dr." Arthur Goldman lived behind his doll repair shop.

The short, chubby man with the electrified hair answered my knock when I went around to a back door. I didn't even have to identify myself.

"Oh, my," he said. "You're the lady who found Miss Bosworth's body."

His hair looked even wilder than the last time I'd seen him, and on that occasion it looked as if he'd just been unplugged from an electrical outlet.

"I'm sorry. Did I get you out of bed?"

"No, no. Won't you come in? I'm in the middle of surgery, but I decided to take a break to have a cup of tea." I didn't even look startled because I'd already seen a dismembered doll and several extra body parts on a workbench. "Would you like some tea too?"

"Sure, why not?" Better to be remembered as the woman who liked tea than the one who devoured cinnamon rolls. Good thing Betty wasn't here, though. She had a deepseated aversion to tea.

Arthur went over and got a cup, poured steaming water in it, and added a tea bag. "I haven't been able to get over the shock of Miss Bosworth's death," he said. "I just keep thinking that the killer is going to come back and get me too."

I tried to reassure him. "I don't think that's going to happen. I think they were looking for something she had." I didn't specify that the item was a dress. "But I was wondering if you had recalled anything more about seeing anyone over at her place the night of the murder."

"No, sorry." He brought the mug to the table and sat down. "It's such a shame. She was one of the nicest people in the neighborhood. She knew I lived here at my shop, too, and she invited me over for breakfast a couple of Sundays ago."

"Oh, really?" I pulled the tea bag out of the water and put it on the saucer under the cup. "Did she say anything about herself or her friends that might be important?"

"No, we mainly talked about me. I told her about losing my wife a few years ago and how lonely it was sometimes without her. She said she knew the feeling. Every time she found a man, it turned out he was married and fooling around on his wife."

Was this something important? Did it mean that she hadn't been in a relationship with the nerdy Michael Morrison, whom I reminded myself I had an appointment with at seven o'clock tonight? Had Evan's innuendos about Michael been fabricated out of whole cloth? From the little I'd seen of Michael, he hadn't seemed Kate's type. Again I thought about Evan. I wondered if he were married and if Kate might have been having a hush-hush affair with him.

It was too much for me, and as I have a habit of doing at times like this, my mind went off on a completely different tangent. Poor, lonely Dr. Goldman. Sweet, motherly Mrs. O'Neal, who had told me at our first meeting that she was a widow.

One of the problems I'd already foreseen about my arrangement for Betty was that I was quite certain she would get tired of Mrs. O'Neal's caregiving attention within a few days. I might have to channel it in another direction after that.

What if I set up Goldman with Mrs. O'Neal? Ah, Mandy, it's another brilliant idea. The doll doctor and Mrs. Santa Claus. It had to be a perfect match.

CHAPTER 16

I was still enjoying the genius of my matchmaking scheme as I headed home. And to think that Mack and Nat had once laughed themselves silly when I suggested that maybe I'd start a dating service by putting a bulletin board inside the call office, like a dry cleaner I'd once read about.

No matter how I tried to divert my thoughts, my mind kept being drawn back to thoughts of Kate and the trailer park. It's strange how things work out sometimes. I'd promised Joanna Sandell, the fire victim, that I'd bring her some clothes, and it was also a good excuse to return to the trailer park and see if the police had it under surveillance. I stopped by the cleaners and sorted through some of the items in our giveaway box.

People brought us clothes throughout the year for our Christmas drive for homeless shelters, and luckily someone had donated a bunch of children's stuff since last Christmas. I eyeballed the clothes and picked out some for the Sandell children as well as for Joanna.

That done, I set forth to the Cottonwood Mobile Home Park with the conviction that I had as much right to be there as anyone. Unfortunately Joanna wasn't home, so I put the box of clothes on her front porch with a note attached and looked around the park for any signs of the police. I didn't see them.

I snuck furtively over to Shirley Sawyer's door and knocked. No answer. I didn't have the nerve to try the door because as I turned around, I saw the curtain drop across the way. The trailer court snoop was at her post, so I went over and knocked at her door.

"Never did find your keys, huh?" the woman said when she finally got to the door on her walker.

"Keys?" For a minute I'd forgotten what I'd told her I'd left at Shirley's. "Oh, yes. I mean no. I wondered if you ever saw Miss Sawyer come home after I was here." Suddenly my eyes began to itch in a repressed reaction to my earlier lie. I was beginning to get better at lying without having my skin crawl, but not when people called me on it and I'd forgotten what I said.

"Oh, yeah, she came home all right." Again, I had the feeling that something terrible might have happened to my only real lead in Kate's murder. The nosy neighbor relieved my mind. "Made a terrible racket in the middle of the night and woke me up. She and that boyfriend of hers threw a bunch of things in their truck and took off."

"So you think they were leaving for good?"

"Looked that way to me. Skipping out on the rent, most likely."

I started to leave, then turned back. "Oh, you mean it was a rental? Maybe I could get someone to let me look around inside—for my—uh—keys." I added that last word a bit too pointedly, and I knew immediately that it probably wasn't a good idea. Conning someone into letting me search the trailer would be stepping over the bounds of what even I saw as a police matter.

The woman confirmed my opinion. "The police were out

here asking questions about her last night, so I wouldn't try to get in right now."

"You're probably right." I was halfway down the steps when I stopped. "You don't happen to know her boyfriend's name, do you?"

"No, and I don't care." She sniffed. "Some of the other people around here might have talked to him, but all I know is what I see from my front window."

I couldn't help feeling sorry for her. The poor woman was on a walker, after all. What else did she have to do? It reminded me of Jimmy Stewart in *Rear Window*. My thought processes were beginning to sound more like Mack all the time.

"Well, thanks for your help." I turned and went down the steps as she moved her walker back toward the window.

As an afterthought I stopped at Mary Lou's, the woman who'd warned me about the boyfriend. She was washing a stack of dishes that looked as if they were left over from last night's barbecue.

"Oh, hi," she said as she came to the door, wiping her wet hands on the tail of the man's shirt she was wearing. "Did you ever track down the woman with the jewelry?"

"No," I said, "but dumb me." If the excuse had worked once, I might as well keep using it. "I realized when I got home that I left a set of keys at Shirley's place, and the woman across the street said she thought Shirley moved out during the night."

"Oh, that old grouch. She doesn't have anything better to do than sit at her front window and watch what everyone else is doing." I felt like defending the woman on her walker, but I didn't have a chance. "If Shirley moved out, it's news to me. But if she did, it's probably to hide from that boyfriend of hers."

"No, the neighbor said he was with her."

"That's too bad. She needed to get rid of the guy. He was bad news."

Mary Lou had finally given me an opening to ask the question I'd been waiting for. "Do you happen to know his name? I thought if I knew it, maybe I could track them down and retrieve my keys."

"No, but let me . . ." She turned from the screen door and yelled down the length of the trailer. "Joey, do you know the name of Shirley's boyfriend?"

"Naw . . ." It sounded like the voice of the teenager who'd been sacked out on the couch the day before.

I heard papers rustle from the other side of the door. "Wasn't it Monty something?" That must be Mary Lou's husband. "Remember that time she came running over here after he'd beaten her up?"

The woman turned back to me. "That sounds right, Monty something."

I had one final thought. "Did he have kind of droopy eyes and light brown hair that he'd cut recently?"

Mary Lou shook her head. "No, that sounds more like her brother, P.T. He was Monty's buddy, which is how she got mixed up with the boyfriend in the first place."

"And what did Monty look like, if you don't mind my asking?"

"A big dark-haired guy. That's about all I can say about him. Drove one of those souped-up trucks with the high wheels."

Aha. I thought I'd finally found the guy with the truck as well as his partner, who'd played Good Samaritan to keep me from seeing Monty's license plate that day in the parking garage. *Found,* of course, was a relative term since I had no idea where either one of them was now that I'd scared them away.

*   *   *

It was nearly three in the afternoon when I returned to my apartment. It took Betty a while to limp to the door and unhook the chain and dead bolt I'd made her lock when I left.

" 'Bout time," she said. "I was getting hungry."

Luckily I'd stopped and bought us both burgers.

"I found you an apartment and a woman who's going to look in on you while you're off your feet," I said as I bit into my hamburger, hoping she wouldn't hear the last part.

"Now, wait a minute, girl. You didn't say anything about no woman."

"She's a very nice lady, who'll see that you get something to eat. . . ." I hoped the lure of food would change her mind, even though she seemed to think that meeting her hunger needs was my responsibility.

"I don't know. Maybe I'll just stay here for a while longer. . . ."

She couldn't get her way with a threat that she was going to remain with me forever. "No, you have to go someplace else. It's too dangerous for you here."

"Then maybe you better come over to this new place with me—if it's so damned dangerous."

"No, Betty. I have to go to work tomorrow, and I can't take care of you. That's why I found this other woman. We'll move you over there tomorrow."

"We'll see. . . ." Betty's voice trailed off ominously.

I wanted to change the subject. "Did I get any calls while I was gone?"

"I heard that answering machine squawking away a couple of times, and there were a lot of hang-ups. Kept interrupting my nap."

I wiped my hands on a napkin, went over to the answering machine, and pushed the playback button.

"You ought to get voice mail," Betty said. "It's better than an answering machine."

I stopped the machine in the middle of rewind. "What do you know about voice mail?"

"They gave me voice mail down in Florida when they were trying to help me find a job. Said that way people could call me and wouldn't know I didn't have no place to stay. Fat lot of good it did."

I resumed the rewind.

"It's me, Nat," the familiar voice said when I rewound to the beginning of the tape. "I'm back from my trip with a story no one else has found out about. Where are you? I was hoping we could get together tonight."

Sorry, Nat, but if you wouldn't go with me on my rounds of garage sales yesterday, why should I get together with you? Besides, I had other plans, and I glanced at my watch. I wanted to try to get the apartment halfway put back together before my seven o'clock meeting with Michael Morrison, and I hadn't had time to even think of any ideas on how to help him with the memorial service.

I was still contemplating that when Nat, never short-winded on the machine, continued, "So where are you? What did you find out at those garage sales you were planning to go to? Give me a call as soon as you get home. I'll be here all day, just waiting for your call. Ciao." There was a long pause, and I thought he'd hung up. "Are you there and not answering because you're mad at me? Hey, I'll make it up to you, and if you don't call me, I'm going to come down to the cleaners tomorrow and bug the heck out of you. Ciao again." This time I heard him drop the receiver.

And Betty was right. There were a lot of hang-ups before a woman came on the machine. I didn't recognize the voice.

"I'm calling for Mandy Dyer," she said. "You gave me your card yesterday." She seemed to be whispering, and it was difficult to understand her, but I thought I knew who it was. I leaned down closer to the machine, willing it to be her. "My name's Shirley Sawyer," she said in a slightly louder voice. "You might not recognize my name—" Oh, yes, I did, and I wanted desperately to talk to her. "—but we met yesterday. I was hoping you'd be home, but I'll try to call you—" The message ended there, as if she'd had to hang up in a hurry. It was followed by the four beeps to indicate that my messages were through.

"Damn," I said, and came back over to the table.

"More trouble?" Betty asked as she finished her burger.

I didn't want to scare her. "No, just someone I wanted to talk to. I hope she calls back." I'd suddenly lost my appetite, and I asked Betty if she wanted the rest of my fries.

She nodded and attacked them with the same vengeance I used to start cleaning up the room. My adrenaline was suddenly off-the-charts, and I might as well not let the new-found energy go to waste. All the time that I was picking up and putting away, I prayed for the phone to ring. It didn't, but when someone knocked on the door, Betty and I both jumped a foot. Betty from the table where she'd nodded off, and me from a trip to the closet with a pile of clothes, which I tossed on the floor. I was definitely going to take them down to the plant tomorrow to have them cleaned before I wore them.

As I turned to answer the door, I nearly tripped on a box, and Spot came streaking out from behind it. He was apparently more startled by my disruption of his nap than by the sound at the door.

I didn't think the visitor was Nat because it was not his knock, so maybe it was Shirley Sawyer who'd checked my address in the phone book and tracked me down. Actually it was neither.

I opened the door to the length of its chain, and there was a stout, middle-aged woman with short gray hair. I'd never seen her before. She peeked at me through the crack from behind thick glasses.

"Are you Mandy Dyer?"

I nodded.

"I'm looking for someone named Florence Lorenzo, and I was wondering if you could help me."

I shook my head in bewilderment. "No, I'm sorry. I've never heard of her before. Was she someone who used to live in this apartment?"

"No." The woman seemed to be trying to look beyond me into my one-room apartment, as if she thought the woman might be here. "I thought I saw you with her at the flea market yesterday. Then I noticed you talking to Luella Anderson, and she gave me your name."

It took me a while to realize the woman was referring to my old acquaintance, Luella Rainey, who sold children's clothes and now had a "married" name.

"Just a minute." I shut the door to remove the chain, but I couldn't help wondering if this was some sort of ploy by Shirley Sawyer and her boyfriend to force their way into my apartment. I glanced around for Betty. She had disappeared.

I held on to the doorknob for a few seconds, then opened the door, still on its chain. "Uh—I'm sorry. I don't know anyone by that name."

The woman wouldn't take no for an answer. "She was about your height, but she was my age or a little older, and she—"

"Look, I apologize, but I'm very busy right now. Why

don't you give me your phone number, and if I ever remember anyone by that name, I'll give you a call." I wasn't handling this well. "Or you can call me? It's just that I have an appointment soon, and I have to get going." That was true. It was almost time to meet Kate's friend, Michael.

The woman said her name was Rose Marino and that she was listed in the phone book under her husband's name, Robert.

"Okay, I'm sorry I couldn't be of more help." I shut the door and leaned my head against it for a few seconds until I heard the woman's footsteps retreating down the stairs. Then I went looking for Betty. It was as if a magician had zapped her out of the room. Bad ankle or no, she had vanished in double time.

I went behind the screen that shielded the rollaway bed from the rest of the room. Betty was standing by the bed, stuffing a few things into the battered suitcase she'd brought with her.

"What's the matter, Betty?" I wanted to try out the name "Flo" on her, but this wasn't the time.

"I suddenly got this urge to be movin' on." She tried to shut the suitcase, but it was too full.

"Don't be dumb. You've got a bad leg. You can't travel now."

She looked over at me. "Sure, I can. I've been out on the streets with worse."

"Look, we'll talk about this later, but I want to know if you think that woman is the person who pushed you down the stairs."

"No." She shook her head vehemently.

"Do you think it has something to do with my friend's murder?"

Again she shook her head.

"So, okay," I said. "I have to go meet someone about my friend's memorial service right now, and—" This might be one of the hardest things I'd ever said. "—and I need you, Betty. Do you understand? I don't want you to leave. I need you."

CHAPTER
17

I was on my way to meet Michael, already a little late for our meeting at the coffee shop. I hadn't even been able to compile a list of Kate's friends for him. All I'd had time to do was talk to Betty and try to persuade her to hang around that night and answer the phone in case Shirley Sawyer called.

"If she calls again, try to set up a time when I can meet her," I'd said. "Tell her I should be free by nine o'clock. I'll call you when I get through dinner, but here's the number for the restaurant in case she calls and wants to meet right away." I copied it out of the phone book. "You can call me there and ask them to page me." I handed her the slip of paper and grabbed my purse. "And put on the dead bolt and chain after I leave. Don't let anyone in except Mack or me."

I didn't have any idea if Betty would do what I said. For all I knew, she might have disappeared by the time I tried to check in with her. She might be gone now. There wasn't anything I could do about it. She was an adult, and if she wanted to go on the run again, it was her choice. I'd find out when I tried to call, but I had one glimmer of hope that she would stay. It had been her response when I'd told her I didn't want her to leave. "Really?" she'd said in surprise. "You need *me*?" Maybe no one had needed her for a very long time.

I climbed out of the Hyundai in the coffee shop parking lot and went to the entrance, where, as I'd hoped, there was no waiting line as there would have been in LoDo.

"May I help you?" The cashier came from behind the counter.

"I'm meeting someone here." I looked around the restaurant. "I see him over there."

Michael was wearing chinos and a wool flannel shirt. It seemed a little warm this time of year for flannel, but wasn't that the dress of choice for computer types?

I, on the other hand, didn't look a thing like a well-pressed dry cleaner. When I finished talking to Betty, I'd only had time to change into a clean T-shirt and jeans, ones that were folded and didn't seem to be contaminated by the burglars.

"I'm sorry I'm late," I said, scooting into the booth across from Michael. "How are Kate's folks doing?"

"It's hard on them, but my parents have come out to be with them."

God, that was going to be tough on everyone if Michael turned out to have something to do with Kate's murder. Even though Shirley Sawyer, her brother, and the boyfriend Monty, might have been involved, I couldn't quite shake the feeling that there was someone else behind it—someone Kate knew personally.

"Have Mr. and Mrs. Bosworth heard anything more from the police?" I continued. "Any new developments?"

It was my only chance of finding out about the case. Neither Stan nor Detective Reilly were going to give me the time of day, much less make me privy to what was going on in the investigation.

Michael shook his head and moved on to what we'd come here to discuss. "We've arranged to have the memorial service on Thursday at a church near Kate's store," he said. "We figured that way more of her friends and customers could attend."

A waiter came, and Michael said he was going to order the liver and onions with salad and mashed potatoes. Well, yuk, I wasn't about to order that. I checked the menu and ordered the fried chicken with the same side dishes as Michael. And one chicken dinner to go. If Betty hung around, she'd need to be rewarded with something to eat.

Then we got down to business. I gave him a list of Kate's friends whom I remembered from the old days. "I have to tell you I didn't know a lot of her recent friends," I added. "In fact I mostly saw her these days when she brought me her vintage dresses to be cleaned."

Michael nodded.

He'd been writing, but now he looked over at me as he pushed his horn-rimmed glasses up on his nose. "We wondered if you would like to say a few words at the service."

My stomach knotted up. Public speaking wasn't my strong suit. I agreed to do it anyway. For Kate. I just hoped I could get through it.

"And I wondered if you could call the people you just mentioned and tell them about the service," he said.

"Sure." I would probably have time to do it at work the next day since we were in the summer dry-cleaning doldrums. It might be hard to locate some of them, though, since they had tended to be a migratory lot. "I'll need the list, though, just to make sure I don't forget anyone."

I watched him as he began to recopy what he'd already written down. He sure didn't appear to be Kate's type. Maybe Michael was just a friend after all, despite what Evan said.

I cleared my throat to get his attention. "Did Kate ever mention someone named Shirley Sawyer?"

Michael shook his head and kept on writing.

"When was the last time you saw her?"

He looked up from his notes. "We went out to dinner last Sunday. Why?"

"Did she seem excited about anything?"

He thought about it for a minute. "She said she bought a dress someplace, and she seemed really pleased about it."

"Did she say where she found it?"

The waitress brought our dinner right then—the salad at the same time as she brought the entree. "I'm sorry about that," she apologized. "They're getting ahead of me in the kitchen."

Michael asked her for rolls, and by then I had to repeat my question to him. "No, I don't think she mentioned that. . . ." He sampled the salad, and when he finished chewing, he continued, "She did say the woman she bought it from didn't look as if she would have a valuable dress like that, and that made Kate suspicious." That was interesting, and now at least I knew the seller was a woman. "Kate said the woman had been too busy that day to answer her questions, so Kate was going to go back the next day and talk to her about it."

That would have been Monday, the same day that she brought me the dress. Had that return trip cost Kate her life?

"Have you talked to the police?" I asked.

He nodded, and I was glad Reilly was covering all the bases.

"Did you mention the dress?"

Michael had another bite of salad in his mouth, and it took him a while to answer. "An officer asked me about it, but I didn't know anything."

"You should tell someone that Kate was planning to go back Monday to where she bought the dress," I said, and began to attack my own salad.

Hopefully Shirley would try to contact me again tonight and I could find out what was going on.

The urgency of getting home made me gulp my food. I'd already finished by the time Michael started on his entree. I watched him as he delicately cut off a slice of liver and carefully chewed it twenty times. I was certain that he was the slowest eater I'd ever seen.

"Will you excuse me for a minute?" I pushed myself out of the seat. "I have to make a phone call."

When I got to the pay phone, I held my breath as I dialed. Would Betty answer, or was she long gone now? It rang four times and the answering machine picked up. Damn, I really had thought she would stay. Just in case, I left a message, "Betty, this is Mandy. If you're there, please pick up." I said it slowly, hoping it would give her time to grab the phone, which I'd pushed as far as the cord would stretch toward her bed. "Look," I continued, "I'm still at the restaurant, so if Shirley Sawyer calls again, have them page me at that number I gave—"

Suddenly I heard the phone pick up. "Yeah, this is me. I've been waiting by the phone all night, and nothing. Finally I had to go to the bathroom, or I was going to wet myself for sure. Then the stupid thing rings, and it's only you."

Relief that Betty was still there was tempered by the knowledge that Shirley Sawyer hadn't called again. I asked her anyway. "So you haven't had any other calls?"

"I already said that."

"Right. Well, I'll call you again before I leave. I have a chicken dinner that I'm bringing home for you."

"Good, I'm hungry. And if anyone should be trying to call, you're holding things up."

"Right again." I returned to Michael, who was in the process of cutting another thin sliver of liver with his knife. Didn't he know that liver was meant to be gulped whole so as not to taste it as it went down? No wonder it took him all night to eat.

He lifted his fork to his mouth and began chewing.

"How long since you moved to Denver?" I asked.

He chewed carefully. "About six weeks."

I probably shouldn't say anything to him, just let him chew, but somehow I didn't know him well enough to have a vacuum in the conversation.

"When was the last time you saw Kate before that?"

I realized I should just ask questions that required a head shake, yes or no, like true-false questions on an exam. Otherwise we'd never get out of here. But now I didn't seem to have any reason to go since Shirley hadn't called. At least I was sure Betty was going to stay now.

Michael finished chewing and swallowed. "Oh, I guess it had been a couple of years," he said. "I hardly recognized her when I saw her with short hair."

I nodded this time. "She finally cut it a couple of months ago because of the way she said I made her look in a mural I did of her down at the cleaners." He looked puzzled as he carefully brought a forkful of mashed potatoes to his mouth. "I used her as the model for a woman in a flapper-era dress," I explained.

It appeared he even chewed his mashed potatoes. He swallowed and took a sip of water, then said, "She'd always worn it long since we were in high school."

Something bothered me about that remark, but I couldn't figure out what it was. It would probably nag me all evening, like a name I couldn't remember. Hopefully I'd wake up in the middle of the night with the answer, as if my subconscious had been working on it while I slept.

But I mustn't get diverted from what I'd been working up to ask. "Do you know anything about a black eye she had about a month ago?"

He blinked, but he didn't seem upset about the question. "Oh, that. She told me some boxes fell out of a shelf when she was reaching up for something, and one of them hit her in the face."

That was the same thing Evan had said Kate told him. Maybe it really was true.

Michael finally finished his dinner. I couldn't believe it. Unfortunately that's about the time I realized that the waitress had failed to bring my order of chicken-to-go. I couldn't very well go home without it. I'd already promised it to Betty.

I hailed the woman, and she said she'd been waiting so that it would still be hot when I got home with it. Personally I thought she'd forgotten and was covering up.

For a few nervous minutes I was afraid Michael was going to order dessert, but after a long deliberation he decided none of the selections from the dessert menu appealed to him.

The waitress scurried away to get Betty's order, and Michael returned to laboriously copying down the list I'd given him. Frankly I probably should have just winged it. More than likely I could have remembered all the names I'd given him, even if I couldn't think what it was that bothered me about Michael's remark.

The waitress brought a Styrofoam box with Betty's order in it, and Michael handed me his duplicate list. "Oh." He reached back and took it from me. "I forgot to put down my phone number in case you want to call me. I'm not in the phone book yet."

Finally, with our business transacted, we went up to the register to pay the bill. I insisted on paying for my dinner and Betty's as well. We said our good-byes at the door, and I went to call Betty one more time, even though she'd had instructions to have the restaurant page me if a call came in.

Wouldn't you know? Both pay phones were busy. I paced, went to the bathroom, came back out in the hall, and fidgeted until one of the callers became so irritated at my eavesdropping that he hung up and left, but not without a parting jab. "If you're that anxious to get to the phone, lady," he said, "I hope your line is busy when you reach it."

Darned if it wasn't. I fidgeted some more, hovering over the phone in fear someone else would want to use it before I could get through to Betty. That's what I got for not having Call Waiting.

After three tries I finally heard the phone ring on the other end of the line. Betty answered immediately. "I'm glad you called," she said. "I've been tryin' to get you at that restaurant, but they kept me waitin' on the phone for so long, I finally hung up. I thought they'd forgotten about me, and I was just gettin' ready to try again."

The cashier had probably been looking for me, but no wonder she couldn't find me. I'd been hiding in the hall waiting to get on the phone. "Did Shirley call?" I asked.

"She did," Betty said. "So you did need me, after all. I thought you were just trying to keep me here."

Happy that she now felt appreciated, I urged her on.

"The woman sounded all panicky," Betty continued. "Wanted you to meet her at—" She stopped to consult a piece of paper, which I heard being crumpled in the background. "Yeah, here it is on some kind of list you made." One of my endless to-do lists, no doubt. "She said to meet her at the Desert Oasis Bar and Grill and that you were to come alone. She said that's where she was when she called, and she'd wait for you as long as she could."

"Did she say where it was?"

"No, I figured you'd know."

Right, like I knew every bar in town. I hung up with the promise that I was bringing home the chicken dinner I'd mentioned to Betty earlier.

Maybe I should have told Betty to call out the troops if I wasn't home in a couple of hours. But what was I thinking? Betty was so suspicious of the cops that she wouldn't want to do that. Maybe I should tell her to call Mack, but he would have a fit if he found out about my late-night plans.

I picked up the phone, ready to call Stan. No, it would be even worse with Stan, especially after his order last night at Adam's Rib to stay out of things. I put the receiver back on the hook and decided I could always call someone from the bar—but first I had to find out where it was.

I grabbed for the phone book hanging from a chain under the phone. Wouldn't you know? There was no book inside the black cover, and I was wasting valuable time. I finally borrowed a phone book from the cashier and found the address on a street that sounded as if it was in LoDo. I almost forgot the stupid chicken as I left.

CHAPTER 18

The Desert Oasis turned out to be in what I quickly dubbed LoLoDo, way beyond the trendy microbreweries and "in" eateries favored by the beautiful people. In fact it was in a downright scuzzy neighborhood, the kind of place you feel uncomfortable visiting in the daylight, much less at night. If it was an "oasis," it was only because it promised a drink to lost souls in their otherwise bleak and blighted surroundings.

A neon sign that was about to burn out blinked from the top of the building. It had a token palm tree by the name of the bar. One of the fronds on the tree had already burned out, as had the word *Desert* and the *O* in *Oasis*. That left only the letters *ASIS*, or "take it or leave it" as I came to think of it. When the *I* went, all that would be left was *ASS*, which is kind of the up-yours way the place looked.

There was a drunk passed out on the sidewalk and another one, still upright, drinking from a paper bag in his hand. My stomach clenched at the thought that this was the kind of life Betty must have endured plenty of times.

A faded sign pointed to a parking lot behind the bar, but I circled the block and parked across the street, not wanting to drive through the dim passageway between the bar and a building next door. I was sure the parking lot would be equally dark and scary.

As I climbed out of my car, I could hear angry voices being carried by the warm night air. Glass shattered somewhere, and I heard the sound of a car backfiring. I wasn't sure cars even backfired anymore, but that's what I wanted to think it was. I dashed across the street to the front door. Luckily there weren't many people inside. Most of them were too far gone on a Sunday night to care about me, but one guy who looked as if he were straight out of *Silence of the Lambs* gave me the evil eye. Now, here was a place that, I would have to agree with Stan, I had no business being.

I looked around for the woman from the trailer park, but there was an obvious scarcity of females in the place. I slunk to a booth as the eyes of the Hannibal the Cannibal lookalike followed me. Damn, I really should have called the police about this and let them provide me with cover. It was the urgency of Shirley's call—"I'll try to wait as long as I can"—that had made me rush off on my mission without giving it nearly enough thought. That and the fact that I hadn't a clue where the place actually was. I guess in my own mind I'd been sure it was in the real LoDo, that sanctuary for partying yuppies and baseball fans.

But the Desert Oasis was beyond the fringe, a place of darkness and dank smells. If Shirley was here, it wasn't obvious. I eased into the booth and wished it had a high back so that I could hide behind it. Instead, with its shoulder-height torn Naugahyde seats, I felt exposed and vulnerable.

At least this way Shirley could see me. Maybe she was hiding someplace, waiting to make sure I was alone. She'd told Betty that I wasn't to bring anyone with me. And I was alone, all right. At least until Hannibal came over, shoved his round, hairless face down toward me, and offered to buy me a drink. He wouldn't take no for an answer, and he was trying to squeeze in the booth beside me when the bartender came over.

You wouldn't have expected a gentlemanly bartender in a place like that, but the burly, bald-headed proprietor, a lot taller than Hannibal, said "Hey, dipstick, can't you see the lady wants to be alone?"

I guess the bartender had figured that out by the way I was trying to push the man out of the booth.

"Damn it, Harvey, can't a guy have a little fun?" Dipstick said, but he went away. I let out my breath as if it were escaping from a helium balloon.

"What can I get you, lady?" the barkeep asked.

"Uh—" I started to speak but discovered that I didn't have any air left in my lungs. I took in a breath and squeaked, "Just coffee—black."

"Sorry, we don't have much call for coffee here. How about a cappuccino?"

Hey, even in my dazed condition I knew he was kidding. I liked a protective bartender with a sense of humor. "I'll take a Coors," I said. After all, we were practically in the shadow of Coors Field.

If not the police, I should have at least called Mack, I realized as I scrunched down in my seat. I hated even to look around for Shirley, afraid that I would catch the evil eye of the dipstick with the Hannibal Lecter look. I finally glanced around, and I didn't see him. He must have gone out the front door. I was facing toward the back and he hadn't gone that way.

Dumb to sit facing the back, but I'd been trying to make myself as inconspicuous as possible when I came in. Ha! I stuck out as if I were wearing mink at an animal rights meeting. Never mind that I was wearing jeans and a T-shirt.

The bartender came back and put the Coors and a glass

on the table. "Enjoy," he said, although he had an amused look on his face and knew full well I wouldn't enjoy it. But at least he didn't ask what a girl like me was doing in a place like this.

The glass didn't look too clean. I opted to drink the beer straight from the bottle. I wiped the top of the bottle, took a sip, and tried to look out of the corner of my eye to see if Shirley had ever appeared. What I discovered is that you can't really see out of the corner of your eye very well. I gave a couple of hurried sweeps of the room. Still no Shirley.

She would have been as obviously out of place as I was in here. Why, "out of all the gin joints" in the world, had she chosen this one? I realized that I was getting giddy, thinking of a line from *Casablanca* at a time like this. Mack would have enjoyed it if he were sitting across from me. Why, oh, why hadn't I called him?

Maybe Shirley had escaped from a house in the neighborhood where her boyfriend was holding her hostage and this was the closest place she could find to call. She wouldn't have wanted to be out on the street for any length of time, not if he were out there searching for her. Maybe she was hiding in the ladies' room. Did they even have a ladies' room? Somehow I didn't have a strong enough desire to find out. I'd come this far. Let her find me.

But perhaps she wasn't going to show. I glanced at my watch. I'd waited fifteen minutes now, and it hadn't taken me that long to get here from Speer Boulevard. So why wasn't she here? I tried to think what she might have wanted to tell me. A confession that had something to do with Kate and the dress, I was sure. But what? Unfortunately my mind had shut down, just the way my body seemed to have done. I couldn't move.

A couple of rowdy guys had come in the bar. I could hear

them. "Hey, look at the chick over there. I wonder if she wants a little action."

I stayed still, like I was a mannequin that had been placed in the booth for advertising purposes. But I couldn't stay here all night. I moved my hands and with an effort lifted the bottle to my lips.

"How about it, chick? Lookin' for a little action?" One of the guys from the rowdy crew who'd just come in was leaning down, leering at me. He had slicked-back dark hair and a pencil-thin mustache, and the only action I wanted was for him to disappear.

"Get out of my face, creep," I yelled.

My voice was so loud, it even got the attention of an old guy passed out at a table nearby. His head rose for a minute, then sank down again.

I'd heard once that if you yelled and swore at an attacker, he was more apt to go away. Surprisingly it worked, although I wouldn't bank on it as a sure-fire method to ward off muggers. Better to know a little karate. I'd put that on my to-do list as soon as I got home.

I think the real reason the guy probably left was that he was three sheets and a couple of pillowcases to the wind already. He staggered away and slumped down beside his buddies at a table up front.

For the moment no one was leering at me, and I decided it was about time to split this place. Two guys had gone away, but I didn't want to ward off a third one.

Shirley wasn't coming. It had been half an hour, and she'd had plenty of time to peek out of the restroom or whatever place she might be hiding. By now it was pretty obvious to everyone that no one was following me as backup.

I'd nursed my beer to the bottom of the bottle, and I sure

didn't feel like having another one. It was definitely time to be moseying along. Breaking into a dead run was more like it. Still, I couldn't leave without one last try at finding Shirley.

I walked across the room, sure that every eye that was still open was following me. Then I bellied up to the bar, so to speak, even though I have to say that the rest of my body gave me a lot of resistance.

The bartender was drying glasses with a dirty-looking towel down at the other end. It made me glad that I'd chosen to drink straight from the bottle. I didn't think I could get to where he was standing without my knees buckling. Besides, I wanted to be as close as possible to the front door in case I needed to make a quick break for it.

"Sir," I said to get his attention. The word seemed out of place here, so I yelled in a louder voice, "Hey, Harvey."

He came down the long bar toward me with a look on his face that seemed to say, *I knew she'd tell me what she's doing here if I waited long enough.*

I put a twenty-dollar bill on the counter, wondering if this was the place where you should offer the bartender a bribe for information. "Could you tell me if there was a woman in here about an hour ago who was waiting in one of those booths?"

"Yeah," he said, taking my money. "She waited around for a while, sitting in that back booth over there." He gave a nod of his head to the rear of the room. "Then it looked as if she saw something she didn't like out front, and she took off out the back door."

"Oh." I'd been standing, and I sat down on the barstool. "Did anyone come in looking for her?"

"Not as far as I saw."

I really should have asked about her sooner instead of sitting in that booth, not telling him what I wanted.

He went to the till and came back with the rest of the money from a single beer.

"Keep the change," I said, even though it was the biggest tip I'd ever given in my life. As far as I was concerned, he'd earned it for running interference for me with the *Silence of the Lambs* guy. To my way of thinking, I was also tipping him for any future aid he might need to render to me.

I say that because no matter how much the thought chilled me, I knew I had to take a look in the parking lot for Shirley. What if she'd gotten so scared that she'd decided to wait for me in her car where she felt more protected? That way she could run at the slightest sign of the danger she'd feared from the street. She might have expected me to park in the lot and thought she could waylay me as I got out of my car.

"Thanks," I said as I forced myself off the barstool.

The bartender pocketed my enormous tip. "Anytime."

"Fat chance," I said, but not so he could hear me.

The hallway leading to the back door was as dark and spooky as I'd thought it looked from the booth. There *was* a door that said WOMEN on it, and I took a quick look inside. There was only a dirty toilet and washbasin, no stalls, so it was easy to see that Shirley wasn't there.

I might have considered locking the door and hiding inside until the light of day, but there didn't seem to be a very satisfactory lock on the door. In fact I wasn't sure it locked at all. I shut the door and continued to the end of the hall.

Don't go outside, the rational part of my brain said. *You have to go,* the illogical side said. *What if she's waiting for you? But what if this is a trap, a setup to grab you the moment you open the door?* My feet agreed with the rational side of my brain. They refused to move. I leaned against the door, trying to get up the courage to yank it open. I couldn't hear anything on the other side. But why would I? I wanted to turn and run through the bar and keep on running to the safety of my car.

As the seconds stretched by, I finally made up my mind. I wouldn't actually go outside, just open the door and take a quick look around. If I saw Shirley, I would give a friendly wave to motion her back inside. Sure, right. Mandy, the human welcome mat that people stepped all over.

I yanked on the door, and that's when I saw the monster truck with the big wheels. It was parked right beside the entrance, and I could see a head leaning against the window on the passenger's side.

Before I knew what I was doing, I rushed over and stood on tiptoe to grab the door handle. The door flew open and Shirley's body fell out on top of me.

CHAPTER 19

I knew it was Shirley. The light came on inside the truck when I opened the door, and I could see her wide-open eyes and the hole in her chest. I wrestled to push her body back in the truck. Then I slammed the door and stumbled through the bar, tears running down my face.

"What the hell's wrong?" the bartender asked as soon as he saw me.

"Call the police. She—she—she's in a truck outside, and she's dead." Well, maybe she was still alive, but I didn't think so.

"Oh, shit." He reached for the phone as the other people in the bar began to do a disappearing act. At least the ones who were still able to walk.

I was shaking as if it were January, not June.

The man poured me a brandy. "It's on the house."

I drank it, hoping it would stop my shakes. I didn't even care if the police thought I had the DTs. All I wanted was for the trembling to stop. I hated the way it made me feel—as if I had no control over my own body, much less events around me.

The bartender held the bottle in the air. "Here, have another shot."

"Thanks." I didn't drink it. Later maybe. I'd just glanced down at the front of my T-shirt. There was blood on it, and I imagined I could feel it staining my skin underneath. I wanted to strip off the T-shirt or cover it up. Something.

"You gonna be okay?" the bartender asked as he continued to watch me shake. The man had a cauliflower ear and looked as if he'd been lifted out of an Elmore Leonard novel, but he'd come to my rescue before. I decided to try again.

"You wouldn't happen to have a coat or something that I could put on?" I asked without much hope.

The bartender went through a door to a back room. He reappeared with a jacket that had seen better decades. "Someone left this here."

I could see why. It was so grungy that, under normal circumstances, I would even have refused to accept it at my cleaners. But these weren't normal circumstances, and I put it on.

I heard a siren in the distance. Thank God, this would be over soon. I wanted to go home and hide.

Two uniformed officers came through the door. In this neighborhood I was glad they came in pairs.

I went over to them. "There's a woman in a truck in the parking lot, and I think she's been shot in the chest." I didn't really know because of all the blood. "She's right outside the back door." I pointed down the hallway to the rear of the building.

"Stay here," one of the cops said. "We'll want to talk to you later." His hand close to his revolver, he started to the back door. The other cop followed him.

I was glad I knew the drill and that I didn't have to go with them. I looked over at the bartender, who acted as if none of this was happening. I was sure the cops would talk to him too, but for now he'd gone back to drying glasses with the dirty towel.

I sat down at a table near him, just for the human contact, and waited for the cops' return. I wanted a cigarette. I'd managed to get through these last few nightmarish days without the desire, but now I craved one. I almost asked the bartender if he had any I could bum or if there was a cigarette machine in the place.

Just then one of the cops came back inside. "Do you know who she is?" the man asked when he sat down at the table beside me.

"Yes." Thank God for the brandy. At least I wasn't stuttering. "I think her name's Shirley Sawyer, but I couldn't see all that well." Actually I'd seen more than I wanted to.

"Is that the way you found her?"

"No." I hated to admit that I'd stuffed her back in the truck, but I did. "When I saw her, I opened the door and she fell out on top of me. I pushed her back inside and went for help."

"Okay." He had a pad and pencil out and asked for my name.

I gave it to him.

"How did you happen to find the body? Is she a friend of yours?"

I shook my head.

"So you just happened to see the body in the truck as you were walking by?"

That's when I finally started my long, convoluted explanation of how she'd called me and wanted to meet me here. I shivered as I told the story. I was cold even in the filthy old jacket. Maybe I would never get warm again. The brandy had lost its warming effect, and I felt frozen inside.

"The bartender over there"—I pointed to where the man was now looking through a newspaper as if he didn't have a care in the world—"he said the woman had been here waiting for me, but she got up and ran out the back door when it looked as if she'd seen something out the front window."

The bartender gave me a dirty look.

"I'll get to him," the policeman said. "Now, would you look over this statement and sign it?"

Another policeman arrived to question the bartender. Meanwhile I saw whirling lights and heard vehicles turning into the dark alleyway that I'd refused to drive through earlier. If I'd chosen to go back to the parking lot in my car, would I have run into Shirley or would I have found her already dead? Or had the plan been to have Shirley get me here and then kill us both?

I didn't think so, because I'd been spared and Shirley had been shot for—what?—calling me or for things that she knew or had done earlier. She'd obviously been on the run, and all of a sudden I had a scary thought. Had that sound I'd heard as I crossed the street been the shot that killed her? I'd wanted to think it was the backfire from a car. I wondered if I'd missed her by just a few seconds. Maybe I'd been parking my car as she fled out the back door; maybe she'd even seen me park and fled, not from the killer but from me. She might suddenly have gotten cold feet about what she'd planned to tell me.

I shivered and realized that I'd been staring at the statement page that the officer had given me to sign. He was watching me with a whole lot more patience than I would have had. *Concentrate,* I urged myself, *so that I can go home.* I read as fast as I could and finally signed my name. I needed to get out of here before either Stan or Detective Reilly showed up. Surely it wouldn't be either one of them.

"We meet again." It was a nightmare coming true. Officer Reilly's hulking lineman frame cast a shadow over the table.

"What the hell are you doing here?" he asked. "I told you to stay out of this. Stan told you to stay out of this."

I wanted to cover up the words on the statement so he wouldn't see that Shirley Sawyer had called me and I'd come running to the rescue. "I can explain," I said.

He took a chair from another table and turned it around so that his arms rested on the back and his legs straddled the seat. "I'm listening. . . ." He sounded like Frasier greeting a caller on the TV show. He ran his hands through his sandy hair in a gesture of impatience that belied the calm sound of his words.

"Stan must have told you about the woman—Shirley Sawyer," I said, looking off at the bartender instead of into Reilly's eyes. "I'm sure she had something to do with Kate's death. Anyway, she called me tonight and said she wanted to meet me.

"I wasn't even home. I was having dinner not too far from here, and the message said she would try to wait for me as long as she could. There seemed to be such urgency about it that I came over here as fast as I could. I was hoping I could catch her while she was still here and convince her to talk to you." I took a deep breath.

"And . . ." Reilly rolled his hand in a circle as if he expected me to continue.

I hadn't planned on saying any more. "That's all. She wasn't here, but when the bartender told me that a woman had been in here earlier and had taken off to the parking lot, I went to the back door and opened it. That's when I saw her body."

"Okay." He grabbed the statement from me and read it, then stood up and swung the chair around to push it under the table. "We're going to take you downtown for a video-taped interview."

* * *

This was serious. It was also the most humiliating experience of my life, being questioned on camera in one of those little interview rooms at police headquarters.

I felt drained when I was through. I like to think the police finally realized I didn't know anything, and that's why they let me go. A uniformed officer took me back to my car. I could still see lights and hear activity in the parking lot behind the bar, but I started my car and drove home without a backward glance. If I never saw Detective Reilly again, it was fine with me. I was sure the feeling was mutual.

At some point during the interview I'd admitted that I found out from a neighbor that Shirley had a boyfriend named Monty and a brother named P.T. I said I believed they were the men who'd had the ticket for Kate's Fortuny dress and had tried to run me down in the parking garage.

I kept wondering if Monty or P.T. killed Shirley. But would a brother kill his own sister? And what about Monty? He'd beaten her, but would he kill her in his own truck? If he'd killed her, I would have thought he would have dragged her out of the truck instead of messing up the interior. Besides, wouldn't he have wanted to use the truck to make his escape from the parking lot?

It was after midnight when I lugged the now-soggy chicken dinner up to my apartment. Betty unlocked my dead bolt, removed the chain, and grabbed for the box.

"It's about time," she said. "I'm starvin' to death."

I pulled back the dinner. "I don't know if it'll be any good now. It's been in my car all this time."

"Oh, for crap sakes, I've eaten food that's been out in the weather a whole lot longer than this."

The image of Betty eating scraps she'd found in trash cans flashed through my mind, but it didn't even phase me after the night I'd had. I shoved the dinner at her, not even sure I would mind if she got ptomaine poisoning.

"Your phone's been keepin' me awake," she complained as she rubbed her sleep-filled eyes and limped to the kitchen table with her haul.

I realized that my own leg was feeling better. It didn't seem to matter anymore.

Betty opened the lid of the Styrofoam box and plucked out a chicken breast. "I quit answerin' after you got the call you wanted, but that guy, Nat, he's been callin' about every twenty minutes. His name should be Nag, not Nat. Nag, nag, nag. Whining for you to call him all the time. I got to tell you, I felt like pickin' up the phone a couple of times and giving him what-for."

"Okay, thanks." I was on my way to the bathroom to strip out of my clothes and take a shower. "He generally quits calling about midnight, so I'll call him in the morning."

Betty stopped eating long enough to add, "And that fancy-smantzy policeman friend of yours called and said you guys needed to talk."

"Stan?" I came back out of the bathroom.

"Yeah, Stan. You really should be more choosy in your friends."

I didn't want to call him if he were going to chew me out, but if there was any chance of salvaging our relationship, I supposed I should. I went over to the phone and punched in his number.

CHAPTER 20

Stan must have been waiting for my call. He picked up after the first ring. "Look," he said, "I was hoping you'd get home earlier. I wanted to talk to you about—well, what we were discussing last night."

Oh, yes, when I'd blown my top and accused him of having a girlfriend whom he met on his secret out-of-town trips.

"Okay?" I wasn't sure I was up to hearing about it tonight.

"It's about that trust thing," he explained.

Well, maybe he hadn't heard about my finding another body yet. And if it wasn't about that, I was willing to listen. Anytime, anyplace. Well, almost anyplace.

"I know it's late, but could I come over to your apartment for a few minutes?" Stan asked.

I turned my head away from Betty. "I still have—company."

"Oh."

I glanced over at my houseguest. She was happily gnawing on a chicken leg.

"Maybe I could pick you up and we could come over

here to my place," Stan said. "It's something I kind of wanted to discuss in private."

I hesitated.

"I wanted to explain about those trips you were wondering about." He sounded like the poor, rumpled guy who'd asked me for cleaning tips when we first met, not the hard-nosed homicide detective of the last few days.

"All right," I said finally, "but I can drive myself. I'll be there soon."

I had to take a shower first. I sure didn't want him to show up while I was in the bathroom and risk having Betty tell him about her tumble down the stairs at the flea market.

We hung up, and I wished I'd suggested that we meet at a restaurant someplace. I didn't particularly enjoy going to his apartment. His dog, Sidearm, hated me, as I've mentioned before. At least Spot the Cat hated everyone indiscriminately—with the possible exception of Betty—and he didn't bark at them.

I looked down and realized I was still wearing the same grungy brown jacket the bartender had loaned me. I tossed it on the floor and started into my big, walk-in closet to find clean clothes.

"Heh, heh," Betty snickered. "That looks like something I woulda found in a garbage can in the old days."

Right, and that's where I intended to throw it as soon as possible. But I didn't feel much differently about my other clothes. Now that someone had gone through them, yanking them off hangers and tossing them on the floor in the break-in, I felt as if they were dirty too. Tomorrow I would gather them up, Betty's included, and take them down to the plant to be recleaned.

"So did you meet that woman who called?" Betty asked. She'd dispensed with the chicken leg and picked up a wing.

"I'll tell you about it in a minute." I grabbed another pair of jeans and a cotton shirt from the closet and went to the bathroom. Then I took off the clothes I'd been wearing when I found Shirley's body and tossed them in my wastebasket. Even a dry cleaner knows that there is no way to remove the stains left by bad memories on your clothes. I didn't stay in the shower as long as I wanted, but it would have taken all night to wash off the horror of finding Shirley's body.

I dressed and came back into the room where Betty was. She was licking her lips, having taken care of the chicken. Spot had appeared from one of his secret hiding places and was licking his chops too. She must have shared the chicken with him before she moved on to the salad and mashed potatoes. I offered to warm the potatoes, but Betty said they were fine the way they were.

"So," she asked, "what about the lady you were supposed to meet?"

"Someone killed her before I could talk to her."

I heard Betty gasp, but I was inside the closet again, looking for my windbreaker. I started going through a pile of clothes, still on the floor, and I finally found a sweater to take with me.

I pulled it on and returned to the living room. Betty had quit eating and was watching me. "Do you really think you ought to be going out again tonight? You seem to attract trouble like a maggot."

I did a double-take. "Magnet. I think you mean magnet."

She shrugged. "Whatever."

Actually now that I thought about it, what she'd said seemed like a pretty apt analogy. Apt, but very, very scary.

"Lock the dead bolt and put on the chain after I leave," I said. "I'll be back in an hour or so, and you can let me in."

She accompanied me to the door.

"And if you hear anything outside," I said, "for God's sake, call the police. Don't just wait out on the fire escape."

She held the door for me. "Be careful."

I wished she hadn't said that.

The roads were eerily deserted at this hour on a Monday morning. I hadn't realized how vulnerable I'd feel to be out in the dark again. I almost wished I'd taken Stan up on his offer to pick me up, but I tried to shake off the feeling. This way I could make a quick getaway, I told myself, if Sidearm attacked me as soon as I got there.

Stan lived in a much nicer neighborhood than I did. His apartment was a second-story unit with a separate entrance from the outside, and as I climbed the stairs, my heart was pounding a whole lot louder than the sound my footsteps made on the steps. The closer I'd come, the more I'd become convinced that Stan was probably going to chew me out, after all. Then good old Sidearm could finish me off.

Still, Stan was the first man I'd cared about in a very long time, and I decided the trip was worth the risk.

The door was open when I reached the landing. No need to ring a doorbell, though. Sidearm announced my arrival with an outburst of yips that were punctuated by him throwing himself against the screen door. Stan had once described the terrier as "the friendliest mutt in the world," but I personally thought Stan was delusional about the dog. "A four-legged terror" was a much better description.

"He'll calm down in a few minutes," Stan said.

Yeah, yeah, that's what he told me the other time I'd been here, but Stan had wound up having to put Sidearm in the bedroom and close the door. Sidearm didn't like it and continued to paw at the door for what seemed like hours. At least cats generally only scratch the furniture instead of doing structural damage to the house.

I could see that Stan was determined to give Sidearm and me another chance to bond. I guess he continued to live with the fantasy that the dog would get to like me if he got to know me better.

"I think he knows that you've been around a cat," Stan said as he grabbed Sidearm's collar to keep the dog from leaping on me. The brown and white dog had an actual brown spot on his rump, and deserved a name like Spot far more than my cat did. He drew back a few paces and growled at me as I entered the room.

Stan gave me one of those endearingly crooked smiles that I'd decided wasn't crooked at all. It just looked that way because the cleft in his chin was a little off center. "Thanks for coming. You look great. I like you without any makeup."

Oh, swell, I'd even forgotten to put on lipstick, and I was sure I looked as tired as Stan did. His blond, curly hair was ruffled, as if he'd been running his hands through it while he waited for me. He was still wearing slacks and a white shirt, but he'd taken off the jacket and tie that were part of his uniform for his work.

I could see that he'd already poured a glass of wine for me, and he had a half-full bottle of beer on the coffee table in front of the sofa, but I wasn't going to fall for that sitting-close-to-him routine. Not with Stan's protector only inches away. Sidearm had gotten particularly incensed when we'd tried to sit close to each other the other time I was here, so I took a position on one end of the couch with Stan at the other end. Sidearm stationed himself so that he could stare at me from just across the coffee table.

Stan rubbed his eyes. "It's been a hell of a day. We had a couple of bodies that were pulled out of City Park lake this afternoon. No ID."

If he'd been busy on another case, then he probably didn't know about the hell of a day I'd had myself. I decided not to tell him about Shirley Sawyer until I heard what he had to say.

He gazed off into space, and Sidearm continued to stare at me. The dog seemed ready to pounce at my slightest movement.

Stan cleared his throat. "You were saying that I was so secretive about what I did sometimes on my days off."

"Look, I apologize. It really isn't any of my business."

"No, please, I want to tell you about it." He went on without giving me a chance to argue. "You see, there's this kid up in Fort Collins—he's thirteen—and I've been going up there to see him. Last Christmas he got into some trouble, and we're trying to see if we can get him straightened out."

"We?" I asked.

"His grandparents and I."

"I see." Well, actually nothing could have been further from the truth.

Stan took a gulp of beer, then looked down as if checking to see how much was still in the bottle. "His mother and I were engaged. . . ."

That's all I heard because, pray tell, where was this fiancée now? I missed some of his concerns about the boy being arrested for vandalism, but when I turned back, Stan was still talking about him. "I guess I feel responsible for him in some way."

What? Was this his son, and if so, why hadn't he told me about the boy before?

"His father left when he was about a year old, and nobody's ever heard from the guy since," Stan continued.

"And the mother?"

"She was killed on the job."

"Oh, Stan, I'm sorry."

He didn't seem to hear me. "We were both street cops back then, but I'd taken off for a few days to go fishing. She pulled my shift one night and was shot when she tried to apprehend a burglary suspect. I should have been the one who got the call."

"I'm sorry." I looked over at him, and he was staring straight ahead again, as if to move might make him lose control of his emotions. I reached over to him, and he grabbed my hand, gripping it until it hurt. Sidearm, ever vigilant, got up on all fours and quivered.

I held on to his hand, but I didn't know how to ease his pain. And I wondered if there could ever be a future for us until Stan resolved his guilt or let go of the love he had for his former fiancée. Maybe telling me was a start, but he had to make peace with himself, and I didn't know if I was capable of helping him do that.

He looked over at me finally. "I guess that's why I get a little crazy when you barge into things the way you do," Stan said. "I don't want something to happen to you too."

I wanted to tell him that it wasn't his fault his fiancée was killed, but I'm sure he already knew that on an intellectual level. And any danger I got into was because I'd brought it on myself. But I couldn't say that either. Not right now. Not when he had that haunted look on his face. And unfortunately I couldn't very well tell him about Shirley Sawyer after all this.

"Jack was really pissed about you going to the trailer park yesterday," he continued.

It took me a minute to realize that Jack must be Detective Reilly and that Stan obviously didn't yet know about my finding another body. If he thought Jack was pissed over the trailer-park incident, he should have seen the detective tonight.

I needed time to think about everything, and I got to my feet. Unfortunately I did it too fast, and Sidearm started barking. I stood very still until he calmed down. Then I raised my hands slowly in a gesture of surrender. "You don't have to worry about me anymore. From now on, the only thing I'm going to do is clean clothes."

After what had happened tonight, I didn't want anything to do with flea markets, garage sales, or especially with clandestine meetings at bars. But what did I do when people broke into my apartment and trashed the place? Not tell Stan, that was for sure, but I did need to get back home to make sure Betty and Spot were okay. "Look, I have to be at work at seven o'clock—so I'd better get going. And I appreciate you confiding in me. . . ." That sounded so callous. "I mean, I'm really sorry about what happened, and . . ." My voice trailed off because I didn't know what else to say.

Stan nodded, and I moved toward the door. The ever-alert Sidearm took off after me.

"Sidearm, sit," Stan yelled. The dog backed off, and his owner tried to reassure me. "Don't worry. He won't bite."

I wouldn't put money on it.

Stan walked me to my car as Sidearm's barks followed us down the stairs.

"Why don't I follow you home to make sure you get there okay?" Stan asked.

"No, I'm fine, really."

"Then call me when you get there. Okay?" Stan reached down and kissed me before I climbed in my car, but I wasn't sure this would ever work out. Spot and Sidearm hadn't even met yet, and look how complicated it was.

*   *   *

It was nearly two in the morning when I got home. On the drive I began to think of all the questions I hadn't asked: How long had it been since Stan's fiancée was killed? Would Stan's guilt recede in time, or was I fighting a losing battle to invest any more time in the relationship? For now I was too tired to think about Stan or Kate or Shirley Sawyer. What I had to do was concentrate on getting a few hours' sleep before I went to work.

And I might have been able to do that if I could have gotten into my apartment. I knocked so that Betty could let me in. I unlocked the dead bolt and opened the door to the length of its chain.

"Betty," I yelled. "Let me in, will you?" Nothing. "Hey, Betty. I'm home. Open the door." Still nothing.

I had a moment of panic, wondering if someone had broken into the apartment again, then escaped down the fire escape. I banged on the door and yelled for Betty some more. Finally I heard her snoring.

You'd think a woman who'd slept on the streets for God knows how many years would have had to be more vigilant than this. In fact you'd have expected her to take little catnaps, always ready to react at a moment's notice to any danger. Strange I should think of catnaps, because just then Spot showed up at the door. He sniffed at me through the crack, but would he meow or go to Betty and scratch her awake? No. He flipped his tail at me as he sauntered away. I could see him jump on my Hide-A-Bed, circle a couple of times, and do a little grooming before he went to sleep.

I felt like crying, but then I got mad. I trudged off to a pay phone on Colfax to call Betty. I wasn't even scared on the walk. On the fourth ring she answered the phone and said she would unlock the door. Then I called Stan and told him I was home so he wouldn't come looking for me. Apparently he didn't hear the street noises in the background.

By the time I arrived back at the apartment, the chain was off its hook, and Betty was already snoring again.

CHAPTER 21

Actually if I'd been thinking clearly, I would have gone on down to work in the middle of the night and slept on the sofa in the break room. I'd done it before, and I did have clean clothes at work.

As it was, the next morning I dragged myself out of bed and put on a cheery red skirt and a red-and-white striped blouse, both only slightly wrinkled from being tossed on the floor by the burglars.

I gathered up a bunch of my other clothes, along with the things we'd bought for Betty at the flea market, to take with me to be cleaned or laundered as the fabric dictated. Then I left a note for Betty that I'd be home at ten-thirty to take her to her new apartment.

It was Mack's week to open up, and most of the crew was already at work when I arrived. At the back door Mack was waiting for me. We always talked over the day's production schedule in the mornings, but today he couldn't resist a jab about Betty. "How's the *woman* who came to dinner?" he asked with a grin.

"Everything's taken care of," I said over the load of clothes I was carrying. "I've found an apartment for her, and

I'm going to move her over to it later this morning." I felt like saying "So there," but I thought it might be premature to get cocky about it.

Mack turned serious. "And everything's okay with your apartment? Did anything turn up missing?"

"No more break-ins and nothing missing." I badly wanted to get on to work-related topics.

"Have the police found out anything more about Kate?" Mack persisted.

"Not that I know of." As with Stan, I just couldn't bring myself to talk about finding Shirley Sawyer's body last night. It wasn't so much that Mack would chew me out, which he would, but he worried about me. "Can we talk later?" I said. "I want to take these clothes up front so Lucille can mark them in for me. They're part of what the burglars threw on the floor."

I dropped off the clothes with Lucille at the mark-in counter. She was irritated that the clothes weren't in a traditional laundry bag with a ticket inside.

"They're all mine," I said, and kept on walking into the call office. Julia and Ann Marie were already at the counter, along with a few customers who'd stopped by on their way to work to drop off or pick up their clothes. I pitched in to help until the rush was over, then told Julia I'd be in my office doing neglected bookkeeping work and answering the while-you-were-out calls that had come in Saturday.

"I don't want to be disturbed unless it's really important," I said.

"Are you all right?" Julia, a mother of three, asked. "You look almost as bad as I feel after I've been up all night with a sick kid."

"Thanks a lot," I said with the hope that I'd get a good night's sleep as soon as Betty was gone.

"Yeah, Mandy, did you have an *exciting* weekend?" the

teenaged Ann Marie asked, convinced that the only reason to be tired on Monday was if a person led an active social life.

I frowned at her and hurried back through the plant. I deliberately skirted the dry-cleaning department so that I wouldn't have to talk to Mack again, and made it to my office with only a few conversations with the rest of the crew. I shut myself inside my office, which was against my usual open-door policy, but today I badly needed to be alone. It helped me concentrate, and I'd actually caught up with my computer work and was halfway through my list of phone calls when someone knocked on the door. It was the kind of knock that sounds like Morse code. *Dum-da-da-dum.* The trademark knock of Nat, the nosy newspaper reporter who'd kept calling all last night. I wasn't sure I wanted to see him, but he was on my list of people to call later that day about the memorial service for Kate, so I let him in.

"How did you get past my guards at the front counter?" I asked.

"Oh, I just charmed them with my sweet talk."

"Don't kid me. I bet you bribed them."

Nat shrugged and came over to the chair in front of my desk. He slouched into it and started to put his feet on the desk.

"Don't even think about it," I said.

"Okay, okay." He thumped his feet to the floor and sat up straight as if that would make me think he was on his best behavior. "You didn't return my calls yesterday." He sounded hurt, but I knew better. Nat was not like Mack, who worried about me. This was a guy looking for a story.

"I had to clean up my apartment." It was true of course, so I didn't itch, even though I knew I was leaving out a lot of my activities the previous couple of days. "My closet was a mess, and I—"

The last thing Nat wanted to hear was a detailed account of my weekend chores. "I'm late for work," he said, waving me off. "So what happened at the garage sales Saturday? Did you find out anything, or was the trip a wild-goose chase?"

I made a quick assessment of what he'd said. If he hadn't been to work yet, his police sources probably hadn't tipped him off about my finding Shirley Sawyer's body and her connection to the garage sale at the trailer park. Still, I had to be careful because he was always devious.

I decided to go on the attack. "I asked you to go with me, remember?" I pointed out. "You wouldn't do it, so now you're out of luck."

He gave me his most ingratiating smile, which he thought made him look like John Lennon. I wasn't buying it. I'd shared a lot of my personal problems with him, but I wasn't about to share anything the least bit newsworthy.

Nat pretended to pout. "Hey, I told you I had an interview already set up, and I couldn't get out of—"

"No, what you said was that you had a lead that none of the rest of the Denver press corps knew about yet. And never let it be said that you would give up the opportunity for a scoop to help out your oldest and dearest friend."

He studied me carefully. "It was a dud, wasn't it?"

I stayed on the offensive. "Okay, you tell me about your big scoop and I'll tell you about the garage sales."

"Sorry, you'll have to wait until Wednesday morning to read about it."

"I bet it's something to do with that woman up in the mountains who was killed a month ago when she surprised some burglars at her house. I already told you that."

The other time I'd guessed we'd been on the phone. This time I thought I could tell by the look on his face that I was right on target.

He pointed a finger at me. "You didn't find out anything,

did you? Otherwise you'd want to tell me about it before one of my competitors got wind of it."

Nat was wrong. The only way I might have considered telling him about it was if I was sure Detective Reilly wouldn't find out about it. Nat would have to get it from someone else.

We were at a standoff, but Nat still seemed unwilling to leave. He fidgeted in his chair, probably trying to decide if one last question would garner him some important information.

I told him about the memorial service as I looked at my watch. It was quarter to ten already, and I'd be late to get Betty if I didn't hurry. So I decided to give him some information that I was sure would be of no use to him.

"Look, I have to go, Nat," I said. "If you must know, Betty the Bag Lady showed up on my doorstep over the weekend, and—"

He didn't let me finish. He collapsed with laughter in his chair.

"Betty the Bag Lady," he said when he'd recovered. "This is great. She always makes things interesting when she's around."

I wasn't amused, although, in Nat's defense, he was the only friend who didn't give me grief about her. "I've found her a place to stay, and I have to move her over there right now."

"You're something else, you know that, Mandy?" He was still laughing as he made his way out the door and through the plant to the call office. I was tempted to follow him, but I refused to let Mack intimidate me with either his questions about my activities or his enjoyment over my problems with Betty.

He was just starting one of the cleaning machines while his assistant, Kim, pulled clothes out of the other one. We consulted on who among the crew didn't show up for work this morning. One presser had called in sick, but Mack said everything was under control.

"I'll be back in about an hour," I said.

"Good luck." I knew he was referring to the Betty-move, but I didn't even think to say "I'll need it." I was actually optimistic that this whole thing would work out.

When I picked Betty up, I remembered to collect some sheets, blankets, and a pillow to take along. I was in need of replenishing my linen closet anyway. I grabbed a few cooking utensils and decided to donate them to her. It was a good cause—getting her out of my apartment. Tonight I would be alone at last.

Betty seemed happy to be moving too. That is, until she met Mrs. O'Neal. The grandmotherly woman hovered over her as if Betty were a patient and Mrs. O'Neal were her nurse in Intensive Care.

"This is the woman I asked to look in on you for a few days while you stay off your feet," I explained to the ex–bag lady.

Betty gave me a dirty look.

I thought of calling her "Flo" to see what kind of response I'd get to the name the visitor mentioned the day before, but I decided this wasn't the time. Betty was still apt to take off if I weren't careful, although why I cared was beyond me.

Mrs. O'Neal—she said to call her Hazel—helped me make up the bed and get Betty settled. She offered us tea to welcome Betty to her new apartment. It was not a move that would endear her to the bag lady. Where were the melt-in-your-mouth cinnamon rolls that Hazel usually made? I'd been counting on them to make points for her with Betty, but I guess Hazel had a different idea of what was the proper way to treat a "patient."

"I even took the liberty of having the phone hooked up,"

Hazel said, "so if she wants anything, she can call me." I didn't know at the time what trouble that was going to cause.

I arrived back at work at noon, just in time to take over for Julia and Ann Marie when they went to lunch. Business was so slow now that summer was here that I even let them take their lunch break at the same time. I really ought to consider running a special on draperies, which always brought in summer business.

Just then the phone rang. "Dyer's Cleaners," I said, picking it up.

"This isn't working out. The woman is like a prison guard."

"Betty, is that you?"

"Of course it's me. Who'd you expect?"

Well, for starters, maybe a potential customer with an inquiry about how to find our plant.

"She made me eat some god-awful bull-yon that tasted like cow shit," Betty said. "*She* said it was good for me."

"Did you eat it?"

"Yeah, and it practically made me barf, and she wanted me to drink some more of that awful tea."

I'd been right about the doll doctor and Mrs. Santa Claus. They'd be perfect for each other with their love of tea.

"It tasted as bad as the bull-yon," Betty continued.

"She's just trying to get you back on your feet."

"Like that's going to help a sprained ankle."

I had turned my back on the door, hoping to muffle this conversation in the event a customer came in. I heard the door open, and turned around. It was Evan Carmody.

"Look, I have to go, Betty. We'll talk about this tonight." I hung up as she continued to protest. "Hello, Evan. What can I do for you?"

"It was in the neighborhood, and I thought I'd stop by

and get some of your business cards," he said. "That way I can give them to our customers when they make inquiries about where to clean the clothes they buy from us."

I didn't even look skeptical. I reached across the counter to a little stand with our business cards in it. "Here, and I'll get you some more if you'll wait a minute." I found the cards in a drawer under the counter and handed him a stack of them. "We appreciate any referrals we get, especially from a high-fashion salon like yours."

Evan nodded and put the cards in the breast pocket of his beautiful blue suit that I was sure had a designer label in it.

I handed him a 25-percent-off coupon. "Your—" I paused deliberately. "—your wife might want to try us sometime. I'm sure she would be pleased with our service."

He looked flustered for a minute. "So Kate told you I was married."

I smiled knowingly, and I had a hunch I was never going to have to honor that coupon. I didn't think he'd want his wife talking to me. Like I knew anything.

Evan seemed anxious to change the subject. "So did you find out anything from those classified ads I gave you?"

I shook my head. "None of them panned out." That wasn't a lie. I'd found the mobile home park because I'd noticed the ad for it myself and it was on a direct route between two of the addresses Kate had circled.

"That's too bad, but I really didn't think they would amount to much," Evan said "I'm sure she found the dress at an estate sale or from a private party, and I told the police as much."

I wondered if he'd come to see me because he knew about the mobile home park where I was now sure Kate had found the dress, or if he really believed what he said.

"The police questioned me about my relationship with

her." He looked at me suspiciously. "As I told you, it was strictly a business venture between Kate and me."

Yeah, sure, fella. I was quite sure now that Evan was the married man Kate had been referring to when she talked to the doll doctor, but I didn't know if it meant anything or not.

Evan had also said that Michael Morrison might have given her a black eye when in fact he was the one who looked as if he had a lot of suppressed anger under those dark good looks. But Michael and Evan had both told me that Kate said she got the black eye when she was trying to get something out of a closet and a box fell down and hit her. Maybe it really had.

"I'm doing an appraisal for Kate's parents so they can sell her business now that the police are through searching the place," Evan continued, "and I ran across a list of recent estate sales where she made purchases."

He reached inside his wallet, and I thought he might be planning to give me the addresses, so I started shaking my head. "You should give them to the police." I was out of the detecting business, but I couldn't resist one last question. "Does everything go to her parents, do you know?" The phone started to ring before he had a chance to answer. "Excuse me a minute." I reached for it. "Dyer's Clean—"

"Now she wants me to take a nap." It was Betty again with a new list of complaints. "The woman tucked me into bed like I was a little kid, and she's waiting outside the bedroom door to make sure I go to sleep."

Well, at least Betty had a one-bedroom apartment, which is more than I could say for myself. She ought to be happy.

"You gotta talk to her," she continued. "She's driving me nuts."

"Betty, I can't do anything right now. I already told you

that. I'll talk to her tonight." Again I hung up. "I'm sorry for the interruption. Where were we, Evan?"

"I was about to give you my business card." Apparently that's what he'd taken out of his wallet. "If you hear anything about what's going on, will you let me know?"

I nodded, but actually that wasn't where we'd been when the phone rang. I tried again. "Did Kate leave everything to her parents?"

"Naturally," he said as if I'd accused him of something underhanded. "With a proviso, of course, to repay my loan."

Well, that answered one of my questions at least: Would Evan inherit Kate's store in some sort of partnership agreement? At least it answered the question if he was telling me the truth, but it didn't necessarily mean that he should be dismissed as a suspect. Maybe he and Kate had gotten into a fight when she discovered he was married, and he'd killed her. That didn't explain why he was so interested in the Fortuny, but what if the dress had actually belonged to his wife, and he needed to get it back? What if he was involved in a burglary ring, and the dress could tie him to a crime? Or what if he simply wanted to find the Fortuny to display in his fancy dress salons? And maybe his wife was the one who'd wanted him to sever his relationship with Kate, which was why he'd denied that it was his idea.

The *what ifs* and *maybes* swirled around in my head so that I almost missed hearing him say good-bye. After he left, I couldn't help wondering why he'd come. Was he satisfied when I said I hadn't found any leads among the classified ads Kate had circled, or had the purpose of his mission been to send me off on a wild-goose chase to every estate sale in the last few months?

Not only was I through looking into where Kate had bought the dress, I was convinced that I'd already found it, just not who was behind her death and the attempt to get the dress back.

When Julia returned from lunch, I told her I was going back to my office. "If anyone calls, take a message and I'll call them back." I had a feeling that was the only way I was going to be able to avoid Betty for the rest of the afternoon.

I needed to think about what I was going to say at the memorial service, and besides, I'd promised Michael I would call Kate's old friends and tell them about it.

I caught Luella at her used-children's store. After I told her the time and place of the service, I asked her if she'd seen Red Berry at the flea market after we talked. She hadn't.

"Do you remember what his real name was?" I continued, still wondering about the coincidence of him showing up just after Kate was killed.

"No, I thought it was Red Berry," she said.

The other people I managed to reach were no more helpful. Several of them thought Red Berry was probably a stage name, but they didn't recognize the birth name he'd given me of Redmond Von Furstenberg.

I wondered if I should call Red's friend, Archie, also known as Bones, and tell him about the service. I grabbed the phone book and had just started to look up the number for Archie's Pawnshop when Julia knocked on the door. "Mandy, I think you'd better take this call."

"Is it a woman?"

"No, it's Detective Foster. He says it's business."

CHAPTER 22

Business? He must have heard about my finding Shirley's body last night. I should have told him about it when I saw him, even though there hadn't seemed to be a suitable opening.

"He's on Line Two," Julia said.

Had he and Detective Reilly talked it over and decided to arrest me for interfering with a police investigation?

"Aren't you going to take the call?" Julia asked.

My hand was poised to punch Line 2, but I felt as if I were floating in a telephone time warp.

"I can tell him you'll call back," she persisted.

"No, I have it." I hit the button, and Julia, looking puzzled, left. "Hello, Stan. What can I do for you?"

"I wondered if you could come down here this afternoon."

By "here" I assumed he meant police headquarters. God, they *were* going to arrest me. But wouldn't they have sent a cop to get me if that were true?

"Right now?" I asked.

"As soon as possible."

"Okay." What else could I say?

I thought I could hear him flipping through some papers. Probably my arrest warrant.

"And could you bring Theresa Emory with you?" he asked.

I was relieved. Maybe that meant I wasn't in hot water for obstruction of justice?

"All right." I looked at my watch. "Theresa comes to work at two, so she should be here now."

"Good, I'll see you in half an hour."

"Could you tell me what this is about?"

"I'll tell you when you get here."

I hung up and went to get Theresa. It had to be about our sketch of the man who'd come to the cleaners, the one who'd supposedly come to my rescue in the parking garage on Friday. Shirley's brother. Had they arrested him for her and Kate's murders?

Our sketch was the only thing Theresa and I had in common as far as the case was concerned. But if that's what this was about, why hadn't Detective Reilly called me?

I collected Theresa and made arrangements with Julia to work overtime in case we didn't get back by four.

"I've never been to police headquarters," Theresa said as if she were looking forward to it. "What's this about?"

"It must be because of the sketch we drew."

"Oh, yeah, maybe they've caught the guy and they want us to try to identify him in a police lineup."

Maybe, but why wouldn't Stan have told me that?

Thunderclouds were beginning to form above the mountains as they do on so many hot summer afternoons in Denver. I didn't know if my nerves could stand a lightning storm right now.

The clouds moved toward us, churning up the sky. I saw a distant flash of lightning somewhere near the foothills, then a few seconds later I heard the clap of thunder. If I could remember how long it took between the lightning and the thunder, I could figure out how far away it was.

The rain hadn't reached us by the time I parked at a lot across from the police building. I had only a twenty-dollar bill and some loose change in my purse, and there was a compartmentalized metal box where drivers were supposed to stick in three dollars for their parking fee. Theresa was no help with the fee because she hadn't brought any money.

I slipped $1.25 in coins through a slot and added a note that I had an appointment at the police station and would pay the rest later. Surely they wouldn't tow the car of a person who was trying to do her civic duty? I led the way across the street and by the side of the headquarters building to the front entrance. I couldn't help thinking of the videotaped interview the night before. I didn't like the place much better today, but at least I didn't have a police escort this time.

There was a granite slab outside the building with the names of all the officers who had died in the line of duty. I couldn't bring myself to stop and look at it. The name of Stan's fiancée must be there. There were also photos of the fallen officers inside the lobby with empty slots for those who would die in the future. In each blank space it said, "We pray that this frame will never be filled."

I remembered the collage from an even earlier occasion when I'd been there, and I was relieved that I didn't have to look at it again. How could Stan handle the stress of seeing those reminders of his fiancée day after day?

He was waiting for us at the information desk, far away from the photographs, and I introduced him to Theresa. He still looked tired, and I wondered if he'd been awake all night thinking about his fiancée and wondering if there was any future for us.

A uniformed officer buzzed us through a door in a

divider that kept the general public from the bank of eleva-
tors to the upper floors. Stan punched the elevator to send it
to the third-floor offices of Crimes Against Persons. Theresa
seemed awed by the whole experience.

"Could you tell us why we're here?" I asked.

The elevator came to a stop, and Stan stood aside to let
us out. "Later," he said. "Follow me." He led us down a hallway to the homicide department. There were several detectives inside, but luckily I didn't see the ferocious Reilly.

"Wait here," he said to Theresa, who was handling all this
far better than I. Stan had her sit in a chair at what I pre-
sumed was his desk. Then he led me into one of the interview rooms, similar to the one I'd been in last night. "I'll be
right back." He shut the door and left me to stare at the wall
with growing apprehension. Was it possible that Theresa and
I weren't here for the same thing? Were the detectives going
to interview me again about finding Shirley's body?

Thunder boomed nearby as the storm rolled into downtown Denver. I jumped as if I'd been hit by lightning, and
just at that moment Stan jerked the door open. I hoped he
wouldn't think he'd scared me.

He sat down and placed a couple of photographs on the
table. "I want you to tell me if you've ever seen these men
before."

I sat down across from him and pointed to one picture
immediately. "That's Shirley's brother, P.T." I recognized the
droopy eyes and thin upper lip. "He's the man in the sketch
that I gave to Detective Reilly—the man Theresa said was in
the cleaners Monday and later came to my rescue in the
parking garage. Did Theresa recognize him too?"

"What about *him*?" Stan indicated the other photograph.

The man in the picture was dark and swarthy-looking
the way Mary Lou had described Shirley's boyfriend.

"He looks like the other man in the parking garage, the one in the truck, but I can't be sure. I wasn't able to get that close a look at him."

"Okay, but you're sure the other photograph is of the man you talked to in the parking garage."

I nodded and looked over at him. "It's Shirley's brother, P.T., isn't it?"

Stan shook his head. "Not P. T. Sawyer."

"It has to be," I argued.

"His name's Perry Terrell, a.k.a. Louie Williams, a.k.a. Sam Louis, a.k.a.—"

"Not Shirley's brother?" I was grasping to understand. "Well, I guess his last name doesn't have to be Sawyer. That could have been Shirley's married name. And she probably just called him P.T. for Perry Terrell."

"You didn't let me finish. He has been going by the name P. T. Sawyer for the last few months, and he has a rap sheet a mile long, mostly for burglary and fencing stolen property."

"Then it is her brother!" I wanted to jump up and down. "I was right." I did get up, but I didn't jump. "Did Theresa identify him too?"

Stan picked up the picture as if he were starting to leave.

"Is that why you wanted us to come down, to identify him?" I continued. "Did you arrest him?"

"No." Stan drummed a hand on the table. "Remember how I told you about the bodies we pulled out of the lake at City Park yesterday?" He tapped at each photo. "The names of the victims were Perry Terrell and Monty Williams."

I sat back down and stared at the pictures. "It can't be." Now all the leads were gone.

"I read the report about your break-in, and I heard about you finding Perry's sister."

"P.T.'s sister," I corrected, still staring at the photos.

He reached across the table and raised my chin so that I had to look at him. "That was a stupid thing to do—going down to a bar to meet her. Why didn't you tell me about it last night?"

"You were upset. How could I tell you about the bar?"

"Look, promise me you won't do anything like that again."

"I already promised."

"Don't even talk to Kate's friends until we find the killer."

"I have to talk to her friends. I'm going to her memorial service Thursday."

"Okay, but we're dealing with a very dangerous person here. Perry or P.T., whatever you want to call him, and his friend Monty were shot execution-style in the back of the head."

I shuddered even though I tried to hold my body rigid. I didn't want to think of any more bodies. The memory of finding Kate's and Shirley's bodies came back to me in vivid detail. I stood up again. "Look, I already told you I'm through, and I just hope you get the bastard who killed them." I jerked open the door and started out to where Theresa was waiting.

Stan grabbed my arm, but he dropped it as soon as I stopped. "Thanks for making the ID on Perry."

I nodded my head, but I couldn't speak. I couldn't even look at him. I wanted to get outside and try to forget the flashbacks of the murders. I rushed into the main homicide room just as lightning lit up the window as if it were an Imax movie screen. Thunder banged less than a second later. The strike had been somewhere very close.

By the time Stan escorted Theresa and me down to the lobby, raindrops were pelting the paved courtyard outside the building. The sky lit up, and another clap of thunder cracked as if it were right outside the door.

"Thanks," Stan said again. "I have to get back upstairs, but I'll give you a call later." He was looking at me, but I glanced away, trying hard to shake the images of Kate and Shirley.

I wanted to rush outside where I could cry to my heart's content, disguising my tears in the rain. Much as I hated the lightning, I felt a compulsive need to leave the claustrophobic atmosphere of the police building.

"Want to make a run for it?" I asked Theresa as Stan disappeared back into the elevator.

"No way," she said. "It's a real downpour." I think she must have realized how upset I was. She didn't say any more.

The two of us stood there watching the rain. It pounded against the door and began to form puddles on the wide expanse of cement outside. Cars splattered water high in the air as they passed on the street.

We stood near the door and stared at the rain. I tried to purge my mind of any thoughts except when the rain would stop. Wind caught the rain and sent it almost diagonally outside the door. Lightning continued to ignite the scene like it was a giant stage. Each flash was followed by a sonic boom of thunder.

A man came through the door, soaked to the skin. "It's a real gullywasher out there," he said, trying to shake himself off like a dog.

After about fifteen minutes the rain let up enough for me to try again. "How about now?" I asked.

Theresa shook her head.

I couldn't stand it any longer. "I'm going to make a run for it. I'll get the car and bring it around in front for you."

I didn't give her time to protest. I set out at a jog and increased to a dead run as I raced to the car. Big mistake. I was drenched when I reached the parking lot, but the rain seemed to take the place of the tears. I felt a little better. Soaked but more alive, and I'd made it without being struck down by lightning. That was a good sign.

We hadn't been caught for being $1.75 short on our parking fee either, and I promised the parking-lot gods that I'd send a check for the difference to the company that managed the lot.

When I drove around the block and picked up Theresa, she was full of questions about the purpose of our trip. I told her that the man we'd identified had apparently been found dead the day before but that we shouldn't say anything about it to the rest of the crew yet.

The minute we walked into the cleaners, me still dripping wet and Theresa only slightly damp, Julia thrust a handful of messages at me.

"There's a woman who keeps calling. She won't believe you're not here, and she's interfering with our work." Julia didn't give me time to respond. "She's on the phone right now. Will you *please* take the call?"

"Okay, tell her to hang on." I brushed the wet hair out of my eyes, but a drop of rain landed on the top message and began to blur the writing. I wouldn't be surprised if my red-and-white striped blouse was running too.

"Where you been?" Mack asked as he spotted me on my way to my office. "You look like Captain Queeg after a storm at sea."

"Thanks, Mack, but I'm going to hit you over the head with my therapy balls if you're not careful."

I closed the door and went to the phone, but I didn't sit down. I didn't want to get my chair wet the way Mack had done when he sat on Betty's melted ice pack in my apartment. I picked up the phone. "Betty, you have to quit calling all the time."

It was probably dumb of me to assume it was Betty, but I did. Unfortunately I was right.

"That woman is going to drive me nuts if she doesn't stop," Betty said. "You'll never guess what she's doing now."

"No, but I bet you're going to tell me."

"She's covering all the furniture with—" Betty paused for effect. "—*doilies*."

"Doilies?" The last few hours had been too much for me. I suddenly felt like giggling.

"You heard me. Doilies!"

Yes, I could just see them. Mrs. O'Neal must surely be the doily queen of Denver, and I remembered the ones that had sprouted around her apartment like clumps of crab-grass growing out of the furniture. Doilies and hundreds of tiny dust-collecting knickknacks and souvenirs of places like the Royal Gorge and Rocky Mountain National Park.

"She says she's trying to make the place look *homely*," Betty continued, "and believe me, it looks god-awful."

I was 99 percent sure Mrs. O'Neal had said "homey," but Betty was giving it her own spin.

"You've got to do something about her, or I swear I'm going to hit the road—bad leg or not."

Oh, yes, lay the guilt on me about the bad leg. "Okay, Betty, I'll talk to her. Is she there right now?"

"No, she went back to her place to get some more *doilies*" —Betty practically spit out the rest of the sentence— "to ugly up the place."

"All right, I'll call her and tell her to lay off, but you have to promise me you won't call anymore today." Betty grunted, which I took as a yes. "And incidentally I think one of the definitions of *homely* is 'suited to the home.' "

"Get out of here," Betty snorted. "I always thought it meant butt-ugly." With that she slammed down the phone.

I changed into a pair of jeans and a sweatshirt with cutoff sleeves that I kept for times when Mack and I had to work on malfunctioning equipment. At least I would be dry until I could get up front to the conveyor and find something more respectable to wear. Then I looked up Hazel O'Neal's number in the phone book and dialed it.

"I'm so glad you called," she said before I had a chance to say anything about Betty's list of complaints. "I was going to call you because I thought I might have a little dinner party tomorrow night to welcome Betty to the building."

I was shaking my head, but of course Mrs. O'Neal couldn't see me.

"It won't be anything fancy, and I'm just going to invite a few other tenants so she can meet them."

"Do you think that's a good idea—until her ankle gets better?"

"Oh, I think it'll do her a world of good. I think her ankle's doing quite nicely, but she seems a little down in the dumps." Probably a more apt description of the bag lady than Hazel knew, and something that might send Betty right back to a life on the streets.

"I want you to come too—about six o'clock."

I was about to refuse and tell her we should wait, but then inspiration raised its evil head. "Uh—I was wondering if I could bring a guest. His name is Arthur Goldman, and he's a wonderful man in his sixties who seems a little lonely. I think he'd love to meet some people his own age."

"Wonderful. There's always room for one more."

Was that quick thinking or what? Of course I'd already thought of the idea the previous day, but I couldn't believe my good fortune in implementing the plan so fast. I would introduce Mrs. O'Neal to the doll doctor, and she would be so busy lavishing attention on him that she would quickly forget about Betty.

"And Mrs. O'Neal." *Be diplomatic,* I cautioned myself. "I don't want you going to a lot of trouble for Betty—just provide her with food for a few more days."

"Oh." Mrs. O'Neal sounded disappointed.

"You see," I tried to explain, "she just returned from a long trip, and she's exhausted. What she really needs right now is peace and quiet—and a little healthy nourishment."

"Maybe I fussed over her a little too much today."

"Perhaps," I agreed. "I think all you need to do is look in on her at mealtime."

"I'll try to give her a little more time to herself now that you've explained it. I know how tiring it can be to travel. I'm always exhausted when I get back from visiting my daughter in Oklahoma."

"Great," I said, "and I'm sure Betty and Mr. Goldman will both enjoy a home-cooked meal."

I didn't get around to calling Betty or the doll doctor until I went home that night. Mr. Goldman was delighted to accept the invitation. Betty was surly about it, but I managed to calm her down by telling her I thought the situation was about to improve.

"If it doesn't, I'm leavin'," she said.

We hung up, and there was blissful quiet in my apartment—all except for Spot, who meowed until I fed him. Afterward he kept hanging around in a most un-Spot-like way. I think he missed Betty.

Maybe I did too. Now that I didn't have all the distractions, the images of finding Kate's and Shirley's bodies returned. I would have thought I was so exhausted that I would have fallen asleep as soon as I stretched out on my open Hide-A-Bed. No such luck. As soon as I closed my eyes, the pictures of their bodies appeared behind my eyelids. I even saw the bodies of Shirley's brother and her boyfriend as if I'd been there when the police pulled them out of the water.

I tossed and turned, but somewhere around ten o'clock I must have dozed. I was awakened later by someone pounding on my door. I groped to my feet, grabbed my bathrobe, and stumbled to answer the relentless knocking.

A sinking feeling told me it was Betty—maybe Mrs. O'Neal had tried to serve her tea before bed and Betty decided to run away. Dang her homely hide.

CHAPTER
23

"Who is it?" I'd already yanked off the chain and unlocked the dead bolt before I thought to ask.

"It's your former friend, Nat."

Oh, damn. Now he knew I was here.

"Let me in or I'm going to cross you off my Christmas-card list."

Nat didn't send Christmas cards, but I opened the door anyway. "You tricked me. You didn't do your standard knock—*dum-da-da-dum.*"

"I figured if I did, you'd pretend you weren't home."

I let him into the apartment. "That's what you deserve when you show up in the middle of the night."

He headed over to the table as if he expected me to entertain him.

"So what do you want that's so important you had to wake me up from my first good night's sleep in days?" I wouldn't for the world admit that I'd been tossing and turning for hours.

Nat took off his Harley-Davidson leather jacket and hung it over the back of the chair. "When I stopped to see you this morning, why didn't you tell me about finding the body of a woman named Shirley Sawyer?"

I shrugged and headed for the microwave to make us both some instant coffee. I wouldn't have done this, but if he insisted on staying until he'd said his piece, I needed some coffee to wake me up.

"Go ahead," he said. "Explain it to me."

"It's simple. Detective Reilly isn't happy with me. I was afraid to say anything to you for fear it would get back to him."

"Ah, geez, Mandy, you know I always protect my sources."

"But you found out about it, right? What's the big deal?"

"I realize that, but I hate to think you're holding out on me. What else do you know that you aren't telling me?"

I put coffee in the mugs of hot water and brought them to the table. "I know that my apartment was broken into Saturday night," I said as I tightened the belt on my bathrobe. "Is that good enough for you?"

His eyes widened behind his round granny glasses. "No kidding?" He looked around at the room, which I still hadn't completely put back together. "How can you tell? It looks the same to me."

I would have liked to throw something at him, but the only thing handy was my sugar bowl, which went with a cream pitcher I had someplace. I hated to break up the set. "You can get your own milk for that crack."

He got up and loped over to the refrigerator with his mug, which he doused with milk from a half-gallon container. "Did they take anything?"

"Not that I've found."

He came back and slouched in the chair across from me. "You think they were looking for the dress?"

I nodded since he'd already promised the police not to release that information.

"So what else do you know?"

"Nothing."

He took a long drink from his coffee, then set it down. "Okay, if you won't talk, I'll tell you what I know and you nod if it's right. That's the way Deep Throat did it in Watergate."

Nat was impossible. I suppose he saw himself as a latter-day Bob Woodward, although I still felt that he would have been more at home back in the newspaper heyday of the thirties.

"This Sawyer woman," he said, "was a sister of one of the men they fished out of a lake at City Park. Right? And she was the girlfriend of the other one. Okay so far? And they all may have been connected to a garage sale that was held a week ago at the trailer park where they lived."

I tried my coffee, but it was still too hot, which is what I get for drinking it black. "How do you know that?"

"I've been doing a little inquiring of their neighbors. They said a woman who matched your description had been out there asking questions Saturday about the garage sale. How's that for investigative reporting?"

I nodded, but only as a response to his explanation.

"What I really want," Nat said, "is some information on the dress."

I shook my head. "That's what the police are keeping quiet."

"Hey, it would be off-the-record. I just need some background for later. What makes you think the dress is so valuable someone would be willing to kill for it?"

Okay, I trusted him on that. If Nat said something was off-the-record, he meant it, and he'd hit on the thing that had been bothering me all along. "I don't think it is *that* valuable—maybe five thousand dollars. There has to be more to it than that."

"So what do you know about the dress?"

I described it and told him what Even had relayed to me.

Nat honed in on my source as any good reporter—or even a nosy dry cleaner—should have done. "Who told you how much it was worth?"

"That's what Kate said, and Evan Carmody, the man you met here the other night, agreed."

"And how do you know she didn't get her information from Carmody? Maybe he wasn't telling either one of you the truth?"

I hated it when Nat was right. I grabbed a Post-It note and wrote myself a reminder. "I suppose I could check it out without too much trouble, and it shouldn't get the police bent out of shape."

Nat finished his coffee and stood up. Now that he was here, I almost hated to see him leave. He'd made me forget all those ghoulish images I'd had earlier, and besides, I wanted to ask him something personal.

"Uh, Nat—" My coffee was finally cool enough to drink, and I took a sip. "Did you know about Stan having a girlfriend on the police force at one time?"

He looked surprised. "No, who was it?"

"I don't know her name, but I thought you knew everything that went on down there."

I could tell I'd hurt his feelings because he began to justify the fact that he didn't know about it. "They must have kept it quiet. The department sometimes frowns on romances between fellow officers." I wished I'd never brought up the subject, because now Nat sat back down, looking concerned. "I could probably do some checking around."

"No, please don't do that." I tried to explain myself. "He said she was killed in the line of duty, and I just wondered why you'd never mentioned it to me."

"Hey, I'm sorry, but it's news to me." He reached across the table and grabbed my hand. "Besides, you shouldn't let it bother you, Mandy. You had men in your life before you met Stan. Why would you think Stan hasn't had a girlfriend?"

I stared into my coffee cup as if I could read the future in it or figure out the past. "It's just that I don't think he ever got over her."

"Geez, Mandy. I'm sorry." I hated it when Nat, of all people, was sympathetic. I began to tear up, which I seemed to do a lot these days, and I was getting sick of it.

He squeezed my hand, but I pulled it away so I could grab a Kleenex and rub my eyes. I'd be damned if I'd cry.

"I was afraid this thing with a detective wouldn't work out," he said. "I never should have helped get the two of you together."

I waved the Kleenex at him. "Don't worry about it, Nat. I'm okay. Really. It's just that I'm on edge about everything—finding Kate's body, the break-in . . ."

"And Betty," Nat added.

"Yeah, and Betty." I couldn't help smiling at that.

"Let me fix us both another cup of coffee." Nat got up, grabbed the mugs, and went to the kitchen. "You know, I have a great idea." He came back to the table as soon as he zapped the mugs in the microwave. "We ought to do something really different to get our lives out of the rut. How about we go up to Sturgis later on this summer?"

I looked over at him as if he were the one who was falling apart. "Sturgis, South Dakota? The motorcycle rally?"

"Yeah, it would be a blast."

"Oh, sure, that's just what I need."

The microwave beeped, and Nat went to fix the coffee. "It was just an idea. When I went up to the mountains Saturday, I was thinking about it."

"So I was right. You were up in the mountains at that woman's house."

Nat still didn't want to talk about his out-of-town

interview. "Hey, I just thought a trip might get your mind off your troubles."

"Don't kid me," I countered. "You just want to make me miserable by having me ride behind you on your Harley all the way to South Dakota. No way."

"Okay." He doctored up his coffee. "But it would have been an *Adventure*."

"So are you going to tell me about the big story you got while you were up in the mountains?"

He looked embarrassed. "Actually it wasn't that big a deal. Not a scoop in the real sense of the word. Just a human-interest story. I don't really want to talk about it."

He sipped his coffee, and I twisted my mug around, waiting for it to cool.

"So you don't want to do the rally, huh?" he asked again.

"No, I went bungee jumping with you. Wasn't that enough?"

"You didn't *go* bungee jumping with me. You watched me go bungee jumping."

"I told you I don't like putting myself in danger unnecessarily." So what was I doing still thinking about Kate's dress?

Nat's visit had helped chase the demons away from my sleep, but I was still tired the next morning. He hadn't left until well after midnight, and by then I was a little jumpy from the coffee—or else Nat's rehash in excruciating detail of his bungee "Adventure."

I helped on the front counter for the first few hours at work, then finished calling people about the memorial service and tried to think about what I would say at the service.

Mack brought me back a salad when he went to lunch, and he dropped down into the chair across from my desk when he delivered it. "Do I dare ask about Betty?"

"Everything's working out fine."

I was feeling more optimistic about that because I hadn't heard from her once today. Mrs. O'Neal must be too busy fixing dinner to bother her. I wasn't about to tell Mack about all the calls yesterday, at least not until we could laugh about them together. I was still a little irritated by how amused he was by the whole thing. I also wasn't going to discuss finding Shirley's body unless he'd found out about it from another source. He would get too upset about it.

"Juan is scheduled for a vacation next week, but he's willing to delay it if he needs to start training Betty." Her name seemed to stick in his throat.

"That would be a good idea. I'm going to see her tonight, and I'll find out if she thinks she can start by then." I doodled numbers on a piece of paper. "How much do you think that Fortuny dress of Kate's is worth?"

"A lot," Mack said.

No help there. "Five thousand dollars maybe?"

"Maybe." He pondered the idea for a minute. "If you're really interested in finding out about it, you should go to the library. They probably have some information about the dress."

Mack must have thought that was a safe and innocuous thing for me to do, or he wouldn't have suggested it. And actually it was a good idea.

Stan called just as I was looking up the phone number for the central library downtown. He wanted to know if I could go out for dinner that night.

"I can't. I'm sorry." So that he wouldn't think I was up to something underhanded and subversive, I explained about getting Betty moved and how her neighbor had invited us to dinner.

"How about tomorrow night?" he asked.

We agreed to meet at eight, and once we hung up, I

dialed the library. A woman on the information desk told me there were several books about Fortuny, and I set out for the library with Mack's blessings.

I'm ashamed to say that I hadn't been to the main library since it was remodeled a few years back. When I wanted to reads, I bought paperbacks.

The original library is now just a small part of an immense new building, which is in a variety of shapes and sizes. I picked up a brochure in the lobby, which is a three-story atrium that looked like the lobby of a fancy hotel. The library had even been the site of the Denver Summit of the Eight, a conference of world leaders, the previous summer.

One of the librarians directed me to an escalator to the second floor, where she said I'd find a biography of Fortuny. Just out of curiosity, I asked her where the meeting between President Clinton, Boris Yeltsin, and other heads of state had been held. She pointed to a reference room just off the lobby.

I made my way to the second floor and found the book. Then I sat down at a desk near a railing overlooking the Summit's conference room. I could tell because the words *United States of America* were painted on the wood just underneath the railing across from me. The names of the other countries in their native languages were painted to the sides under the bannister.

In a spot where momentous decisions must have been made, you'd have thought I might have uncovered some world-shattering information of my own. Nothing. As I read the book on Fortuny, everything that Evan Carmody had told me appeared to be true. In fact he'd apparently taken the information from the same source as I now had in my hand.

I spent the next hour intermittently staring out at the room below for inspiration and looking at the book. There were color photographs in the book that showed some of the shimmering fabrics Fortuny used in his gowns. The colors were so vibrant that you wanted to reach out and touch them.

Other pictures were of the famous women who had worn the gowns through the years—an Italian countess, early-day movie star Dolores Del Rio, socialites Gloria Vanderbilt and Peggy Guggenheim, actress and set designer Natasha Rambova, who had been married to silent-screen idol Rudolph Valentino—even Julie Christie and Lauren Hutton posing for fashion magazines in Fortuny gowns from private collections.

No revelations here or indications of how much a Fortuny was worth. One thing Evan Carmody hadn't mentioned to me was that many of the Fortuny gowns had tapered overblouses with Venetian glass beads at the bottom. The original design had bat-wing sleeves, and it wasn't until the late twenties that any of the designs were sleeveless. So the only thing I learned was that Kate's gown with its almost invisible cap sleeves probably qualified as a later version.

There was another photograph from an auction at Christie's in New York, and I got out my telephone calling card and found a pay phone before I left the library.

I called Information for the 212 area code and then called the number for Christie's. After being transferred several times I connected with a man who said I'd need to send a photograph of my gown if I wanted an appraisal.

"No," I said. "I just need a ballpark figure of how much a Fortuny gown would sell for today."

"Anywhere from two thousand to thirty thousand dollars," the man said. "It all depends on the condition of the garment, who owned it, and the intricacy of the design."

I thanked him for the information. Even a thirty-thousand-dollar-gown didn't seem as if it was worth killing for, but Kate's gown probably hadn't been worth that much. It wasn't as intricate as some of the ones I'd seen in the photographs, but I wondered who had owned it.

With more questions than answers, I headed home to change for my matchmaking dinner with Mrs. O'Neal, Arthur Goldman, and of course Betty.

CHAPTER 24

The doll doctor was all dolled up in a suit and tie when I collected him from behind his toy-repair shop. I should have told him that it wasn't a fancy-dress affair. I was wearing a pair of brown slacks and an ivory-colored silk blouse with some gold earrings Kate had given me in her jewelry-making days.

When we arrived at Hazel O'Neal's apartment, she was in a flowered shirtwaist with an apron over it, and her cheeks were rosy from her work in the kitchen. I introduced my perfect couple to each other and left them to get acquainted while I went to fetch Betty.

"I think your friend must be feeling better today," Hazel told me before I left. "I've been trying to let her get some rest, and she hasn't seemed as"—she lowered her voice as if she hated to speak badly about anyone—"grouchy today."

I'd brought Betty some of the outfits we'd bought at the flea market, all freshly cleaned and pressed. I thought she might want to wear one of them, but she was already dressed in her bilious green pants suit.

"Hazel," she complained, "insisted on washing my clothes, and she shrunk my best outfit."

I noticed that Betty was hardly limping as we went to Mrs. O'Neal's apartment. Having a nursemaid hovering over her was apparently a good incentive to get well, and I decided it was time to bite the bullet and discuss career opportunities at the cleaners. I wanted to do it before she used up all my money for upkeep, so I told her she could start work Monday morning. "And the clothes and the rent are coming out of your salary," I added.

She shrugged. "Be good to get away from the jail warden."

See, that was smart of me, after all, having Hazel look in on her. I had feared that Betty was having such a good time at my place that she'd lost whatever zeal she ever had to become a productive member of society.

I handed her a bus schedule, which I'd marked to show her how to get to the cleaners. I wanted to quash any thoughts she had that I might be willing to pick her up on my way to work.

When we returned to Hazel's apartment, Betty nodded as we were introduced to two of her neighbors who had arrived while I was gone. They were both women about Hazel's age, so Arthur Goldman seemed to be the hit of the party.

Everyone vied for his attention until Hazel called us to the table and told us where to sit. It was an unfortunate seating arrangement. Our hostess had her two women friends sit on either side of her, and the doll doctor was seated between Betty and me.

"So you're a doll doctor," Betty said. "That takes the cake."

He began to explain to her about how he repaired dolls and other toys, restoring them as close to their original condition as possible. "Today I had to put a new wig on a Barbie doll that was in good condition except that some child had whacked off its beautiful long blond hair."

Why did his remark about the doll with the long mane of

hair bother me? It was the same thing that had gnawed at me when I had dinner with Michael. I lost track of the conversation for a few minutes while I tried to remember what it was. When I tuned back in, the doll doctor was explaining to Betty that some dolls could "fetch handsome sums" from collectors.

"I know," she said. "I found a doll one time, still in its box, that someone had thrown in the trash. I got ten bucks for it when I took it to a pawnshop."

This was kind of like bringing Liza Doolittle to the ball in *My Fair Lady*. I wondered if she was going to start regaling the dinner guests with other things she had found in the trash cans of Denver.

Fortunately Hazel asked the doll doctor if he would mind carving the turkey she'd prepared. I felt as if it were Thanksgiving in June. Or actually Christmas. Surely Mrs. Saint Nick and Santa's helper would realize they were a perfect match, providing Betty stopped monopolizing the doll doctor's attention.

Conversation stopped for a while as he carved the turkey.

"If you don't mind telling me, what kind of a doll was it that you found?" Arthur asked Betty when we finished passing the food around the table.

Betty was already busy eating, and it took her a while to respond. "It wasn't no Barbie or nothing. It was a doll that was supposed to look like Esther Williams. Remember her? She used to swim around to music in those old-time movies."

I thought I saw Arthur pale. "Dear me," he said. "There weren't many of those made, I don't think. You know, it might have been worth a lot more than ten dollars."

Betty shrugged. "I was happy to get it at the time."

"Well, if you ever find another doll like that, you come to me first. I'll make sure you get a fair price for it."

"Don't figure I'll be finding any more. You might say I'm changing professions."

At the other end of the table I could hear Hazel and her friends discussing a pattern for a needlepoint pillow. Arthur started eating, but before long, he turned to Betty again. "What do you do, by the way, Miss—uh, I didn't catch your last name."

"You can just call me Betty." She looked over and gave him a wink. Or maybe she was winking at me because she had successfully avoided revealing her last name again.

Arthur blushed, I guess because he thought the wink was for him. "So what do you do for a living—Betty?"

"I'm going to be helping Mandy out at her cleaners."

Oh, God, that she would really be of help.

"Would you like any more turkey, Mr. Goldman?" That was Hazel from the end of the table.

"Not yet, but it's very good." He wiped his lips with a napkin and turned back to Betty.

"I could use some more," Betty said as she stretched her arm across the table and speared a piece of white meat from the tray.

"And what exactly will you be doing at the cleaners, Betty?"

"Oh, I don't know, Art. Maybe I could be a seamstress." She looked over at me with a gleam in her eye.

I started shaking my head, but Betty had gone back to her food.

"I used to be one in another life," she said.

Was this a clue to her former identity or just another way to taunt me with a tall tale?

"Do you think you could make some doll clothes?" Arthur asked. "Sometimes I need to provide a gown for one of my dolls."

"Why not? If I can clothe the hoi polloi of New York City, I ought to be able to put clothes on dolls in Denver."

This was really getting out of hand, and all the time the queen of doily-making and needlepoint was sitting at the other end of the table making small talk with her female friends. I was sure she would be a much better choice to help Arthur with dresses for his dolls.

Meanwhile Betty was telling Arthur about a man who had once wanted her to make a cowboy outfit for his dog. "The guy didn't have any thread on his bobbin, if you know what I mean."

Arthur, or Art as Betty had decided to call him, laughed until he began choking and had to grab for a glass of water. I was surprised at Art's reaction. The remark sounded like something that only my late Uncle Chet would have appreciated. Art, however, seemed to be having the time of his life.

When the meal was finally over, we moved to the living room, where Mrs. O'Neal served peach cobbler and ice cream, which went against the holiday theme, but who cared? Things weren't working out the way I'd planned anyway.

But I never give up. I hoped maybe there'd be a different seating arrangement when we moved so that Art and Hazel would have a chance to get acquainted. Arthur, however, followed Betty over to the couch. She continued to tell him stories about her handiwork with a needle, including the time she'd accidentally sewn a man's pants to his underwear.

"I was trying to make an emergency repair after he split a seam at"—she looked over at me with a twinkle in her eye—"well, you might say it was a social occasion." What kind she didn't mention, and it was probably just as well.

Even when Hazel served tea, instead of coffee, Arthur

failed to realize that the two of them were meant for each other. At least Betty didn't make some nasty remark at the offer of tea, but she got up suddenly and said she had to go back to her apartment because her leg was beginning to hurt.

"I think I'll have to pass on the tea," she said.

"I'll help you." I jumped up to escort her down the hall. Arthur looked disappointed, because I was sure he wanted to do the honors.

"What was that all about—you saying you were a seamstress?" I asked as soon as we were out the door.

"I been thinking about it," she said, "and I decided I might as well tell you about my dressmaking skills."

"You know," I said, "you're going to have to give me a Social Security number if you're going to come to work for me."

"I figured I would—so I guess I'll have to start using my real name, huh?"

"And is it Florence Lorenzo?"

"I'd prefer you call me Betty."

"But was that woman looking for you when she came to the door and asked for Florence Lorenzo?"

"I been thinking about that too, and I guess those bad vibes I was havin' at the flea market was because she recognized me from a long time ago."

"Are you going to look her up?"

"I'll have to do some more studyin' on that. . . ."

For the time being, I guess that was enough for me to know. "So I'll see you Monday."

"I ought to be up to it—if that lady friend of yours will leave me alone." With that, Betty—er, Flo, went into her apartment and closed the door.

I returned to Hazel's apartment and drove Arthur back to his toy shop.

"That Betty," he said on the way home, "she's really some-thing, isn't she? Do you think she'd go out for dinner with me sometime?"

Why ask me? Mack and Nat were right. Playing match-maker didn't seem to be my strong suit.

All the same I tried to smile. "Give it a try, Arthur. Betty would probably jump at the chance."

I stopped at a Safeway to get some aspirin for my headache. On the way out to the parking lot I saw the early edition of the *Denver Tribune*. I couldn't resist buying one. I would go home, take a couple of aspirin, and read Nat's "scoop" that he seemed to be embarrassed about.

It wasn't even on the front page. I changed into my sleep-ing attire, another long T-shirt like the one I'd donated to Betty, took my pills, and made myself a cup of decaf. I must be getting old because I was giving up on "regular" in hopes I wouldn't be as jittery as I'd been the night before. At least tonight I had less nightmarish things to think about: How could the doll doctor be enamored of Betty when I'd found Mrs. Santa Claus? And what had Nat written that he didn't want to talk about?

I opened up the Hide-A-Bed, plumped up a couple of pillows so that I could read in bed, and started thumbing through the paper. I found the article on pages 10–11, and I'd been right. It did have something to do with the woman, Mavis Emerson, who'd been killed when she apparently sur-prised burglars in her mountain home last month. But it wasn't what I would have expected from a hard-news guy like Nat. It was an interview with the victim's daughter, who was at the house to inventory the estate, and it was mostly about her grandmother.

Nat had written, "Mavis Emerson, the murder victim, was the daughter of silent screen star Zelda Coolidge, and had lived a reclusive life for the last twenty years in a mountain retreat known as the Warwick Castle."

I had never heard of Zelda Coolidge, but I was sure Mack would be able to recall her.

Nat's article continued: "Emerson's neighbors said they had no idea the victim was related to the film legend, who was one of the few actresses to make the transition from the silent screen to the talkies.

"Emerson had always lived in the shadow of her famous mother and had continued to do so even after Coolidge's death in 1965, according to Linda Berrigan, Emerson's daughter.

" 'My mother saw herself as the guardian of Zelda's movie memorabilia,' Berrigan said in an interview this week. 'She even had one of the turbans Rudolph Valentino had worn when my grandmother appeared with him in one of his sheik-of-the-desert films.

" 'I think that's why Mom protected her privacy so much. She didn't want anyone to know she had all these valuable items from the silent films. I don't think the people who killed her realized what they had stumbled into because they don't appear to have stolen any of the collection.' "

Nat's story went on to mention that jewelry and cash, plus Emerson's purse, were the only things that appeared to have been taken in the break-in. He then chronicled the career of the silent-screen star and some of the items in her collection, but by then my heart was doing flipflops.

The killers may not have stolen much of Zelda's collection—except maybe for the Fortuny gown and the long silk chiffon scarf that had been with it. The scarf Kate had given me as a present.

CHAPTER
25

I skidded to the counter by my kitchen table and grabbed the phone. "Be there," I said as I punched in Nat's number. "Please, Nat, be home."

At the same time I was trying to analyze my jump of logic. But that's what it could be. The Fortuny gown. A dress so unique that it could tie the people Kate bought it from to the murder of a woman in the Colorado mountains.

Nat didn't answer, so I left a message for him to call me as soon as he got home. Then I called the newspaper. He had already departed for the night.

Okay, maybe my idea was a little far-fetched. I probably wouldn't even have thought of it if I hadn't whiled away the afternoon looking at the book on Fortuny at the library. All the photographs of the famous women who had worn Fortuny gowns came back to me. Even the wife of Valentino himself. What had seemed like an unproductive few hours could be the key to everything.

I spent another restless night, decaf or not, waiting for the phone to ring and studying my first reaction to Nat's story. I supposed I could be wrong. I certainly had been about the doll doctor and Mrs. Saint Nick. But this was different, and it was definitely worth a shot.

When I climbed out of bed the next morning, I dressed for work in a two-piece blue dress and called Nat. So what if I woke him up? He'd done it plenty of times to me.

"Yeah," he said when he answered the phone. I could hear the sleep in his voice.

"Why didn't you call me last night when you got home?"

"Mandy?" He really was sleepy, not to recognize my voice.

"Yes, why didn't you call?"

"I figured you'd bought the early edition and were going to rag me about my *scoop*."

"Okay, it wasn't hard news," I said, "but that's not why I called. I think Zelda Coolidge could have owned the Fortuny that Kate bought."

"What?" I could tell Nat was awake now.

I explained how many of the famous actresses and socialites in the early part of the century had owned Fortuny gowns. "The dress could have belonged to Zelda Coolidge, and the people who sold it to Kate could have been the ones who killed her daughter, Mavis Emerson."

I could tell Nat was picking up on my excitement. "Hey, I'll give the granddaughter a call."

"Listen, Nat, I have a crepe chiffon scarf that Kate gave me. It had been in the box with the dress."

"Better yet. I'll swing by this afternoon and get it. I can take it up to the castle and show it to the granddaughter."

I didn't know if I wanted to give up the scarf. "Okay, but I'm going with you."

Nat hesitated, and I could tell he was reluctant to share the possibility of a real scoop with anyone, even me.

"It was only a human-interest story, Nat," I reminded him, "unless my idea turns out to lead somewhere."

"All right," he said reluctantly, "but I have to go to work first. I won't be able to get away until later today."

"That's okay. I have things to do myself. I'll meet you down at the cleaners."

Nat didn't show up until nearly three. I'd occupied myself by filling in for my presser, who was still out sick. I'd also called Bones at his pawnshop on the pretext of telling him about the memorial service. I wanted to ask him if he'd heard any more from Red, but he wasn't at work. I even thought of calling a locksmith about my door, which I'd been planning to do since Monday. I decided that could wait as long as I had the dead bolt and chain to lock me in at night.

I also considered calling Detective Reilly and dumping my idea in his lap. But what, really, did I have? A vague feeling from a book I'd read at the Denver Public Library.

We were caught up on work when I finally heard Nat at the back door. He was wearing his leather biker's jacket, which should have given me a clue that things might not go well on our upcoming trip. I guess I didn't pick up on it because I was intent on keeping him from telling Mack about our plans.

"Mandy and I are going up to the mountains," Nat was saying.

"Good," Mack said. "An outing might do her some good." I think he was so anxious to get me away from the temptation to investigate—especially after I'd told him the trip to the library was a dud—that he didn't stop to consider the time. Then he looked at his watch. "Isn't it a little late?"

I rushed over to them. "We're not going that far," I said.

"Yeah, I thought I'd take her up to some of the casinos in Black Hawk since she's never been there." Nat never even twitched when he lied.

I whisked him away to my office before Mack realized that I had in fact been to Black Hawk on a couple of occasions—the last time with him and some other people from the plant.

"I have to get the scarf," I whispered to Nat as we reached my door.

"You have to change clothes too."

I looked down at my two-piece dress. "What's wrong with my clothes?"

"They're no good on a Harley."

"No, absolutely not. I'm not going to Sturgis with you, and I'm not going up into the mountains on your bike. We'll take my car."

Nat laughed. "That tin can of yours doesn't have the oomph to get where we're going. Besides, there was a wash-out on the road from all that rain when I was up there Saturday. I don't know if anyone will have gotten around to fixing it yet. Most of the people up there have Jeeps like Linda does."

I wasn't sure if Nat was telling the truth. He might just want to get even with me for insisting that I go along. I was not a fan of riding shotgun on the back of Nat's bike, and I'd done it only once. On that occasion I'd vowed never to do it again.

I began to voice my misgivings, or perhaps I was just trying to weasel out of a very unsatisfactory means of getting where I wanted to go. "Maybe we should just tell the police about my idea and let them follow up on it."

Nat wasn't having any of that. "Look, if you don't want to go, just give me the scarf, and I'll go myself."

No way would I do that. I shooed him out of the office and changed into jeans and a yellow cotton knit shirt. In case the temperature dropped as we went up in elevation, I grabbed a sweater, plus the scarf, and tried to look as if I were off for an afternoon of rest and relaxation.

"You don't need a sweater," Nat said as I came out of the office. "I brought you a helmet and one of my old jackets."

"I prefer the sweater, thank you."

"You ever heard of 'road rash?' "

"No, only roadkill and road rage. Why?"

"Well, leather helps to keep you from winding up as roadkill when someone with road rage cuts you off and you take a spill off the bike."

This was sounding more and more ominous all the time, but I put the scarf in my shoulder bag, put the bag's strap over my head so I wouldn't lose it, and left the sweater behind. Then we made our way past Mack, who apparently hadn't noticed Nat and me bickering.

"Have a good time," Mack yelled, "but be careful."

"Yes, Mom." I don't think he realized we were going on Nat's Harley, or he'd have had a fit.

I've heard it said that Denver is a city just waiting to head out for the mountains on the weekends. We were doing it on a weekday, but I couldn't even take pleasure out of escaping from work. Sure, I was hopeful that Zelda's granddaughter was going to recognize the scarf, but the idea of being on the back of a motorcycle reduced the anticipation considerably.

"Look," I said, thinking of my date with Stan. "I have to be home by seven o'clock. Can we get back by then?"

"No problemo." Nat handed me the jacket and helmet. "Here, put them on."

As soon as I did, I began to perspire, even when Nat took off and the wind was blowing in my face.

"Some women think riding on the back of a Harley

is better than sex," he yelled at me. "You know—all the vibration."

I didn't think the remark was worthy of a response.

"I've been mulling it over," he yelled a mile or two later, "and I don't really think that's where the dress came from. Linda Berrigan said she'd been inventorying her grand-mother's collection and nothing seemed to be missing."

I didn't bother to argue with him about that either. Besides, I wasn't sure my voice was strong enough to carry forward as he zoomed across town on Eighth Avenue and hit the Sixth Avenue freeway heading west. It seemed as if he was going more than fifty-five miles an hour, but I didn't want to know.

I clung to him as if my life depended on it. I hated feeling like a biker's old lady, and the vibrations were giving me a headache. Better than sex? I didn't think so.

We went through Golden, where Coors brews his beer, and Nat turned west on Highway 6 through Clear Creek Canyon, which leads to Black Hawk. Nat had better have been lying about stopping off to gamble. Even when I tried to duck behind him, the wind blowing across my face and into my mouth nearly took my breath away.

The two-lane road seemed to have narrowed since the last time I'd been on it, and the steep canyon walls whizzed by just outside my reach. Not that I was going to reach out to touch them and break my grip around Nat's waist.

I could see the creek running over its banks from the runoff of winter snow and the recent rains, but the water was only a cold, churning blur on the other side of the road. And to think that I often dreamed of setting up my easel by a quiet mountain stream so that I could paint.

The rains and saturated soil sometimes dislodged rocks on the sheer cliffs above us, and I had read of huge boulders tumbling down on a passing car or a casino bus. A motorcycle helmet hardly seemed like adequate protection in the event one of the rocks came tumbling down about now. I ducked my head even lower behind Nat's back.

He didn't take the turnoff to Black Hawk but went zooming on through a tunnel and finally connected with Interstate 70 near Idaho Springs. I don't know how much farther we went, because I finally closed my eyes and quit trying to squint at the passing terrain. Nat had on his motorcycle goggles, after all, and I figured he could see.

He eventually pulled off the interstate, and we were on a gravel road. I opened my eyes and might have enjoyed the pine trees zooming by on either side of us if I didn't feel that I suddenly had double vision. My body was being shaken apart from the inside out. The upheaval started in my internal organs and worked its way out to my skin. My cheeks burned. My head continued to sweat under the heavy headgear.

We bounced over the ruts in the road, but they were nothing that my Hyundai couldn't have handled. Then we came to a mini-arroyo that Nat managed to avoid by going halfway up the side of a hill to our left. It was preferable to going over the drop-off on the other side, however. Okay, so maybe my Hyundai would have had trouble with that.

The road got better again as we rose up the mountainside, and since we were going slower than we had out on the highway, I tried for conversation. "Did this Linda Berrigan live with her mother?"

"What?" Nat yelled back at me.

"Did Linda Berri—" We hit a bump that made the bike airborne for a minute. "—gan," I continued when we settled down to earth. It was a few seconds before I finished my sentence because I'd just had a strange thought. I tried to reject it.

"Did she live with her mother?" I yelled.

I could see Nat's helmet move back and forth in front of

me, which must have taken an effort. Mine seemed capable only of bouncing up and down, rattling my teeth and keeping my eyes out of focus.

"No, she and her husband live in L.A., and she's just here for a few more days."

"So maybe she didn't know everything that was in her grandmother's collection." I guess the air whizzing by me must have sent my words away with them.

Nat didn't respond.

Another arroyo. This one was more like a tiny canyon where the road had eroded away as the rain rushed down the slopes. From such things was the Black Canyon of the Gunnison created. Nat took a run and jumped his bike across it. I felt like Evel Knievel in free flight.

"We're almost there," Nat yelled.

And not a moment too soon. My insides hadn't quite bounced out of me yet.

Nat turned into an even narrower roadway, and we drove through an open gate. The road, now only two lines where tire tracks had cut a path up the hill, turned sharply as we continued to bounce over rocks that jutted out of the ground. At last I could see the stones of a big gray building through a stand of quaking aspen. Nat came to a halt and put his foot to the ground.

"How you doing?" he asked.

"Quaky," I said, looking at the aspen. The only thing I needed now was for another thunderstorm to roll across the mountains this afternoon. Then we could enjoy the unprotected challenge of the rain in our face and the lightning crackling around us as we made our way back to town.

I climbed off the bike and felt as if I had just dismounted from a mule—at the top of the Grand Canyon this time. My legs were trembling, and my left knee had tightened up.

"We'll walk the rest of the way," Nat said.

I removed my helmet and tried to shake out my hair. It was damp with sweat and plastered to my head.

"I wish you'd let your hair grow out again," Nat said. "I always liked it better when it was long."

The hair thing again, and then I remembered what had nagged at my subconscious since Saturday. Red Berry had said he preferred to remember Kate the way she was—with that long mane of beautiful auburn hair. Had that implied what it sounded like? That he'd seen her after she cut her hair a couple of months ago? But he'd said he hadn't seen her for the last ten years.

And suddenly the idea that had bounced—literally—through my head seemed more important. What if Red Berry had lied to me about his real name being "Red" for Redmond Von Furstenberg? What if it had been "Berry" for Red Berrigan instead? What if he were even the *husband* of the woman we were going to see? It couldn't be, but still . . .

"Maybe we'd better think this over a minute," I said, "before we go up to the door." I wasn't sure if the bike ride had shaken up my brain to the point that it had turned to mush or if it had actually loosened important data from my subconscious.

"Can't," Nat said. "I see Linda coming to meet us right now."

"You called her?"

"Of course. I had to make sure she was going to be home."

I tried to smile as the woman approached. She had blond hair and was rather plain. Not exotic the way her grand-mother had appeared in the photographs that accompanied Nat's article. More like her mother, whose picture had been printed too. Short and very thin. She was wearing jeans and a cableknit sweater and was harmless-looking, really. Definitely not Red Berry's type, at least not from what I remembered.

"I've been curious ever since you called," she said after we'd been introduced. "What was it you wanted?"

Nat jumped in before I had a chance to collect my scattered thoughts. He said that an antique dress had shown up at a garage sale in Denver, and we wondered if it might have been stolen from her grandmother's collection. He deferred to me for a description of the dress.

"It was a long gown with tiny pleats and a shimmery blue silk fabric that almost seemed silver sometimes," I said.

Linda thought about it for a minute, then shook her head. "I'm afraid I don't remember a dress like that, but Mom never would let me even touch any of Nana's things."

"Show her the scarf," Nat said.

By now I'd begun to think I was reacting to the stress of the trip up here. I opened my purse and pulled out the long scarf in the swirl of pastel colors. "Do you happen to remember this? It came with the dress."

She looked at it for a moment. "It doesn't look familiar, but come on up to the house and have some lemonade. I'll check and see if Mom had it listed on her inventory." She pointed up the steep, rocky road to the house.

"We're not interrupting anything, are we?" I asked. Personally I'd just as soon conduct our business here in the road and be on our way.

"No, I've been going through Mom's papers all day, and I could use a little company." She motioned us to follow her as she stomped over the rocks in sturdy hiking boots.

Nat took off with her. I still wasn't sure I was satisfied, but there was only a Jeep Cherokee up close to the house, and Nat had said she had one. I lagged behind and studied the house for any sign of movement.

When people called the place a castle, they were right. It was of gray stone that didn't look as if it came from around this area. And it even had turrets. The only thing lacking was a moat, and I couldn't help wishing that we could pull up a drawbridge in case any other people showed up at the last minute.

An entryway had what looked like a genuine marble floor and a wrought-iron chandelier with tiny bulbs screwed in it at various places. It had probably held candles at one time, but the flame-shaped bulbs that had replaced them didn't cast much more light than candles would have.

Through a doorway I could see a living room with dark paneling on the walls and a massive fireplace across from us. The room had big bulky leather furniture. With this gloomy atmosphere I was sure there must be a dungeon somewhere.

"Let me see the scarf again." Linda took it over to the light from a window near the fireplace and stared at it. "It does look a little familiar, but I can't be sure." She returned and handed the scarf to me.

"What about this?" I asked. "The dress was meant to be stored in a round little container that looked like a hatbox. Do you remember anything like that?"

Her eyes lit up. "A hatbox? You know I do think I remember one that used to be in the hall closet."

She motioned us to follow her to the entryway. I tucked the scarf into my purse first, and that's when I thought about the scarf Kate had in her hand when she died. What if—I needed time to think about this—what if Kate had grabbed a red scarf from the pegboard by her bed as she was being strangled, not to keep from falling but to leave a clue that her killer was Red Berry? And if that were true, Red had to be the person behind the murder of Linda's mother.

The light of the chandelier didn't reach to the closet, which was still in darkness. Linda was inside the small space, and I could hardly see her. "There's a string in here that turns on an overhead light," she said, "if I can just find it."

I thought I heard a noise from the back of the house. "What's that?" I asked. "Are you expecting company?"

Linda was reaching up to the ceiling for the string. "Oh, don't worry," she said. "It's just my husband. He and a friend have been locked up in the den all afternoon talking over old times. They won't be bothering us."

I felt as if every nerve ending in my body had gone on alert. I wouldn't be surprised if my still-damp hair had lifted off my head the way the doll doctor's always did. Just then I heard a door slam somewhere. Had someone been listening to our conversation?

"Oh, here it is," Linda said.

The closet erupted in a glare of light from a bare bulb hanging on a cord. Linda pushed some coats aside to look behind them. I don't know what she found. All I saw was a Burberry coat hanging on the rail. It had a mustard stain on the left lapel.

CHAPTER 26

I was sure that Nat and I needed to get out of the house as fast as possible.

"I can't see a hatbox in here," Linda said from the back of the closet. "I thought I remembered seeing one, but I can't find it now. Maybe it's in the closet upstairs."

"That's okay," I said. "We need to get going. I'm sorry we took up so much of your time."

Nat looked at me as if I were crazy. "Let her look some more, will you? If it isn't here, then maybe that means the dress really was stolen from her mother."

"No, I have to go. I think I'm going to be sick." And it wasn't far from the truth. My stomach was churning up a storm.

Linda came out from among the coats. "It's probably just the altitude. Why don't you lie down for a few minutes? You'll probably feel better, and that'll give me a chance to look in the other closet."

"No, but thanks." I tugged at Nat's leather jacket. "Come on, Nat. I need some fresh air."

I thought I saw a shadow pass by a window in the living room by the fireplace, but I couldn't be sure. I waited for the sound of someone starting the Jeep, but when no sound came, I yanked on the door. It wouldn't open.

Linda brushed back a strand of hair. "Oh, I must have locked it without thinking," she said, coming over to the door.

I would have liked to look through a window first before we burst outside, but the heavy wooden door didn't have any opening in it, not even a peephole to look through.

Was Linda in on a plan for Red and his friend to kill us? She pulled the door toward her, and I couldn't see anyone outside. I felt a momentary relief. Better to leave and take our chances in the outdoors than to stay and have Red discover us here. I was trying to convince myself that Linda wasn't in on the murder of her mother and that Red didn't yet know we were in the house.

"What about going for a walk?" Linda asked. "That might make you feel better, and it would give me time to look upstairs and also check through some of Mom's papers. She had a list of everything in Nana's collection, but it isn't in good order."

Nat eyed me curiously. "Want to do that, Mandy?" I could tell he thought it was stupid to leave, but he must have caught the panic on my face. He answered his own question. "No, I guess we'd better get back to town. If you find anything, you can call me."

For a second I wondered if I should tell the woman my suspicions about her husband, but I rejected that idea. She seemed innocent enough, but on the other hand, she did seem to want to keep us here. And if she didn't know anything, why would she possibly believe that her husband was connected to the murder of her mother and his old girlfriend? I could hardly believe it myself.

"Are you ready?" Now Nat was tugging at my arm. "Come on, let's get going." He thanked Linda as I barged through the door and down the stairs. He hurried after me.

Luckily Linda didn't accompany us. She closed the heavy door, probably totally bewildered by our sudden departure. Or not. Maybe she preferred not to be around when her husband and his pal accosted us.

"What was that all about?" Nat asked, trying to catch up with me as I started down the hill.

I stopped just long enough to warn him. "I think her husband is Kate's old boyfriend, Red Berry." I turned and plunged on down the road.

"Hey, wait up."

"Did you see her husband the other day?" I asked over my shoulder.

"No, she said he was still in L.A. and wouldn't be getting here until late that night."

That computed. Red Berry had said he just got into town when I saw him at the flea market.

"Dammit, will you wait up?" Nat yelled.

He was making a valiant effort to catch up with me, but I wasn't about to stop. I half ran and half slid my way down toward the motorcycle. Nat finally came abreast of me and grabbed my arm.

"Why the devil do you think that?" he asked.

"I ran into Red at the flea market Saturday, and I accidentally squirted mustard on his trench coat. There was a coat in the closet with a mustard stain on the lapel."

"Are you sure it was the same coat?"

"Trust me on this, Nat." I was puffing as I continued to plunge down the hill with Nat holding on to me. "There's more—Berry and Berrigan, and Kate had a red scarf in her hand when she died. I think it was her attempt to tell us who killed her."

"Holy shit." Nat's hand tightened on my arm.

I pulled away. "You'll make me trip if you keep hanging on to me."

"Okay." He let go and dropped behind for a minute. "As soon as we get out of here, I'll call the sheriff's department."

"You have your cell phone?" It gave me hope that maybe we could save ourselves yet.

"Yeah, but I couldn't get any signal Saturday until I was farther down the mountain."

He passed me, now in as much of a hurry as I was. Unfortunately I was actually having to hold myself back so that I wouldn't fall. I could feel the muscles in the front of my legs protesting the rapid descent.

We reached the Harley, and I looked around. There was no one behind us, but I heard the sound of a car running somewhere back up the hill. Probably the Jeep Cherokee.

We put on our helmets, and I climbed on the Harley behind Nat. I pulled my bag's shoulder strap over my head with the scarf tucked away inside.

Nat tried to kick-start the bike. It didn't catch on the first attempt. He hit it again. This time the engine caught, and I put my arms around his waist. We began to bump our way along one of the tracks in the road. I could hear the vehicle behind us more clearly now. Someone was definitely following us down the hill.

The Harley began to fly, a dangerous practice when it wasn't equipped with wings. I felt as if I might be launched over Nat's head into outer space as we plummeted downward.

He took the last turn before the gate we'd seen on the way into the property. Once we passed through the gate, we'd be on a public road, which didn't necessarily mean we were out of danger. I wouldn't be able to breathe easy until we were on the paved highway, and maybe not even then.

Nat leaned into the turn, and I felt the wheels skid on gravel as the bike took the corner. I was afraid Nat was going to lose control, but he righted the bike as he made a run for the gate. I guess I had my eyes closed by then because suddenly I felt the bike begin to go into another slide.

I opened my eyes as we tilted dangerously to the left. That's when I saw us coming up on a heavy metal gate. Someone had closed the gate, and the motorcycle was skidding out of control.

The bike pitched to the side, and we both sailed into the dirt and gravel that had accumulated at the bottom of the hill. I lost my hold on Nat and slid across the road into some bushes to the left of the gate. Thank God for the helmet and leather jacket. I could see what Nat meant by "road rash" now.

I looked back and saw a balding man with a ponytail and a beer belly lumbering toward me. It was Bones, Red's buddy from Archie's Pawnshop.

As I started to crawl out of the bushes, I saw Nat on the ground not far from me, and he was just beginning to move. His helmet had come off in the accident. I scrambled toward him as the Jeep I'd seen at the house slammed to a stop in front of us.

"Are you okay, Nat?" I asked.

He nodded and managed to get to a sitting position, but he still look dazed.

Red Berry was out of the driver's seat when I noticed that my shoulder bag had opened up as I slid across the expanse of dirt and gravel. Its strap was still around my neck, but the contents were scattered everywhere. Kate's scarf, a corner of which was still stuck in my purse, had unfurled to almost its six-foot length. One of the therapy balls was at my feet, and I reached down and picked it up once I helped Nat to his feet. The left knee of my jeans was in shreds, and my leg was bleeding.

"Hello, Mandy," Red said. "You and your friend shouldn't

have come snooping around." Apparently Red didn't remember Nat. "We're going to have to get them off the property." He had turned and was talking to Bones.

"So what we going to do with them then?" Bones asked.

I began to reel in the scarf, but it must have caught Red's eye. "Put your hands behind your head, Mandy, and don't move."

That's when I noticed that he had a gun. I did what he said. Red stared at me, probably trying to decide how to kill us. Finally he glanced at Bones. "We'll have to tie them up and take them somewhere else to dispose of them. There's some rope in the back of the Jeep. Get it."

Red held the gun so that it seemed to be pointed squarely between my eyes as he waited. When Bones returned with the rope, Red waved the gun in Nat's direction. "Now tie him up." Nat still looked as if he were out of it, and he offered no resistance when Bones tied his hands behind his back. "Okay, now get him on the floor in the back of the Jeep and tie up his feet."

Bones gave Nat a push toward the Jeep, but as he opened the back end, Nat tried to wrestle with the much larger man. It was no contest. Bones shoved him to the floor behind the backseat.

"And you better behave like a good boy or I'll kill your girlfriend," Red yelled, moving the gun back to me. "The same goes for you, Mandy. I'll shoot your buddy if you give me any trouble."

"I got him tied up, Red," Bones said as he came back to us, "but I used up all the rope. What are we going to do with her?" He tossed his head in my direction.

Red glanced at me. "Use the scarf she has and cover them both up with those blankets in the back of the Jeep. That should work until we can get rid of them."

Bones came over to me. "Okay, you nosy bitch, put your

hands behind your back." It went against every instinct I had to submit to being trussed up for the kill, but I didn't have a choice. Red had the gun trained on me, and I knew my legs were too shaky to make a run for it. Besides, I couldn't abandon Nat.

I felt Bones wind the scarf around my wrists a couple of times, give a yank on it, then give me a prod in the direction of the Jeep.

"Now get inside." He opened the back door on the driver's side. When I was halfway in, he pushed me down onto the seat facefirst. Then he bent my legs up toward my arms and wound the scarf around each ankle and tied them together. When he'd completed the job, he tossed a blanket over me and slammed the door shut, but I could still hear the two men outside.

"You better hide the bike in the bushes so no one will see it until we get back," Red ordered. "I'll pick up all the junk from her purse."

The voices faded as the men moved away from the Jeep.

"Are you okay, Nat?" I whispered.

"I feel like a damned steer in a roping contest."

I listened for the men's return. I didn't hear them. "I'm going to try to get my hands free," I whispered again.

"Lots of luck," Nat said.

"They tied me up with Kate's scarf, and the material stretches."

"Glad you know about things like that." He was silent a minute. "And just what are you going to do if you get untied?"

"I don't know. I haven't thought that far ahead." I heard the crunch of footsteps on the gravel, and both of us quit talking.

"Open the gate before you get in," Red yelled.

I heard him open the door and get in the driver's seat. A

moment later I heard Bones climb in the other side. I tried to shake off the blanket to see what was going on, but all I could see was Bones yank on his seat belt as he fastened it. On the other side there was no responding click as Red put on his seat belt. I didn't think he'd bothered with it, and it gave me an idea—if I could just get free.

"Dammit, Red," Bones said, "you never should have had lunch with that dumb broad."

Red started the Jeep and pulled out, making a sharp left turn to the main gravel road. "Shit, we wouldn't be in this mess if your two buddies hadn't botched up the break-in."

"Jesus, Red," Bones said. "They had to make it seem authentic if they were going to kill the old lady and have it look like a burglary."

"Yeah, but they didn't have to stash the stuff with P.T.'s stupid sister, who'd decide to sell it. The greedy bitch."

"Like you aren't greedy too." Bones was fighting back, which surprised me after the way he'd followed Red's orders earlier. "If you hadn't been living so high on the hog out in Hollywood, you could just have waited for the old lady to die and then you and Linda would have inherited. But no, you thought some guys were going to kill you if you didn't come up with what you owed them."

Red and Bones were so busy hurling accusations and blame back and forth that they weren't paying any attention to Nat and me. I twisted my wrists, trying to stretch the chiffon enough to get one of my hands free. It wasn't working as well as I'd hoped.

"Hey, I told you those guys play hardball," Red yelled, "and I couldn't wait. Besides, the plan would have worked if P.T.'s idiot sister hadn't sold the dress to Kate."

"But did you really have to kill Kate for it?" Bones sounded as if he might break down in tears.

"I didn't have any choice after you and those punks

screwed up. Especially when Kate showed up at the trailer park and ran into me and Monty."

So that's how Kate found out about Red's connection to the dress. I felt as if I were going to be sick, but I didn't dare. I had to concentrate on getting loose.

"You should have let me handle it, not gone barging out there to scream at Shirley for selling some of the stuff." That was Bones again.

The scarf seemed a little looser around my wrist, and I continued to tug on it.

"Yeah, sure, just like you handled getting the dress back from the cleaners," Red yelled. "I wouldn't have been out at the damned flea market either, if you'd been able to get the dress back from the cleaners."

I continued to wiggle my wrists against their binding until I was sure they were bleeding.

"You said I wouldn't be involved in no killings," Bones whined.

"You jackass. You couldn't even handle Mandy at the flea market. You pushed some old lady down the steps—"

"She was wearing the same raincoat," Bones said. "Besides, if Linda ever finds out you had me hire P.T. and Monty to kill her mother, you won't get no money nohow."

Red's voice showed no emotion. "Linda isn't going to find out. P.T. and Monty are dead, and this is the last loose end."

I gave my right hand a yank and was able to squeeze it up to the knuckles. I pulled at the fabric some more, but just then we hit a dip in the road, probably where the second washout had been. I gave another tug on my hand, and it came free. My arm slammed against the back of Bones's seat.

"What's the matter back there?" he yelled.

"I hurt my head," I cried. I was afraid he'd look over the seat, but he must have been cinched into his seat belt so tightly that he couldn't turn around.

Bones seemed satisfied. "How far we going?" he asked Red.

"Not far now. It's off this road a couple of miles."

Damn. They weren't going out to the pavement. I hoped I could get free before they turned off onto another private road. It was easy to slip my other hand out of its noose, and I started to work on the scarf where it was bound around my ankles. Pain shot through my reinjured left leg as I tried to bring it up closer to my hands. I finally eased my legs to the floor, still under the blanket. My wounded knee throbbed as I worked at the knot. My hands felt prickly from where the scarf had cut off the circulation, and it was difficult to get them to move on command.

The Jeep veered to the right. I was knocked against the seat this time, but Bones didn't even ask about me. I hadn't been able to get free before they'd come to the road Red had been talking about, and I had to do it before he reached his destination. I clawed at the knot and finally managed to untie it.

I had no idea what the terrain was like outside the Jeep, but I felt that we were climbing again. At this point I was beyond caring. I brought the scarf around in front of me and wound it around my hands as if it was from a ball of yarn.

"I didn't count on it turning out this way." Bones picked up where he'd left off earlier. "You said there wouldn't be no killings—except for your mother-in-law."

"You moron, I suppose you wanted Shirley and them to go to the cops and spill their guts."

The Jeep banged over the washboard of ruts, muffling the sound as I wiggled around so I was facing forward. It took every bit of strength I had to push myself up in one painful motion with the scarf raised above me. Red obviously wasn't looking in the rearview mirror. I brought the scarf down over his head and pulled it taut against his neck. I didn't think it would strangle him, but it was tight enough to make him lose control of the Jeep. He took his hands off the wheel to paw at the scarf, and the Jeep careened wildly from side to side.

"You damned bitch," Bones yelled, and tried to work himself out of his seat belt to reach back and grab me.

The Jeep veered to the side of the road, and we careened down the mountainside through the trees.

CHAPTER
27

The Jeep didn't stop until it plowed into a Ponderosa pine. I lost my hold on the scarf. Red's head slammed forward into the windshield. So did Bones's now that he was out of his seat belt. I tried to brace myself on the headrest of the driver's seat, but my body sailed forward. My head rammed into Red's shoulder before I fell away into the backseat.

I'd heard poor Nat banging around on the floor behind me. "What's going on up there?" he yelled. Of course he couldn't see, but his voice reassured me that he was alive and mad as hell that he didn't know what was happening.

I managed to pull myself up again, and I could see that both Red and Bones had been stunned by the impact. Red's gun must have slipped off of his lap, and I spotted it on the floor between his feet. If I could just grab it before either of the men regained consciousness . . . I started to get out on the driver's side of the Jeep, but my legs wouldn't support me. I went down on one knee, and by the time I stood up again, Bones had come to and was stumbling out the door on the other side. He started to stagger down the hill, and I needed to stop him. I didn't think he'd grabbed the gun. I ran around the Jeep to grab it through his open door before Red roused, too, but Bones was getting away.

Fine. Let him go. Just get the gun, I told myself. But I couldn't resist one final gesture to stop him. I didn't even realize I was doing it. I grabbed the therapy ball from my shoulder bag and hurled it at his back. It was like throwing a handful of sand to stop a tidal wave.

To my amazement he lost his balance. His arms flailed in the air and he fell as he reached a trail just below me. I would have liked to think he slipped on my therapy ball, but more likely he tripped over a rock jutting out from the ground.

It didn't matter. I scrambled across the passenger seat and grabbed the gun. I climbed out and raised it in the air.

"Stop or I'll shoot." Whoops, I shot anyway.

Bones raised his arms over his head as soon as he managed to clamber to his feet. So did a middle-aged man who'd just appeared on the trail in hiking shorts and boots, a walking stick, and a safari helmet.

Oh, good grief. "Get out of the way, mister," I said as I scooted down the hill toward my prey. "Now put your hands behind your head, Bones, then turn around *slowly* and come back up here to the Jeep."

Bones obeyed. So did the hiker, who looked as if he'd just been charged by a rhino on the Serengeti plain.

"Sir," I said to the stranger. "Could you help me? This man and the guy up there in the driver's seat"—fortunately Red still hadn't stirred—"were trying to kidnap my friend and me."

The man looked dubious, but he lowered his hands.

"My friend's a reporter on the *Denver Tribune,*" I said. "I'm sure he has a press card in his wallet. You can check it out. Then maybe you could untie him for me."

The hiker did better than that. He took off a backpack and removed a *Crocodile Dundee*–sized hunting knife and started up to the Jeep.

"You're going to cut the ropes off of him, right?" I asked to assure myself that he wasn't going to use it as a weapon.

The man said he was.

Meanwhile Bones was almost adjacent to me, and I told him to keep his distance as he stumbled around me. "Now get down on the ground, flat on your stomach, and put your hands behind your head again."

Apparently the hiker had satisfied himself that Nat and I had been legitimate hostages. He cut Nat loose, and Nat grabbed his cell phone and managed to get a call through to the local sheriff's department. A dispatcher said he would send some deputies to assist us.

We were a motley crew who greeted the deputies when they finally arrived. All except the hiker, who introduced himself as Roger Cavender and looked quite dapper.

I'd been relieved when Red Berry finally came around, but despite an ugly knot on his forehead, I ordered him down on the ground with his friend Bones. Nat and I were somewhat the worse for wear with the signs of road rash on our tattered jeans and leather jackets. Nat's knees were scraped too, and our ankles and wrists bore ugly marks from being tied up.

It took an hour to explain everything to the deputies, and then Nat insisted on going back to Linda's property to get his Harley. I went along to recover my billfold and the other things that had fallen out of my shoulder bag. After that, one of the deputies went up to the castle to talk to Linda. I opted to ride back to the sheriff's office with another deputy and meet Nat there. We spent another hour or two going over our statements and being checked out by a doctor, who cleaned the gravel out of our knees and patched us up.

I didn't have to worry about calling Stan and explaining about why I'd broken our date. He and Detective Reilly showed up from Denver to sort things out about Red and Bones and who had killed whom. We'd already told the sheriff we didn't think Red's wife had anything to do with it, but the sheriff wanted us to stick around and talk to the Denver police.

Stan seemed relieved that I was okay, but he wasn't a whole lot happier to see me than Detective Reilly was, and when they finally finished talking to us, Stan said it was over and we could go. He made it sound as if *Stan and I* were over, not just the interview.

As soon as we were outside, Nat used his cell phone to call in his "exclusive" to the *Trib*. Then I climbed onto the back of the Harley, which was not something I was anxious to do, especially now that it was dark. However, the bottom line was that I couldn't figure out any other way to get home.

"What's Stan so mad about?" Nat asked before we started.

"I promised him I'd stay as far away as possible from the investigation," I said. "I guess he doesn't think this is far enough."

Maybe Nat felt he owed me one for finding him the best story of his career, not to mention saving his scrawny neck. "I'll tell him I talked you into coming up here with the scarf," he said. "Besides, this shouldn't count. We're miles away from his jurisdiction."

I had a feeling that, jurisdiction or not, it was going to be hard to resolve the "trust" issue between Stan and me after this. Even if I spent the rest of my life doing nothing but taking care of clothes, I wasn't sure I could mend the tattered remnants of our relationship.

But I couldn't deal with it now, and I turned my thoughts to Kate as we headed back to Denver. It may have taken me a long time to realize the significance of the red scarf Kate had been holding when she died, but at least we'd caught the men who'd killed her.

As soon as I got home, I'd have to prepare something to say at her memorial service the next day, but I said my own private good-bye to her on the back of the Harley and with my body screaming out in pain at all the abuse I'd put it through today.

Tears rolled down my face. Nat never even knew. The wind dried them off my cheeks or blew them away into the clear night air.

MANDY'S FAVORITE CLEANING TIP

Take careful aim when putting mustard on a hot dog. Mustard's one of the hardest stains to get out of clothes, so you should probably heed the advice (Chapter 10) and take any garment with mustard on it to the cleaners. Otherwise, you can try vinegar or peroxide to remove the stain, and if that doesn't work, it's either dye or dry clean.